Magick Unveiled

ALEX POLAK

Published 2020 by Your Book Angel
Copyright © Alex Polak

The characters are all mine, any similarities with other fictional or real persons/ places are coincidental.

Printed in the United States
Edited by Keidi Keating
Layout by Rochelle Mensidor

ISBN: 978-1-7341814-9-4

This book is dedicated to my darling wife Melanie.

Introduction

Hi there, my name is Gavan Maddox and I'm a thirty-two-year-old shop owner living in South Yorkshire. My shop, to the average customer, appears to be just another ubiquitous "New Age" boutique, selling the same crystals, incense, dream-catchers and "spell book" diaries for teenaged girls as every other. We've all seen them, both on high streets and in town markets, and usually dismissed them out of hand as hokey, and only fit for tie-dying, canvas-sandal-wearing hippies.

Now please don't get me wrong, I have nothing against hippies and New Agers. Those granola munchers account for about ninety-nine percent of my sales, enabling me to keep a roof over my head and the lights on. I pride myself on the fact that I only stock the highest quality items, at least as far as possible. The crystals are all genuine with no coloured glass or red spinel labelled as ruby; the incense is in multiple forms and will actually smell of what it is supposed to when burned, the dream-catchers don't start unravelling the first time you dust them, and the books, although not teaching real magick, are at least well bound and printed, and won't fall apart or smudge when touched.

At this point, the more attentive and observant among you are no doubt asking, "Hang on, what about the other one percent, what do you mean by 'real magick', and why the hell do you spell magic with a K at the end?"

All valid questions, dear reader, and ones I will endeavour to answer to your satisfaction. I say endeavour, as there will always be some sceptics and non-believers who will never be satisfied with my explanations. If you are one of those, then I would advise you to stop reading at this point and find yourself a nice historical biography. If, however, you are gifted with imagination and even the slightest degree of belief in the impossible, then please stick with me. I know you'll have found my story safely tucked away in the fiction section of your local bookstore, but that's only because most people refuse to believe in powers they can't explain, and phenomena they can't analyse in a lab.

Those are the kinds of people who, when confronted with a child who has an absolute, unshakeable belief in psychic abilities and other magick like I had, would diagnose them as "reality-challenged" or having a "schizo-typal personality disorder" and start putting them on medications and into counselling, rather than encouraging them to explore what makes them happy. (Sorry for the rant, I'm still a little resentful as you can probably tell.)

The few who know, deep in their souls, that there are greater powers in this world if only they could tap into them, are where my other one percent of sales are made and where my story begins.

Welcome to Dinas Affaraon. Please do not touch the labelled displays —you break it, you buy it!

PART 1

The Quest

Chapter 1

I was walking away after a somewhat disastrous date which had ended early (I mean seriously, who hates books?!) and decided to stop and get a sandwich as I hadn't eaten much at dinner. To be honest, I had been glad for a reason to get out of it as it had been a blind date set up by my friend and assistant and I'd only gone in the first place to stop her nagging me about my lack of a social life. I stopped into Subway for a meatball marinara and ordered a six-inch on wheat.

"Are you sure you don't want a footlong?" asked the cute brunette behind the counter.

"No thanks, six inches is quite enough. I don't need to over-compensate," I replied with a wink, making the guy next to her manning the salad section turn away and start coughing as he tried not to laugh. She, on the other hand, just blushed and grinned cheekily back. At six-foot-one with light brown hair and what I have been told are striking green eyes, I was used to garnering at least passing interest from women, although I rarely had the inclination to follow up on it.

I had been told by my shrink as a child (thanks Dad!) that I had an "Avoidant Personality Type" as I was always afraid of looking stupid in social situations. I had learned to flirt but only if I knew it was innocent, it would go nowhere and I could walk away afterwards.

I got my sandwich (extra cheese, just like me) and headed out, hearing the two laugh as the door closed. I hunched my shoulders instinctively, momentarily thinking that they were laughing at me, rather than with me.

I relaxed after a second, then unwrapped the end of my sub and took a bite, savouring the taste as I walked. Clearly I should have done one or the other as I managed to stumble on a cracked paving stone, drawing the attention of a passing community patrol officer. Those guys always irritated me, acting like police without the actual authority.

"Have you been drinking sir?" he asked haughtily, looking me up and down. I finished chewing my bite of sandwich and swallowed, then let him have it, already uptight from my farcical attempt at a date and my subsequent anxiety from the sandwich shop.

"OK, let's review. Number one I'm walking not driving, in a pedestrian zone so who cares if I have been drinking? Number two, I stumbled on a cracked paving stone and didn't fall over –if I have been drinking, I'm clearly not inebriated or lacking control. Number three, even if I was totally wasted, what the hell were you planning on charging me with? Being drunk in charge of a sandwich?!"

As I was talking, I got more and more worked up and my gestures got wilder. As I asked my final snide question, the hand holding my warm, fragrant sandwich moved just a little too far from my body. Out of the corner of my eye I spotted a local stray dog creeping up, attracted by the enticing aroma. Too late, I felt a tug and watched as my beautiful sandwich ran off down the street hanging from the mutt's mouth.

"Oh, perfect!" I shouted. "That just sums up my entire damn night! That's your fault, you ass!" I added heatedly. The toy cop turned away, laughing obnoxiously, and walked off with his head held high. I stuck two fingers up at his back and my shoulders slumped, then I slouched off to the nearest taxi rank to catch a cab home. I decided to write the entire night off as a ridiculous bust. That would teach me to go on a blind date!

The next morning I arrived at the door of my store, reaching for my keys with a wry smile of amusement as I remembered the events of the night before. The old-fashioned, spring mounted bell above the door chimed brightly as I entered the shop, and I breathed in the welcome aroma of incense and books. I always made sure to keep the incense and scented candles near the door, so the smell never got too overpowering but merely added a gentle perfume to the air. It also helped the fragrance permeate out onto the street luring the occasional passer-by in for a browse. I used to have them by the checkout, but within a week I'd had to move them owing to the massive headaches I was getting, and the constant sneezing. Now the counter was taken up by display cases filled with some of the more expensive crystals and jewellery pieces. The bell was a style choice, both to fit with the shop and because I'd loved the idea after seeing one in the magic shop on Buffy the Vampire Slayer.

"Morning, boss! Any luck?" The cheerful voice sounded behind me before the door even closed, heralding the arrival of Summer Rain, my only employee and long-time friend. Summer, or as she was legally known Betty Michaels, was the most cheerful person I knew. Despite being only five-foot-two, fifteen pounds overweight, with messy brown hair tied into a ratty-looking plait, and having to wear glasses that looked like they came off a cartoon character, Summer had a smile and Devil-may-care attitude that could light up a room and instantly endeared her to any customers. She was the reason we sold as much of the routine merchandise as we did, as she was also a skilled saleswoman who could talk an Eskimo into buying ice. She had chosen her new name when she came to work for me as she had decided to style herself as a hedge witch, although she had never made a potion in her life.

Her somewhat unusual opening sally was a running joke between us, referring to whether I had managed to finally unlock the potential I knew resided deep in my core (a belief that meant I still had to see a community psychiatric nurse once a month, the latest one being a paunchy overly sympathetic guy named Frank).

I had become convinced of this latent power when I was a child, and the memory of the incident still remained as fresh as ever. I had been sitting in the back of my mother's car, waiting for her to pick up the last kid on the pooled school run, and I had been looking at my old Speak and Maths machine. This was a big plastic console with buttons like a giant calculator and a green LCD display that was made to help kids learn basic arithmetic. My dyslexic sister had had the Speak and Spell version.

I must have been about six or seven at the time, and we had been learning about atoms and molecules in science class that week. I had a piece of string threaded through the handle at the top of the console, which was solid plastic and about an inch and a half thick. I had been thinking that if the molecules were all arranged in a regular lattice as my teacher had said, and if most of the molecule was almost empty space –the electron cloud surrounding the nucleus –it should be possible to align the nuclei in the string with the empty space in the plastic handle and make one pass through the other (hey, I was a kid, gimme a break here!). With the naivety of youth, and the absolute conviction of a child, I promptly yanked on the string –and pulled it through the handle!

The handle wasn't cracked (I checked), the string wasn't broken (I pulled it as hard as I could), and I hadn't let go of one end and then caught it again as the string was actually wrapped around my hands. I had stared at the string, tested everything as I say, and then tried again. At this point, I had already thought "I don't believe I just did that!" so doubt had already taken root in my mind. Naturally, it never worked again.

A few years later, my mother joined a Spiritualist church, where they did psychic evenings, there was a spiritual and psychic healing group, and I had been informed of the power of my aura and my extreme potential. It was probably just a sales tactic, but I chose to believe it.

As I grew up (or should I say got older –I'm not sure I ever really 'grew up'), the fascination for those interests stayed with me. Some called it "New Age", some called it "The Occult", some said "Psychic", and many simply called it weird and labelled me a "freak", a term which I gleefully embrace to this day –freak and proud. I'd rather be a freak than conform to others' expectations and be miserable; I'd seen far too many people do that.

Also, I was determined that one day I would release my power and finally prove to my CPN that it was real –maybe then they'd leave me alone! I had always resented my diagnoses and the stigma that was associated with them, as with any mental health issues. I had discovered when I was younger that the medical profession used the Greek letter 'Ψ' (pronounced psi) to denote psychiatric services. I had always thought it looked like a pitchfork such as was carried by Satan, which to my mind was another reason that such conditions were vilified and feared. Just one more driver to try to free myself from being under their surveillance.

"Nope, still as mundane as ever!" I replied to Summer, completing the second half of our morning routine. "I guess we're still stuck with Frank for now." She gave me her standard pitying look, heading into the small kitchen area to start the coffee while I opened the shutters. We were in a city centre, on a main pedestrian street, but we still had some pretty pricey goods so the insurance companies wouldn't have touched me with a bargepole if I hadn't had the shutters and used them every night. Even so, they tried to re-classify the shop as a jewellery store every time I was due to renew the policy.

I walked back inside to the welcome sound of the drip machine burbling away, and the ambrosial smell of Cafegeddon wafting through the shop. Cafegeddon was my own personally created blend of coffee, made up of equal parts Death Wish, Valhalla Java Odinforce blend, and Throat Punch coffees. All my friends who tried it wanted the recipe, and that had even led to Throat Punch expanding their shipping from the UK to worldwide for a time, due to the sudden demand from my American friends and colleagues. I poured a cup of caffeinated bliss, savouring that first sip of the day with a contented sigh.

"Perfect as usual, Summer. What would I do without you?"

"Put the pot on yourself and wait an extra thirty seconds for your first cup!" she laughed at me. "Stop trying to butter me up and tell me how it went! I've been dying to know. You never go on dates, and it took me weeks to set this up with Karen —she's harder to pin down than you are, with all your 'issues'. Gods only know why you have them —is your mirror busted or something? Anyway where did you take her? It better not have been some cheesy Nando's or something. I know how good business has been going, especially from the special orders, so you better have at least made sure she got a decent meal out of this! Well come on, don't just stand there all tight-lipped, how did it go?!"

I just smiled and sipped my coffee, waiting for her rapid-fire questions to slow down long enough for me to get a word in edgewise. I knew from experience that there was no point starting to talk until she slowed down to breathe, or she'd just steamroll right over me.

"I took her to the Japanese place in the centre of Doncaster. I remembered you saying she liked sushi. You can close your mouth and wipe that amazed look off your face! Yes, I actually listen when you talk." I savoured my own chance to laugh. "We had some saké, sushi and sashimi, and teppanyaki, and sat there and chatted for a couple of hours. Everything was going quite well until I asked her about what books she read. She actually said that she didn't 'waste her time reading' —yes, I physically threw up air quotes in my disgust —and that if the story was any good, it'd be made into a film or a TV series, so she'd watch it and save herself 'hours of ploughing through some boring book'! How could you set me up with someone who hates reading?!"

The look on Summer's face was priceless. It was clear she'd had no idea of her friend's disdain for the written word, as she knew my love of reading would eventually bring the conversation around to books.

"Oh my gods, I'm sooo sorry!" she apologised, raising her hands to her cheeks. "She always talks about films she's seen, and I know you love films, but I never knew she was actively against books! I'll have to try and get her into Audible in the car or something."

"Great, let me know when she's developed beyond the kiddie pool of culture." Which was my standard description for people who didn't like books. Now I don't want you to think I'm a snob, I have no issue with anyone who has trouble reading, either because of time constraints or educational difficulties such as dyslexia —my own sister is dyslexic, so I have every sympathy —but there are still ways to adapt to that, like Kindle with dyslexia open font, Audible, or even getting Siri to read to you.

On the other hand, to genuinely disdain books as a waste of time really stuck in my craw, as Summer well knew. I had been known to ask customers to leave if they turned their noses up at even the idea of perusing the books in my shop. They were my favourite items, and I had spent many an hour chatting to customers about books, segueing into novels after we'd discussed their original enquiry regarding some volume or other on my shelves. Summer giggled, and then immediately looked crestfallen.

"I can't believe I never knew that about her. I never would have set you up if I'd had any idea. And after I pestered you for so long to finally go on a date, then you finally screwed up your courage and agreed! I feel like such an ass!"

"Don't worry about it," I relented. "I know it's not your fault. Some people just don't get it the way we do. But if she asks, don't give her hope of a repeat. I was polite after the bombshell and walked her home but refused her invitation of coffee or a nightcap. I told her that I'd had a pleasant evening but wasn't sure how compatible we'd be long-term, so hopefully she got the message."

"Ah, ever the gentleman" -Summer smiled -"and then you wonder why I'm in love with you! Yet more proof that you're a lovely guy with no reason to be afraid of what people might think of you. I swear, if I didn't prefer clams to sausage, and I wasn't happy with Emily, I'd have been chasing you around the stock room years ago!"

"You never know, I might even have let you catch me!" I winked at her, flirting in the comfortable way that only old friends can when they know nothing will ever come of it. "And that's such a lovely, ladylike way of putting it, by the way! Anyway, enough about my failed date and non-existent love life. What's on the cards for today? We finished the inventory check yesterday, so that's done for the quarter, and all the orders have been emailed to the suppliers, so it should hopefully be a nice easy day."

Summer looked at the computer behind the counter, which she had been booting up in her usual efficient manner while we were talking.

"You've just got one appointment at half past nine with someone wanting to commission you to find a particular item for them. Doesn't say what item and doesn't give a name, so I can't tell you more than that I'm afraid."

"How did we get a booking with so little information?" I asked, puzzled. "I'd have never taken one like that, and I know you wouldn't, so where the hell did it come from? When did it get put in the calendar?" I was amazed; we always tried to get as much information as possible, so that I could do some preparation for any meeting and give the client an idea of potential costs, how long it might take to obtain their item, or if there was no chance in hell I'd be able to help. Sometimes that was because I didn't have the appropriate contacts to find what they wanted, or because they were asking for something from the "darker" side of the line —my own personal line, across which I refused to step. I knew magick was intrinsically neither good nor evil, it was the intention of the user, but some things were clearly aimed more in one direction or the other. One such example was blood magicks, which generally had a darker slant to them, and even for a good outcome could require a significant price.

I also regularly arranged my appointments for later in the day, as we were usually just finishing opening up by nine-thirty so I wouldn't have had a chance to review any advanced research that I might have done —which was my standard prep for an appointment, and why we normally booked at least a week to ten days ahead.

At this point, I think I should explain the difference, in my mind, between magic and magick. To me, magic was what stage magicians employed to entertain, consisting of essentially special effects and sleight of hand. Magick was where authentic power was tapped into, with the potential to genuinely affect the world around us. There were many rules that people had come up with over the years for magick use, but I had tried to boil them down to just two:

1. Do no harm (borrowed from many sources, including the Hippocratic oath)
2. What you send out will come back in multiples

Now, they may sound simplistic, but they had their limitations. For example, if you were able to work a spell to win the lottery, that meant you were taking that win away from someone else who might need it more, and they might lose their house when they otherwise wouldn't —"The law of unintended consequence", as I'd once heard it referred to. That was why I often preferred "intend no harm", rather than do no harm. So long as your intentions were pure, I felt it was unreasonable of the universe to expect a mere human to know every potential outcome of any given action. Then again, when has the universe ever been fair?

The second was easier, basically consisting of another description of Karma. I'd heard many variations —what you give out you get back, the rule of threes (what you give out comes back three-fold) and the rule of sevens. Whichever way you sliced it, it came to the same thing: act like an ass, and yours would get kicked in turn.

"It was put in ten minutes ago by an anonymous source," Summer said, looking at the booking details of the appointment. "The system was powered down at the time, and the virus software shows the firewall as fully intact when I just did a scan. I have no idea how it got on there, except by…" She trailed off and glanced over at me, and I knew exactly where her mind had gone, because mine had gone there too –magick. Either that, or there was a seriously talented hacker out there with mad skills to jump over our firewall and add an appointment to a system that wasn't even turned on. Bearing in mind the circles we worked in, and the items we dealt with, I somehow doubted the latter.

We were still looking at each other somewhat uneasily when the bell chimed to announce our mystery appointment, and we turned as one towards the door.

Chapter 2

"Mr Maddox, I presume?" The cultured vowel sounds and smoky, almost sensuous tone of our visitor's voice exuded class and screamed old money, while the self-assured delivery spoke of someone used to getting their own way. The tone immediately set me on the defensive but I mentally shook myself, thinking that this was my shop and I refused to be intimidated by a tone of voice.

Once my ears were done, my eyes took over, and definitely did not go wanting. The floor-length black silk shift, belted at the waist with what looked like an obsidian chain, rose up over a generous bust emphasised by three gold chains draped over it with different pendants on each. The first was a symbol commonly seen in my circles –a pentagram in a circle. The second looked to be a rose quartz bound in wire, and the third was a symbol that, from a distance, could have been the Seal of the Archangels, or something obscure from The Key of Solomon or some other magickal text (I couldn't tell exactly without a closer examination, which even my social ineptness told me wasn't exactly appropriate, given where it was hanging). All three pendants shifted in unison as she sensuously peeled off her black opera gloves, holding them loosely in her left hand rather than forcing them into the small clutch bag under her left arm.

As my eyes rose further up, they encountered curls of hair so black it had the almost blue sheen of a raven's wing, which immediately made me think it was either a very high-quality wig, or an equally expensive dye job. The skin visible above the demure neckline of the dress was also too pale to belong to a naturally dark-haired woman, unless she spent all of her time indoors (or was a vampire, but she had walked in off the street in full sunlight, so I doubted that). She was clearly shooting for, and totally nailing, the whole goth, Morticia Adams vibe. The outfit simply confirmed what my ears had already detected —there was money involved here, and lots of it.

The mystery woman's face then captured my complete attention. Individually, each feature could potentially be wrong. Her eyes were slightly too large, the nose was aquiline with a slight bump on the bridge and the jaw line was fractionally too strong. Her chin was slightly too pointed, and she had a tiny gap between her front teeth that must have been murder to keep clear when she ate. However, when taken as a whole, the effect was of a strong, confident woman who was handsome and strangely attractive, rather than classically beautiful. When taken as a whole, she reminded me strongly of a young Angelica Houston combined with hints of Monica Bellucci.

Realising I had been staring with my mouth open and my coffee cup stalled halfway to my lips for a good five to ten seconds, I cleared my throat, set my mug on the counter, and stepped forward with my hand out.

"Please, call me Gavan. Mr Maddox was my father." I smiled as I delivered my customary greeting, designed to set people at ease and help me feel a sense of control in the situation. Not that she appeared to need any help, standing there surveying the shop as if it were her own and she its undisputed queen, holding court. "And you are?"

"Representing a party interested in acquiring a unique item that we believe you may be able to obtain for us." She deftly sidestepped giving me her name, while immediately making the point of who she felt was in charge here. She did, however, take my hand in a cool, soft grip, squeeze briefly and then let go, almost as if apologising for her lack of decorum in refusing to reveal her name after I had given mine. In my mind I had already dubbed her Angelica, given my initial impression.

"I see," I replied, tilting my head slightly. "I have to say, this isn't how I normally work. I prefer to know who I'm working for and what they're asking for before the first meeting, so I have a chance to do some research. That way, I know if I'm likely to be able to help, how difficult it will be, the costs involved, and most importantly, if it's something I want anything to do with in the first place. As I'm sure you are aware, there are some items that no respectable person should have anything to do with, which should remain locked away or lost to the sands of time. I'll tell you up-front, if this is something too dark, my answer will be no, regardless of how much money may be involved. I have my standards and my code, and I violate them for no one." I finished, mentally sticking my tongue out in defiance.

'Angelica' smiled at this point, the first genuine smile she had given since she had entered, and her face immediately transitioned into beautiful. She appeared to relax, and took a deep breath, which caused some interesting movements of her pendants (dammit man, eyes up, this is business!).

"I'm glad to know our information on you was correct," she replied. "It does make things so much easier when dealing with a man with principles."

"Wait, your information on me? What, do you have some kind of dossier on my work?" I asked, wanting it to be a joke but my suspicious nature already setting alarm bells ringing.

"Of course not." I began to relax, only to be whiplashed back to tense at her next words. "Our information is far more comprehensive than just your work. Incidentally, I agree with you, anyone who thinks movies and TV can replace a good book wants slapping firmly across the face. You extricated yourself from the situation very adroitly." At this, I felt the blood drain from my face, and goose bumps sprang up over my entire body.

"Are you telling me you've been spying on me?! Even watching my date last night?! Just who the hell are you people, and where do you get off invading my privacy like that?" I was fuming at this point, and about to throw her bodily from the shop, gentleman be damned, and to hell with the money. My nerves were also making me want to run and hide in the stock room and I had to take a deep breath, clenching my fist behind my back to stand my ground.

"Now, now, don't be hasty." She held her glove-free hand out placatingly. "We haven't been spying on you. I got that from your mind. Call it a demonstration to show you we're for real. I have a gift for accessing people's thoughts. Some call it psychic, more scientific types prefer telepathy, but either way, I've got it. It's a useful tool in negotiations, as I'm sure you can appreciate, which is why I tend to be the liaison chosen for this sort of thing."

The admission stopped me cold. That meant we were dealing with, potentially, an entire group of people with access to genuine magick. No wonder they were able to get the appointment onto our system.

"Exactly," she said. "I'm glad you understand." Her response to my unspoken thoughts raised my hackles and anxiety still higher.

"OK, miss," I replied, somewhat heatedly, "let's get a few things straight from the outset. Number one, stay out of my head or you can get out of my store right now! If I want you to know what's going on in there, I'll tell you. Beyond that, you start peeking where I don't want you and I'll make sure you regret it, because I have a fairly vivid and twisted imagination and I'll not be held responsible for any mental scarring you gain from experiencing it. Second, if you have access to those kinds of resources, why do you even need me? There's no way I'm getting involved in some deal only to find out I'm someone's patsy and I've been hung out to dry when everything goes tits up." Dammit, my gaze dropped again and short-circuited my mouth. That wasn't meant to come out quite that way. But you know what? I was gonna start my imagination running and see just how much she wanted to watch before she changed the channel.

Vivid images of the two of us entwined in various poses from the Kama Sutra (£34.99, illustrated edition, second shelf down, left hand end) immediately began to fill my mind fuelled by my prolonged celibacy, rapidly moving on to leather, handcuffs, toys, sweating, writhing, hands, breasts, lips, tongues, moaning, begging... Damn, this was getting hard in more ways than one, but I could see I'd already had the desired effect. Her eyes had widened, her breathing was more rapid, her whole face and neck flushed rose pink, and she shifted where she stood. She looked away and closed her eyes, biting her lip, at which point I immediately switched tactics (mostly for my own sanity, and the integrity of my underwear) and began imagining torture scenarios. Flesh peeling off, insects, spiders, snakes, flames, being forced to watch Love Island on a continuous loop

—the most horrific things I could imagine. Her eyes flew open, she stared at me, and then she immediately looked at the floor.

"OK, OK, enough, I've closed my mind, I swear." She looked back up at me and I saw that something behind her eyes looked different, as if she had genuinely shut herself off. "I'm sorry, I usually keep my mind open, both for information and my own protection. It's much harder to sneak up on someone who can hear you coming. It takes a concentrated effort for me to shut it off." She gave me a very sly smile and flushed again. "Some of those first ideas of yours, though…"

Aaaand BAM, my underwear was too tight again! Still, her admission did more for my self-esteem than almost two decades of psychiatric treatment and counselling ever had.

"Shall we make this more formal, and go to the office?" I asked, desperate to try to reintroduce some semblance of control and normalcy to the proceedings. I looked at Summer, who had stood watching the back and forth between us like a Wimbledon tennis final. From her expression, she was still clearly irritated at the liberties our strange visitor had taken. "I'll take the usual precautions." She nodded at me and moved behind the counter to get on with the day.

"Good. Make sure she knows about them too. Best to be clear," she said, irritated on my behalf as any good friend would be. Our client, if indeed that was to be the case, looked quizzically at us, clearly on the back foot now that she couldn't read our minds.

"I record all business dealings in the office, for everyone's protection and complete clarity. A copy of the recording and the full transcription will be sent to you after our meeting. Another copy will be kept by me, so we both have a record of everything that was said, and there can be no arguments over what was agreed." She immediately stopped following me, pausing midstride.

"I'm not sure I'm particularly comfortable with that," she said. "Some of what we discuss is, by its very nature, sensitive." I hurried to reassure her.

"It's not for distribution, it's for mutual insurance. After our business is concluded, I will destroy the recording, and the transcript will be filed in the vault. No-one else will see it, and if there's nothing illegal involved, you should have nothing to worry about. I also use this as a bit of a litmus test. People asking me to do something shady always baulk at this point, which tells me all I need to know, and they are asked to leave with no recourse to appeal. Please bear in mind that with your group's obvious resources and… abilities, I'll be making multiple copies and storing them in multiple locations, one of which is warded with a significant number of inscribed protection runes." She smiled, and continued walking.

"Fair enough, Mr Maddox −Gavan," she quickly corrected herself. "I'll provide you with a post box address where you can send our copies." I was almost unreasonably happy that she agreed, since for some reason, I wasn't ready for her to leave. It probably had something to do with my rapid-fire mental porn film from just a few moments ago, and I was looking forward to talking about her… needs.

Chapter 3

The office was my ultimate pride and joy, my sanctuary from the stresses of the day. As such, it housed some of my personal collection of books and artefacts and was decorated more like a library or study in a stately home than a workplace. I had surrounded myself with things that either confirmed my belief in magick, (which annoyed Frank interminably, but I didn't care) or helped me to calm down when things got too much for me.

There were bookcases on three walls, each starting a quarter of the way up the wall, with the bottom quarter taken up by a cupboard, the doors fronted with oxblood leather, crossed by an X of the same wood as the bookcase. The wood itself was a medium tone oak, so as not to be too dark, and the front columns were engraved with various mystical and arcane symbols, stained a couple of tones darker to make them stand out. I had designed them myself and got a friend who made furniture to build them for me to my specifications. He had also built the matching antique-style desk that dominated the floor space, the set of drawers on each side engraved with the same arcane symbols, and the client side also faced with a square of oxblood leather and wooden X. The two client chairs were antique-style swivel chairs, the seat, back and arms covered in matching oxblood leather.

My own chair was covered in the same leather, but was a thoroughly modern high-backed chair that had originally started out as a high-end gaming chair. It was the best constructed and best shaped swivel chair I had been able to find. The floor was polished oak boards. The effect was incredibly luxurious, looking like it had cost several hundred thousand to create. In reality my friend had used all reclaimed wood, been given a great deal on the leather, and had done the work as his thanks to me for introducing him to his wife. He'd been wanting to do something for me for years, as I had set them up together at a party I'd thrown for the first anniversary of my shop opening. This had been his ultimate chance, and they had both been overjoyed at the opportunity.

The ceiling had four square panels of pale marble, also reclaimed, with a central light fixture that had a wooden circle with six spokes, each ending in a bulb with a green glass shade. I don't mean to sound virtuous by having used reclaimed wood and marble. It was just vastly cheaper, and the wood immediately imparted the antique look I wanted.

The shelves on the left and right of the room were filled with books, either pertaining to my work –arcane and mystical volumes, including 3 different versions of The Key of Solomon, along with dozens of historical and other reference texts –and simple fiction for relaxation. Everything from Anne Rice to Tom Clancy, to Douglas Adams, to Calvin and Hobbes was represented, to account for any particular mood that might take me.

The case behind me was occupied by various artefacts, mostly high-quality reproductions as I had neither the money nor the magickal ability to afford or use the real things. "Maybe one day" was what I always told myself, meaning both the money and, to my mind almost more importantly, the magick.

I also had a decent climate control system to keep the room at a nice comfortable temperature while keeping the moisture level to a minimum to protect the books. Overall, it was a place I could work in comfort, meet clients, or simply kick back and relax. It was not unusual for Summer to arrive in the morning to find me asleep in my chair, having simply kicked off my shoes, reclined the chair and put my feet up on the desk. She often asked me why I didn't just have done with it and move into the apartment above the shop, which we currently used for storage (or an occasional shower and quick change if I hadn't been home), but I preferred to have my home further from work, to make the transition away from business at the end of the day more definite.

I held the door open and motioned for 'Angelica' to go in first – purely as a gentleman. I in no way wanted to see if her rear elevation compared to the front (it most certainly did, thank the gods). As she entered, she looked around and smiled in such a way that I could tell she approved. She immediately moved to look at some of the arcane volumes on my shelves, and I stepped around the desk to take my seat and watch her perusal of my collection. She ran her finger along the shelf, stopping at my three volumes of The Key of Solomon, then moving along to a couple of Kabbalah texts.

"For someone who can't use magick, you have a very impressive collection, especially as a private citizen outside of any of the major groups. It must have taken you quite some time to accumulate it all." She turned to me, and stepped over to one of the visitors' chairs, sitting down with the poise and decorum of someone completely at ease and used to being in charge of a situation.

"Thank you. It's kind of you to say so, but being in this business actually made it much easier than you might think. The only reason it takes time to accumulate is the cost. I simply don't have the resources to go out and buy the entire collection I'd like to acquire." I smiled. "Maybe someday I'll win the lottery and be able to buy any volumes I fancy, then have the time to just sit and read them," I joked.

"Maybe we can help you along that road," she replied, completely serious. "We're prepared to offer you a quarter of a million pounds to look into our request. The money is yours, regardless of the outcome of your research, but all details of your investigation remain confidential and we own any information you unearth. If you are eventually able to obtain the artefact for us, we will cover the price, then pay you whatever it cost to obtain, plus an extra two million pounds on top."

I sat there, stunned into silence for the first time in years. I swallowed a few times, and my mind raced to try to process the information. I desperately tried to moisten my suddenly dry tongue, as she looked at me in amusement, clearly able to see the effect her offer had had on me, even without resorting to her psychic abilities. My self-doubt threatened to rise up and choke me but I took a deep breath and focused on my professional persona to help drive it back down.

"And is there..." My voice came out as a whisper through my suddenly dry larynx. I cleared my throat and tried again. "And is there a maximum amount your 'group' is willing to consider for whatever this mystery artefact is? I don't want to start promising someone a billion pounds to find out you can't cover it," I said sarcastically.

"Also, am I going to find out what this 'mystery artefact' is? Between your group remaining anonymous, dealing with an anonymous liaison, an unnamed item, no idea of a maximum price range, no clue of a time frame, and no way to contact you to ask for more information if I need to, I've got crucial unknowns at both ends of this, when I prefer to have none. I can accept your group remaining anonymous –for now, at least –but I can't find out anything about an artefact if I don't even know what it is."

She sat back in the chair and steepled her fingers –a sure sign of someone who knew they had the upper hand and felt superior as a result.

"Of course you'll get more information, but only if you decide to accept our offer and look into our enquiry. If not, there's no reason for you to know any more than you already do."

I immediately understood what she was doing. She was using my own curiosity against me, making my desire for answers push me into accepting her case. Annoyingly, I knew it was going to work because I knew how much I hated mysteries. If I let her walk out, I'd hate myself for two reasons –first because I'd be turning this over in my mind, trying to figure out what the artefact might be and who she represented; and secondly because I'd have lost the chance to see her again, and I was starting to realise that she was intriguing me almost more than her case. There was no way I could possibly tolerate the first situation, but more importantly there was no way I could allow her to know there even was a second factor. I would simply have to focus on the case and ignore my growing fascination with her, a result of both the purely physical attraction I felt towards her and the fact that her abilities gave me some further confirmation of my long-held belief in magick.

"Obviously I'm both intrigued by the mystery, as I'm sure you knew I would be, and attracted by the money, which is more than generous. That in itself does however raise more questions. I'm just some small-time shop owner. Why would you be offering such obscene amounts of money to me, rather than paying less to someone with more experience and more contacts in these sorts of matters?"

"The money is to show you we're serious, and the initial payment will be in your account within ten minutes of you agreeing," she replied. "As to 'why you' —we had, as you're already aware, checked you out and found that you were honest in your dealings with clients, and had that ethical code you mentioned so wouldn't be involved in anything you weren't comfortable with if it turned out to be too dark. Also, to be honest, we have already been to others in your field, and they simply laughed at us and told us to stop being stupid."

That pronouncement immediately made me prick up my ears and feel some trepidation. Clearly what they were after was something legendary that most people were convinced didn't exist, so I might never get beyond research.

"So, if I find out it's turning dark, I can simply pass my research to that point over to you and walk away, no questions asked?" I wanted to clarify that point right off the bat. "Because you're right, I won't be part of anything that isn't the right side of the line. Also, if I find out that what you want does exist, I won't be involved in strong-arming the owner into selling if they don't want to, nor in helping you obtain it by illegal means. I'll make them an offer up to your group's stated maximum, and if that's not enough I'll simply walk away." She smiled, realising that these were the thrashings of a fish that was already firmly on the hook.

"Of course you can walk away if things start crossing the line and contravene your code. However, we would want evidence of that. A quarter of a million pounds surely buys us the right to be sure that you're not just taking the money and running."

"Certainly," I replied. "If you've done your research, you'll know I always follow through to the best of my ability. I have my own reputation to consider, after all."

"Then you're agreeing to the terms?" She showed the first signs of excitement I'd seen on her since we'd come into the office. At this point, the mental porn film from earlier threatened to make a reappearance, and I shifted uncomfortably in my seat.

"Yes, I'll look into it for you." She immediately reached into her bag and pulled out a smart phone. She swiped it awake, went to the contacts and tapped an entry.

"Send the money. He's agreed." She disconnected and placed the phone back in her bag. I eyed it with hope; maybe that would be the contact number I'd get for future enquiries!

"OK, so how about filling in some of those blanks I mentioned," I prompted. "How about introducing yourself, and telling me who you – and by extension who I am about to –work for? Then we can start filling in the blanks at the other end of this, and we'll discuss what you want me to look for." She smiled at me in a way that had me thinking that she, too, might still be remembering my erotic mental firewall.

"Let's just call them a multi-national group with interests in a wide range of areas, including more esoteric topics. As to who I am, I am simply a liaison. This is my number for any future enquiries relating to your investigation." She passed me a business card with a mobile phone number on it and nothing else. I promptly pulled out my phone and entered it into the contacts, under the name Angelica.

"Fine. You read my mind when you walked in, so you know who you reminded me of, so I guess Angelica will have to do for now."

"It's a lovely name," she remarked, smiling broadly. "Also a very useful herb in times past. Just remember, Angelica is poisonous until it's been cultivated for at least two years." I laughed at her sudden tack, making me think she had an idea of my growing fascination with her.

"I guess I'll just have to draw out my enquiries then," I said, only partially joking, as our interaction had made me interested in pursuing a relationship for the first time I could remember in over a decade.

"That might not be such a good idea," she replied, turning serious. My heart immediately sank in fear of yet another personal rejection but I held my breath as she continued. "As you know, we've already approached others who told us there was no chance, or that the item simply doesn't exist. Our enquiries may, however, have prompted some of them to start looking into it themselves. Time has therefore, unfortunately, become a factor." I released my breath and relaxed a couple of notches as I realised that she was talking about professional concerns rather than personal ones –at least, so I hoped.

"Then why waste time with all this cloak and dagger stuff? Why not just ask me to find whatever it is?" I asked.

"We wanted you to understand how serious we were first, so that when we tell you what it is you won't simply dismiss us out of hand like all the others have," she replied.

"Fair enough. Well, you've just paid me two hundred and fifty thousand pounds, so I promise to at least look into it carefully and build a comprehensive report. If everything I find points to the conclusion that your artefact doesn't, in fact, exist, I will at least have justification rather than a snap decision." I tried to sound reasonable, but I was already becoming concerned that this might be a wild goose chase. Still, I was getting paid well to chase this particular untamed bird. "So what is it I'm looking for?"

"The Veil of Isis," she replied simply.

Chapter 4

Angelica's pronouncement sat me back in my seat in surprise and my mind immediately began racing. The last of my personal issues faded into the background as my professional fascination took over. Of all the relics I had imagined I might be sent after, that certainly wasn't one of them. I could immediately see why her group had had so much trouble getting anyone to investigate their case, and I was afraid I might end up in the same camp.

"You are aware that the Veil is considered to be allegorical, and is simply an artistic device to convey the inaccessibility of nature's secrets, I take it? There has never been even any legendary tale of the Veil as a true physical relic, at least as far as I'm aware. The whole idea of 'lifting the veil' simply refers to revealing great truths, and the magickal ceremony of 'rending of the veil' is a ritualistic representation of ascending to a higher state of spiritual or magickal awareness and/or power." I wanted her to understand exactly where we were starting from, and that I might not get any further than that in my enquiries. "I'm going to have significant problems finding an item if it doesn't actually exist."

"I see you are already acquainted with some of the lore regarding the Veil," she responded with a smile such as a promising student might receive from a teacher after getting a difficult question right. "But at least you haven't done what some of your colleagues did and laugh in my face while asking me to leave and stop wasting their time."

"Hey, for a quarter of a million, feel free to 'waste' my whole day if you like!" I laughed in response to her honest admission of the difficulties she had encountered thus far. "Speaking of which, if we're going to keep talking, my throat's getting dry. Can I offer you some coffee? It's my own personal blend."

"Coffee would be lovely," she said with a grin. "Is that the blend I smelled when I came in?"

"Absolutely," I replied, "we always put a pot on to start the day. I'll be back in just a moment. Feel free to continue your perusal of my collection in the meantime." I smiled, and walked around my desk to the door, heading into the kitchen to get the refreshments.

"Everything OK in there?" Summer asked as I came out, hovering as usual in case I needed her. "She's not playing any more of her psychic games, is she? I'll happily apply some 'cognitive recalibration' if she is!" She gleefully quoted Scarlett Johansson's Black Widow from the film Avengers Assemble (her personal heroine, and significant celebrity crush).

"Not necessary, Miss Romanov," I replied with a laugh, as I usually did. "We've moved past that, and we're actually getting down to brass tacks now. While I make some coffee, just log into the transaction database record, and see if her deposit has cleared, would you?" I thought I might as well take the opportunity to check I wasn't being taken for a complete fool.

I set up a tray with a cafetière of Cafegeddon, two cups, cream, sugar and sweeteners. As I went to pick it up I heard a gasp and a yelp from Summer.

"Holy crap!" She swore loudly. "What the fuck are you doing for her for this?"

"Language, Summer, we have a client in the office." I struggled valiantly to keep the laughter out of my voice. "I take it the transaction cleared then, and the bank account is correspondingly healthy?"

"That's one way of putting it!" she almost shouted "I can't wait to see my Christmas bonus this year with this taken into account!" I couldn't help it, I had to put the tray back down to laugh at her audacity. Her tone had completely changed after such a lavish demonstration of intent from our new client.

"Trust you!" was all I could sputter after I managed to draw breath. "Right, I'm going back to the client now. Keep an eye on the shop." I picked up the tray again and went to head into the office.

"Oh, no problems, boss. For that, she can stay all day. Just remember, the customer is always right, so whatever she wants she can have. Don't forget, the bed upstairs is fully made up if needed!" She fired that parting shot as she closed the door behind me and I was left staring at Angelica, who was over by one of the bookcases with a Calvin and Hobbes compendium in her hands (gotta love a woman who appreciates fine literature!). I felt my face flush as she raised her eyebrows at Summer's final quip.

"Well, there's an offer I didn't expect to hear from your assistant!" she remarked with as wide a smile as I'd yet seen from her, "but I think we should keep this professional for now, don't you? Still, it's nice to know she's warmed up to me a little." I nearly dropped the tray as I tried to keep from laughing.

"I think her potential share of the retainer your group very kindly deposited has had more to do with it than anything!" I laughed finally, having safely negotiated the tray onto my desk. "How do you take your coffee?"

"Cream and one sweetener, please," she replied.

"I'll just give it a few minutes to brew, then I'll pour," I said, trying to get back into my safer, more professional mind-set after Summer had effectively derailed my equilibrium. "Good coffee should never be rushed. Meanwhile, let's address your enquiry again. Have you come across some documentation that leads you to think the Veil may be a genuine physical item? At least something that might give me an idea of where to start digging?"

At this, Angelica almost looked relieved that someone was listening to her and addressing her case with the appearance of interest and reason, not to mention a degree of professionalism that, from what she had said, had been sorely lacking in her previous attempts to set someone on this trail.

"The group has come into possession of a diary, written by a member of the Theosophical Society who went on a pilgrimage. In it, he talks about following the movements of Helena Blavatsky, the founder of the

Society, as she moved to various cities throughout her life. He says at the end of the diary that although he never saw it himself, discussions had with what he called 'the Keepers of the Veil' had impressed him to a degree he had never thought possible. He states that they had a reverence for it akin to Christians discussing pieces of the True Cross, and they were just as protective of it and reluctant to let anyone touch or even see it. He also mentions that he was told it was 'no simple piece of spun fabric, but a veil the goddess would have been born already possessing.' Several members of our group therefore feel that this indicates it might be what in later times was called a caul." She had referred to notes on her smartphone several times during this recitation, especially for the quotes from the diary. This latest piece of information stopped my thought process in its tracks, and then sent it at high speed down an entirely different route. One which had a potential positive outcome for all concerned.

"I see," I temporised, pouring the coffee as a way to give myself a bit more time to absorb and process the earth-shattering revelation that had just been dropped on me. "That certainly changes the playing field. Of course, you realise that if all the so-called 'True Cross fragments' in the world were joined together, there would be enough wood for about a hundred crucifixes. Charlatans sell fakes to believers every day. It could still be the same with this, if the Veil were even in the possession of the group the writer met. It could just as easily have been an empty reliquary, or if there was something inside, it could have been a fake. That doesn't change the significance to the believers, but it would obviously be important if your group were looking to acquire it and become its new keepers. I doubt you'd be willing to spend millions of pounds for a piece of goat stomach lining! Speaking of which, what is the maximum you'll authorise me to offer if I find this group, and if I think there's a chance it might be genuine?" I was thinking on the fly, but I could certainly see enough avenues of research to justify a retainer, although my usual fee was nowhere near what they had already paid. Their generosity meant that even travel around the world in pursuit of this was on the cards. Who knows, I might be able to make some new contacts and line up new suppliers for the shop while I was at it –two birds with one stone, and all that.

"I'm so glad to see you're at least taking this seriously and addressing it logically. Many of the points you've raised are arguments that several members of the group have already pointed out and are not without merit. We appreciate that it may not actually exist in the final analysis or may be a fake. The potential gain if it's real, however, cannot be ignored. It could open up whole new areas of study and be the gateway to new levels of understanding of the world around us, both scientific and magickal!" Her enthusiasm shone through in this statement and she leant forward in her chair as her arms became more animated in her excitement. When she finished, she reached for the coffee cup I had placed near her and took a long sip to steady herself. As she did, her eyes flew up to meet mine and I watched her pupils dilate in pleasure at the taste.

"That's delicious!" she exclaimed. "You say it's your own blend?"

"Mm-hmm," I replied distractedly, both due to the outpouring of information I was trying to process, and the thought of her eyes dilating in pleasure from other reasons. "I can give you the recipe before you leave, if you like." I clung to the coffee conversation as a means of grounding myself.

"Oh, yes please," she enthused. "I know the group members would appreciate that as much as I would."

"I'll write it down for you before you leave. Now, back to the matter at hand. How much are you prepared to authorise me to offer any potential seller? Bear in mind that you've offered me the same again plus two million, so the more I offer, the more I get for myself. Also, please keep in mind that the unique nature of this item will make it exceptionally desirable to anyone and an object of worship to many, so it won't come cheap. Just how deep are the pockets of this group you represent?"

"Fair points all, but we are confident that your reputation for honesty and fairness are well earned so you'll make the best deal for us you can. That being said, you are absolutely correct in your assessment of the desirability of the Veil and the potential cost involved. As such, you are authorised up to fifty million. Beyond that, you'll need to get in contact to discuss things further."

The cool, nonchalant way in which she threw out such a figure had me reeling. If it cost that much, it would mean my fee would be fifty-two million, on top of the quarter of a million they had already advanced me! I could retire if I wanted. I could get rid of the 'New Age' rubbish from my store and concentrate on the genuine magickal side. I could even employ people with confirmed magickal ability to try and help me unlock my own powers and teach me to use them! Of course, all that depended on the Veil turning out to be real and on my being able to acquire it.

"That's... very trusting of you. I hope I can prove worthy of that trust." I barely avoided stammering in my excitement. "Just one final question regarding the enquiry in general, before I ask a few specifics. You mentioned that there might be others looking for the Veil. Any idea who?"

"There was a man we approached early on in our attempts to find someone to look into this for us, a well reputed doctor of occult studies. His name is –"

"Dr Ciarán Heffernan" I interrupted her with a sinking feeling in the pit of my stomach and a rush of fear at having to deal with him again. He and I had had previous dealings and I had always felt a sense of inferiority due to his abilities, plus his resultant greater success and acclaim, despite my superior intellect and height. "I can understand why you went to him; he's the foremost accredited expert on occult and magickal phenomena in the UK. It's made him extremely wealthy and extremely arrogant. Coupled with his total disregard for other people's feelings and almost obsessive need to accumulate rare and powerful artefacts, it's no surprise to me that he refused to help you but used your enquiry as a starting point for his own search. Knowing him, with his resources, he's probably three steps ahead of us already." My mind was already racing with ideas on how to potentially catch up with Heffernan's head start.

"How much did you tell him before he said no?" I asked. "I need to know where he's starting from."

"Just that we were searching for the Veil of Isis," she replied, already looking disheartened by my knowledge of the man and my description of his less than stellar personality traits.

"Thank the gods for that!" I exclaimed. "Did you mention the Theosophical Society or Madam Blavatsky?"

"No, fortunately he laughed me out of his office simply for mentioning the Veil," she said, "so he'll be starting from scratch. I also know that the group has agreed to keep the diary totally confidential and locked away until all avenues of enquiry have been exhausted, so there's no way he'll be able to get access to it."

"In that case, we have a chance to get ahead of him. Without the diary to point him towards Blavatsky's life and movements, there's nothing to indicate that the Veil is even a real artefact. Plus, with the comments from the diary, there are a few places we can rule out from the outset, like the Society's London headquarters. It's far more likely to have been located in Eastern Europe or even the Far East, where Helena fully awakened her psychic and spiritual abilities." I was skimming through Wikipedia on the Microsoft Surface on my desk for information on Helena Blavatsky's life for clues while we were talking.

I noted that she had suffered a fall from a horse in Mingrelia which had led to a spinal fracture and a coma lasting several months. It was on reviving from this coma that her paranormal abilities had fully awakened, and her spiritual odyssey to gain better control had begun. This, then, would be my starting point. While I was online, I downloaded a copy of Blavatsky's seminal work titled Isis Unveiled to my Kindle for further reference on my quest. I relayed to Angelica what I had found and my reasoning behind my chosen beginning, and her excitement was evident.

"It sounds as though you've already made some important strides in your search," she enthused. "I look forward to hearing more as you update me. For now, I'll leave you to plan your trip."

"Before you go," I halted her departure, asking something that had been bugging me about this whole thing, "may I ask why you need to pay someone to look into this for you? I've done about five minutes of research on the internet and I already have a starting point. How is it that such a clearly well-funded organisation can't spare one of their own staff to do the searching for them?" She nodded at my logic and smiled at my insight. I was also proud of the fact that my attraction to her and my excitement at the prospect of the money hadn't dulled my common sense.

"The group has sent a few people but they didn't get very far," she replied, "and they don't have anyone else who is familiar with this kind of research and investigation who they feel is competent enough to be trusted with something this important. They also decided to get someone dispassionate without any ulterior motives to assess things for them." I nodded in understanding and felt a sense of challenge to succeed where others had either failed or refused to believe.

She stood up and accepted the business card I handed her, looking amused as she did so.

"Surely you've realised by now that we have all these details," she remarked, amused.

"Turn it over." I smirked in return. She did so, her superior expression immediately converting to a beaming grin as she read the list of different coffees that made up my blend.

She inclined her head in thanks and turned to leave. I heard her wish Summer a pleasant day as she passed, and my eyes fell on her gloves, forgotten on the corner of my desk. I grabbed them and hurried after her, asking Summer which way she had headed out of the door.

"Left," she replied, looking on in amusement as I almost stumbled in my haste to catch up. I pulled the door open, hearing the bell chime brightly as I did so, and turned to my left to search for the distinctive outline of my client, but she was gone. As I walked back into the shop, I felt a lump in the left glove. I shook it out and found the rose quartz pendant she had been wearing, along with a note:

"Wear this during your search. You may find you need it."

Chapter 5

"Did you catch her?" Summer asked from behind the counter. When I didn't answer immediately, she looked up from the computer and asked, "What have you got there?"

"She left her gloves on my desk," I replied distractedly, turning the pendant over in my hand and wondering why Angelica would have left it, and what her cryptic note might indicate. I knew rose quartz was often used for protection, but it had no inherently magickal abilities as far as I knew. Unless... had this been provided by her group? She had said they had magick users in their midst, as evidenced by her display when she arrived, and they knew what they were sending me after and who I would be up against. Could they have imbued it with a genuine protection charm? Suddenly, one of the dusters we kept by the register to give crystals a quick polish when we sold them came flying towards my head.

"OI, CLOTH EARS!" I jumped, realising I had been standing in the middle of the shop lost in thought and had completely ignored Summer's questions. "I said, I can see the gloves. What's that in your hand?"

"She left her rose quartz pendant for me in one of the gloves and said I should wear it while I search for the artefact they want," I replied. "I'm not sure why." Summer's eyes rose to the heavens, as if asking why men were so stupid, why I in particular was so unbelievably dense, and why it should be her cruel and unusual punishment to try to beat some sense into my skull.

"Well duh!" she replied with a long-suffering sigh. "It's perfectly obvious why she's done it!" I hated when she used feminine logic against me –there's not a man alive who truly understands women and their various thought processes. We can come close occasionally, but as soon as we think we've got it nailed they'll change direction and do something we never expected, so we're suddenly back to square one again.

"OK, oh wise and powerful oracle of all things X-chromosome'd, enlighten me with your Sapphic wisdom!" I laughed, wishing I was being sarcastic, but in reality looking for a glimmer of hope that I might see Angelica again.

"The rose quartz pendant will be for protection. She said her group has magick users, so there'll be more to it than meets the eye."

"Yeah, even my Neanderthal male brain worked that one out, genius!" This time the sarcasm was very real. I didn't want her to think I was a total moron. "But why leave the gloves? Why hide the pendant where I might have missed it?"

"Men!" Summer said, in that classically female way that indicates all the millennia of exasperation felt by their gender. "No subtlety at all. She left the gloves as an excuse to come back and see you. She likes you, in case you missed the glaringly obvious. Leaving the pendant inside the glove ensures you find it with the note, and it's more romantic and mysterious, so you start thinking about her again, just like you've already done. Get out of your own way and see that you're a gorgeous, smart guy. She saw it too and she's interested because of it."

"I was out of the room for two minutes getting coffee. She thought all that up in two minutes?" Summer shook her head at my inability to grasp even the simplest concepts.

"She no doubt had the pendant from the group already, to provide help to whoever accepted their commission. The rest was decided when she met you."

I felt like I was back in school, asking my friend if he thought a girl liked me. I had the same fluttering in the pit of my stomach, the same giddy feeling of euphoria, the same sense of unreality. But I had to set all that aside for now. Summer saw the smile slip from my face and my resumption of 'work mode'.

"So, what are they sending you after, or can't you say?" she asked. She was well used to requests to keep an enquiry confidential, knowing that I fully believed that the more people who knew a secret, the less likely it was to remain secret. She also knew I had absolute confidence in her discretion and trustworthiness, but it was a point of pride with us that if a client asked for discretion and confidentiality, that was what they got.

"Not this time, hun," I said apologetically. "They want this kept close to the vest. And to be honest, you're probably better off not knowing. I'm up against Heffernan again on this one, and we both know he's got no scruples when it comes to getting what he wants. I doubt he'd come after you, but if you don't know anything, he's got no reason to. He knows well enough how we work, so he wouldn't be at all surprised that I kept this from you. I'll tell you once it's over." She nodded, but her eyes had widened at the mention of the doctor.

"You know, I looked his name up once to see what the Gaelic meaning was," she remarked. "With him being in your field, and being such a nasty piece of work, I wanted to know a bit more about him. His first name, Ciarán, means 'little dark one', and Heffernan apparently means 'descendant of little demon'. Put those together with his interest in the occult, and you've got an interesting mix that is more than a little disturbing. Watch your back, and for gods' sake wear that pendant. Wire it to that stupid Thor's hammer that you never take off or something."

I lifted my necklace out from under my shirt and looked at it. It was a pewter Mjolnir with Odin and his ravens on it, something I'd been wearing for a number of years now. It was on a heavy silver chain, in the style called a king's chain, and I was very fond of it. I only took it off to go through airport security checkpoints, as the pewter set off the metal detectors.

"Fine," I said and unwound some of the wire making up the loop at the top of the pendant. I threaded it through the top of my Mjolnir and snugged the crystal up behind the hammer. I then used the rest of the wire I had unwound to encircle both pendants, binding them together firmly with the rose quartz resting against my skin. Summer looked on in approval.

"Right then. Are you starting with the books, or do you already know where you're heading?" she asked, getting into logistical mode. I swear, if the army ever got hold of this girl, they could plan a successful invasion of the entire Middle East in three hours —and be ready to leave in four!

"I did some research while we were talking," I replied, "and her group has already provided some, too. Airport, here I come. I Just need to dash home and get a few essentials. My bag is already packed with most of it, as always. I'll book my ticket on my phone on the way to the airport, that way you can't even be made to tell someone where I've gone to start searching. The shop's in your hands 'til I get back, as usual."

I ducked back into the office to grab my Surface. I much preferred it to my old laptop, as it was smaller and lighter. Then I headed out again. I waved on my way out the door and headed to my trusty little Suzuki Jimny. I already had my keys in my hand and was reaching for the door handle when I heard the oily voice I'd been dreading.

"So, they really scraped the bottom of the barrel. I guess no one reputable would take their commission. Still, if you've got no scruples and you're desperate for money, you can justify searching for something that doesn't exist and getting paid for it." My heart sank. How the hell had he found out I'd been contacted, and how the hell had he gotten here so fast? "It's called magick, dear boy. You must have at least heard of it in your line of work, even if you yourself are so pitifully mundane you can't even manage a simple tracking spell."

"Heffernan," I began, knowing he hated people forgetting his PhD.

"That's DOCTOR Heffernan, you jumped-up librarian!" he hissed. "Why they ever came to you is beyond me. Well, actually it's not. As I said, they must have exhausted all the qualified professionals, so resorted to the dregs of the business." My stomach clenched as he belittled my professional standing, my own neuroses threatening to rise up in agreement.

"Then why are you watching me and following me?" I retorted, mentally shaking off my negative thoughts and fully prepared to spend a few minutes with him to piss him off. It was also greatly reassuring to find him here —it meant he'd found nothing in his literature searches, so had no idea where to start. I was in with a shot! I just had to find a way to stop him from following me. As I thought that, the rose quartz grew warm against my skin. My eyes flew over to Heffernan, to see him staring at me and mouthing something under his breath. His frown deepened as the crystal grew warmer, and I laughed as my suspicions regarding the pendant were confirmed.

"Ehhh, what's up, Doc?" I asked cheerfully, channelling my inner Bugs Bunny while leaning back against my car. I suddenly realised that he must have been lying –if Angelica had been wearing this pendant, he'd never have been able to put a tracking spell on her. He'd have failed the same as he just had with me. He must have resorted to tracking her car or something else just as mundane, which I knew would have infuriated him, as he felt himself to be above such things. I made a mental note not to use my own car once I got home. He practically snarled at me in his frustration and spat on the ground near my shoes.

"So they gave you some kind of protection charm. Big deal. You'll never find the Veil; it doesn't exist!" He sniffed dismissively.

"Then you have nothing to worry about," I replied calmly. "And yet here you are, following the so-called 'dregs of the business' like some stray mutt hoping for scraps." I relished the chance to turn the tables on him with my insults, knowing that he hated anyone to get the better of him. Also, from what I had studied on magick usage, any kind of precision required a degree of clarity of thought that his rage would make difficult, if not impossible. The only thing possible without that clarity, according to the books I'd read, was battle magick, but I doubted he'd resort to that before he at least knew what I knew regarding the Veil, or better yet had it physically in his possession. A nasty piece of work, yes. Stupid? Unfortunately not.

"Anyway, I have another appointment to get to, so if you don't mind..." I turned my back on him, now more confident with the protective wards on the quartz pendant. I had completely underestimated Heffernan's willingness to resort to the mundane, however. He grabbed my shoulder, spun me around and shoved me back against my car.

"Don't you turn your back on me, you piece of shit!" He was almost screaming in my face in his frustrated anger. "You're not going anywhere until you tell me what I want to know. What did that bitch tell you that convinced you to go scuttling off after her bullshit story? Where the fuck are you going?"

"Careful Doctor!" I cautioned him. "Your painstakingly maintained façade of manners is slipping. If you keep this up, people might get the idea that you're not the high-born gentleman you profess to be. I'm sure you'd hate for people to find out you were born in the East End of London out of wedlock to a mother on the dole." This was the final straw for him, as I knew it would be. He'd kept his origins a closely guarded secret, but I'd done some digging on him when he'd stolen a series of clients from me several years ago, just to let me know he could. I'd found out about his birth mother, where he grew up, how he'd dragged himself out of poverty by winning a scholarship to a decent school but had never lost the chip on his shoulder regarding his lowly background. That had twisted him, resulting in the selfish, self-entitled bastard of today.

He completely lost control at my final verbal jab and swung a wild punch at my head. I, however, had never had the benefit of defending myself with magick, so I had started learning karate at the age of twelve. I'd loved it, and had kept training ever since, resulting in the wiry, well-muscled physique that I currently enjoyed. I executed a simple but well-timed grabbing block, pulled him in and stepped through, finishing with the second part of my two-part personal move which was an elbow strike aimed straight at his face. I stopped a millimetre from his cheekbone and watched him stumble backwards in shock at the realisation that without his magick, I could take him apart without breaking a sweat. I felt a swell of satisfaction at getting the better of the bullying little shite.

"Now go away, you obnoxious midget," I taunted him, relishing his helplessness and knowing it infuriated him that he had to look up to me, at least physically. "And there's no point bugging Summer; I've deliberately not told her anything, to protect her from you. Plus, she'll be sleeping at the shop, protected by its wards –which you've tested before –until I get back. Meep meep!" I finished, this time calling on my inner Roadrunner as I continued the cartoon theme, just to piss him off. Heffernan ground his teeth in frustration as I closed off every avenue I could think of. I then simply got into the car and drove away. As soon as I turned the corner, I hit the voice dial button on my Bluetooth headset. "Call Summer, mobile." As soon as she answered I told her what had happened.

"Call Emily and get her to bring enough clothes for both of you for a couple of weeks. You stay at the shop, use the shopping app to get groceries delivered, and you both stay safe until this is done. I don't want that bastard getting near you." I thanked the gods that my friend who'd made the shelving for the office had gotten his wife to engrave the symbols. She was a low-level general magick user. I'd met her when she had come into the shop asking about a certain volume she needed and we'd become friends as a result of her ongoing studies into the arcane. Her true speciality, however, was in protection spells, and she'd used all her talents to provide the shop with wards against everything she could think of. As long as you had no aggressive intentions, you were fine (hence Summer repeatedly being able to throw dusters at my head when I ignored her or zoned out), but gods help you if you came in with mayhem in mind. You'd get zapped but good, and probably walk out with a permanent afro and singed nasal hair, or worse. The feedback was proportional, and could literally knock you out, from what she'd said.

"We'll be fine, Gav," she reassured me. "I know the drill. Now get going and get that whatever it is before that bottom-feeding scum-sucker. Oh, and I'll keep the champagne on ice for when you get back –if we don't drink it in a nice bubble bath first!" She giggled and I laughed, knowing her plans for the night had just been set.

"I'll keep in touch," I promised and hung up, heading for home.

Chapter 6

I soon reached home, which was a nice two-bedroom apartment in a discrete new development in a small village less than half an hour's drive from Doncaster. I'd gotten it cheap by being the first to sign up before they were even finished. The company had been allocated cash incentives from the local council to get people moved in as they were trying to revitalise the area. My neighbours were mostly new couples in their first home, or single professionals like myself who worked in the city. Some of my favourite features were the secure underground parking with bays numbered for your unit so there was no fighting for a space, and the key-operated lift to get into the building. If you didn't have a key fob you couldn't get into the garage, and if you didn't have a key you couldn't get into the lift. It was a small complex so we all knew each other at least by sight, and if you didn't belong here no one would just let you up to "drop in on a friend".

I raced out of the lift on my floor, unlocked my door and headed inside, making sure to shut the door behind me. Despite the security of the building, I was still paranoid about being burgled. I grabbed my bag, threw in my shaving bag which also had my toothbrush and other necessities – what my father had always called his 'wet pack' when he went on business trips –and grabbed my passport. Fortunately, as Brexit hadn't happened yet, I didn't need to worry about a visa for Eastern Europe. Furthermore, I doubted the flights would be overbooked as it was still term-time for schools, so peak holiday season was still some weeks away.

I called a taxi and told the driver to take me to the train station. Call me old-fashioned, but I still didn't have an Uber account. Once at the station, I bought a ticket to London on the next train, which was in just twenty minutes, and used the time to buy myself a Subway sandwich to eat on the way.

I went to the platform to wait and used the time to look up a cheap flight to Georgia. Thene best-known airport was Tbilisi, but Batumi airport looked to be closer to the historical state of Mingrelia, so I booked my ticket for that destination. I had always had to fly economy before, but with the money from Angelica's group, I wanted to avoid 'cattle class' if I could. I couldn't justify first-class, or even business class, but a slight upgrade to World Traveller Plus seemed reasonable, and the extra space would be very welcome. I paid for the ticket on the company card and made a note which terminal of Heathrow I needed. The next available flight was a night flight, so I had about eight hours to get to Heathrow and check in, then get through security. Having made the trip numerous times before, I knew I could be sitting in the departure lounge in about five hours from now, so that worked out nicely.

The train pulled in and I quickly found my seat. I'd managed to secure a table seat, so I set up my Surface, plugged into the train's power, signed into the free Wi-Fi and was researching more on Helena Blavatsky's movements from Mingrelia before the train even left the station.

I was glad that I took the time to do so, because I came across a snippet that I had missed while skimming through earlier. Although she'd fallen from her horse in Mingrelia, she had been in a coma for several months, so she had been moved to Tiflis into what would these days be called a spinal injuries unit. Tiflis was now modern-day Tbilisi. I immediately went online and changed my ticket to a direct flight to Tbilisi International Airport and started researching healthcare in the city. I quickly found they had no specialist spinal injuries unit that Google could locate, so I changed tack.

I looked up medical museums and found that there was one located on Uznadze Street. I could already see I was going to have fun trying to pronounce the names of where I was going –I really hoped the taxi drivers spoke English! The museum had recently been restored and reopened in November 2018. Although it had apparently been established in 1963, and Helena had had her fall in 1864 almost a hundred years earlier, the museum would be my best chance of finding out where she would have been likely to be sent for treatment of that kind of injury, so it would be my first stop.

That decided, I made a couple of notes on her next stops, which according to Wikipedia were in Italy, Transylvania and Serbia. I could definitely see the frequent flyer miles racking up on this trip. I then decided to download a copy of Blavatsky's Isis Unveiled: A Master Key. I opened my Kindle to look on the store, saw the copy I had downloaded earlier, then laughed at myself for being so taken with Angelica that I had lost track of my own actions. I found that Blavatsky had originally titled the work The Veil of Isis, and there were two volumes. The first apparently dealt with the more mystical side while the second was more theological, concerned with the comparison between Christianity and other Eastern religions. I decided that only volume one would be likely to give me any useful answers regarding my search, but I would read both volumes in case there were references of importance in the second volume. Also, I'd be in the air a lot over the next few days, so I might as well have something to read.

I could be a bit of a snob when it came to my collection, especially for mystical and occult volumes. I think there is an intrinsic magick in physical volumes that can't be replicated digitally, but for times such as this, e-books were a gift. The ability to carry hundreds or even thousands of books on my reader meant I always had something with me. For research it was also beyond useful, with the ability to do word searches in a text speeding up the process. I still always read a couple of pages either side of a reference, as you never knew what nugget of information you might miss. Bearing in mind the care with which the Theosophical Society had pored over this manuscript for the last century, I doubted I'd find any obvious clues, but in light of the information from the diary, I might be able to put a new interpretation on some of the references. As such, I was probably going to have to read it all if I wanted to be sure not to miss anything important.

By this time, we were getting close to London, so I shut my Surface down and got ready to negotiate the maze of London's Underground. I had used it several times, but the variation in schedules, different lines running through the same stations and different branches running through the same platforms, all combined to make it a place where one wrong turn could have you ending up on entirely the wrong side of the city. As the train drew into Kings Cross, I made a snap decision: I had the retainer now so I was going to take a black cab. They were always lined up outside and it would be direct to the terminal. It would also be harder to follow me than on a crowded tube, where a potential tail could simply hide in the crush.

I stepped down from the carriage and as I did so, I felt someone grab my bag and try to drag it from my hand. I tightened my grip and turned to see someone in a green hoodie. The guy had long, greasy black hair hanging out from under his hood, and cheap plastic sunglasses obscuring his face. I assumed he must have seen my Surface when I was on the train, then thought he'd grab it to make a quick buck.

I had no intention of just letting some scumbag run off with my stuff, so I yanked my bag towards me to break his grip. This clearly wasn't his first time, as he quickly pulled out a knife. Whether he was planning to cut me, or just the handle of my bag, I had no idea but I didn't wait to find out. I started pulling the bag in different directions to throw him off balance and keep the knife away from me, then as he staggered I stomped on his knee, hearing a crack as it flexed the wrong way.

He let out a high-pitched, piercing shriek which quickly drew the attention of the platform guard. The guard rapidly sized up the situation and radioed for the transport police, telling me to stay put and also asking some of my fellow passengers to wait as well, as witnesses. Most just kept their heads down and kept walking, clearly wanting nothing to do with this, but one elderly lady agreed to say what she had seen.

The police officer grasped the matter very speedily, taking us to his office in the station. I gave my statement, corroborated by the woman with me who was apparently on her way to see her new grandson. The station cameras also verified everything we said, so there was no question that I had acted in self-defence. I also showed the officer my karate club membership card to explain the effectiveness of my actions.

With the overwhelming evidence in my favour, the asshole who had tried to mug me was quickly arrested. The new grandma and I said our goodbyes, and the last I saw of my would-be attacker was of him crying in pain as he waited for the ambulance to take him to the hospital in handcuffs.

It had taken a couple of hours to get everything straightened out, but I still had plenty of time to catch my flight. I walked out to the taxi rank and waited my turn, soon enough reaching the front of the line and climbing into a cab decorated blue and pink.

The cabbie was a cheerful old guy, and we chatted about the disgraceful state of the English cricket team as we wound through the back streets and short-cuts known only to those blessed with "The Knowledge". This is the teaching all black cab drivers have to go through to learn those routes not usually taken by the masses that cut down on journey time to maximise their profits. That was why, in London, I never used any other taxis.

As we went, my memory suddenly prodded me with the reminder that the recording of my meeting with Angelica hadn't been transcribed, and I didn't want Summer doing it as it would immediately put her in possession of knowledge I was deliberately trying to protect her from. I quickly rang her on the shop phone.

"Dinas Affaraon, how can I help?" Summer's cheerful voice immediately reassured me that Heffernan hadn't attempted to get to her after I'd left.

"It's me," I replied, knowing she'd recognise my voice, "I just remembered something. Can you pull the recording of the meeting this morning off the system and store it on a USB stick please? Make three copies: one for the safe, one for the vault, and you hide the third. Don't listen to it, but make sure it's secured. Thanks sweetie."

"No problem. I'd already copied it to a drive and wiped it from the system after you left –I figured you wouldn't have had time to do it. I'll just make the duplicates and get them locked away."

"You're an angel!" I told her. "I'll catch up with you later." I hung up and relaxed, one more problem off my mind. I briefly considered whether my attempted mugging had really been just a simple random act, or whether Heffernan had somehow had anything to do with it, but I quickly discounted the idea. As far as I knew, he was just an unpleasant guy with a doctorate. He wasn't some underworld mob boss.

I thought about what Angelica had told me about the diary, and how the writer had described the owners of the artefact as the "Keepers of the Veil". The description was of a religious reverence bordering on fanaticism, which didn't fit with a medical facility. I was beginning to think I would be wasting my time in Tbilisi, but I had no Idea where in Italy she had gone from there. I was hoping that by finding out where she had been treated, I might be able to track down more information on her next port of call.

The drive to Heathrow passed in a blur as my mind raced down various possible avenues of research, but none seemed overly promising. I decided to simply go to Tbilisi, go to the medical museum, see what I could find and go from there. I looked out of the window, satisfied that my plan at least had a degree of merit, however small, and saw that we were just coming off the motorway to head to the airport. We drew up to the terminal drop-off point, and I paid the cabbie, thanking him for a smooth ride.

As I entered the air-conditioned comfort of the terminal, my skin crawled and it had nothing to do with the cool air. Heffernan was standing near the automated check-in machines, and he was looking right at me with a self-satisfied smile on his smug face. How had he known? I had left my car at home in case he had tracked it, I knew his tracking spell on me had been repelled by the pendant, and he couldn't have put anything on...

My mind flashed back to our encounter, and his uncharacteristic attempt at violence. I reached up to my shirt collar and sure enough there was a small GPS dot, widely available on the internet or at spy shops, tucked underneath. The bastard had tagged me when he grabbed my shoulder, meaning that the rest had just been an act to distract me. He must have seen where I was headed, then beaten me here thanks to my two-hour delay at the train station.

I was fuming, and I threw the dot to the ground and stamped hard, looking at him as I did so. His smile simply widened, and he shrugged, indicating he didn't care about the dot now that he'd tracked me this far. I was going to make sure he didn't get near me or my bag again, and I'd be looking out for anyone he might have hired to try to tag me, too.

Resigned to the fact that he knew I was leaving the country, I walked over to the machines but stopped short, and looked over towards the airport employee stationed near the end machine to help those newbie travellers and tech haters who were unfamiliar with the process or just struggled with technology in general. I could play that role.

I walked over to him, and played the whole 'I hate machines, what happened to personal service' bit to the hilt, told him how nice it was to see someone prepared to help, and had him laughing along with me in no time. I always found it easier to talk to men, as there was no worry about the kind of judgement or rejection that there could be with a woman. I made sure not to mention my destination out loud and was careful to block the screen from Ciarán's sightline. I wanted to be sure he wouldn't be able to follow me, but as I walked away, I looked back and cursed. Heffernan had walked straight up to the assistant and used his psychic abilities to read his mind, immediately finding out where I was going. He turned to look at me, mouthed "See you soon," and headed off to the ticket desk, no doubt to buy a first-class ticket on the same aircraft as me. As soon as we were airborne, he'd certainly do a search to cross reference Tbilisi with the Veil of Isis and rapidly come up with Helena Blavatsky's name, the Theosophical Society link, and the title of her work. My heart sank.

It immediately lifted again as I remembered the one crucial piece of information he didn't have: the diary! How could I have forgotten that? I immediately sent Angelica a text message explaining what had happened with Heffernan. I also asked her to go to the group to get permission to look at the diary. I wanted her to go through and find out which exact locations the follower had visited. It would also be helpful to know when in his travels he encountered the Keepers. If I could cut out some of the steps in the journey, I could still stay one step ahead of that slimy bastard Ciarán! I asked her to email me the results, and to double-encrypt the message for security. I told her to use the name I had given her as the first password, and the name of the book that she had been reading when I returned to the office as the second password. Hopefully that would be secure enough.

I relaxed, getting out my Kindle and deciding to read a novel rather than Isis Unveiled, and chose to reread The Inheritance Cycle by Christopher Paolini. I loved the books and liked to read the descriptions of some of the main character's magickal training, in the hope that one day I might be able to put some of it to use. Fortunately, with Heffernan refusing to mingle with 'the common folk', he would be in the first-class lounge until boarding, so I wouldn't have to see him until Tbilisi. I was always reluctant to go through security too early, as then I would be stuck in the departure lounge and at the mercy of airport prices. Instead, I always did most of my waiting before the checkpoints, only checking my bag and negotiating security when absolutely necessary.

I was deep into my book when I became aware of my phone vibrating. I pulled it out of my pocket and swiped it awake, unlocking it with the print of my left ring finger. I didn't use the fingerprint lock most of the time but had taken the precaution of engaging it in the cab in case Heffernan got hold of it. I had also decided not to use my right index finger as an added layer of security. I refrained from taking off my shoes and socks and using a toe print as that just made using the phone for routine things next to impossible, or at best a serious pain in the ass, not to mention looking completely ridiculous.

I saw that I had an email from Angelica and immediately felt my heart skip a beat. Then I remembered that I'd asked her for information so this would be work, not personal. The corresponding dip in my excitement told me all I needed to know about how infatuated I already was. I would have to work to stay professional and not let those feelings develop. Man, maybe I just needed to go and get laid! It had been a while, and I'd cock-blocked myself last night with Summer's friend. Or more accurately her astounding attitude had removed any trace of lead from my pencil!

Putting my hormones aside for the moment, I got my Surface out of my carry-on and set it up. I checked that I was at the back of the waiting area, so no one could peer over my shoulder. I went into my emails and saw the one from Angelica was password-protected. Damn, that woman worked fast. Then I mentally kicked myself and realised they had probably already been through the diary for exactly this information and were astounded it had taken me this long to ask for it. I put it down to my excitement at a potential financial windfall and the interest in a previously undiscovered arcane artefact of immense power and significance (my frustrated testosterone had nothing to do with it!). That was my story and I was sticking to it.

I entered the two passwords, smiling as I remembered her standing in my office reading Calvin and Hobbes, then opened the body of the email.

Chapter 7

There was a brief message and an attachment, which I hoped had some useful information. I must confess, I was more interested in seeing what Angelica had said to me than I was in reading the information from the diary. All she had written, however, was that the group had indeed gone through the diary, but it had not yielded any clear indications as to the location of the Veil. The only information she could give me was that it wasn't until after the writer had reached Tibet that any religious or mystical language had crept in. She had received permission from the group to scan and send the pages from that time until the mention of the Keepers, starting from the arrival in Tibet. Those pages were the attached document.

My heart sped up for an entirely different reason now. Once again, I was in with a chance to get ahead of Ciarán. I shut down my computer and stowed it back in my carry-on, then raced to the desk and immediately asked about flights to Tibet. There was one leaving just half an hour after the Tbilisi flight –thank the gods that London was such a major international travel hub! I cancelled my original ticket, getting no refund as it was too close to the flight and I had already checked in. The computer was updated that I would not be on the flight, so that at least made sure there would be no calls put out for my name, which might alert Heffernan that I wasn't on board. I handed my now useless ticket to the brunette behind the counter and she shredded it. I then purchased a ticket on the Tibet flight. I again upgraded, although this time to business class as the flight was smaller so the World Traveller Plus option wasn't available.

I took my ticket and elected to go through security immediately as it was now closer to the departure time. I checked my main bag, keeping hold of my carry-on with my electronics. I negotiated security without needing, as a friend of mine often put it, "pre-lubing with lavender-scented gel for extra soothing". I had felt curiously vulnerable when I removed my necklace with its new quartz addition, so retrieved it and put it back on as soon as possible. As I put it back on, I could swear I felt a comforting warmth settle over my shoulders. I was a little excited at this, as it was the first time I had been aware of the presence of magick in an object, although I then second-guessed myself into thinking I was just imagining it. I had obviously felt it warm up when Ciarán tried his tracking spell, but I had felt nothing from it when I first held it. Then again, I had been more concerned with Angelica at the time.

I went from security down the escalator to the departure lounge and decided to wander around some of the duty-free shops while I waited. As I walked, I looked up towards the balcony where the entrance to the first-class lounge could be seen. Standing there, looking down on me with all the superiority he could muster, was Heffernan. I waved at him and smiled, which immediately wiped the smile off his face in response. I knew he was annoyed that he hadn't unsettled me by his presence, but I was savouring the thought of him stuck in Tbilisi with no idea where I had gone once he landed and found I wasn't on the plane.

With that cheerful thought in mind, I went to the nearby shop and bought a couple of bottles of flavoured water, then sat down and got my Kindle out to continue reading. When I saw the Tbilisi flight was getting ready to board, I checked which gate the Tibet flight was going to be boarding and nearly laughed out loud when I found it was at the next gate. I made my way there, to find that the sitting area was shared between the two gates, so I was in the right place to both wait for my own flight and make Heffernan think I was waiting for his.

Right on cue, the smug bastard sauntered past me to board with the rest of the first-class passengers, making sure to be heard as he called out his derogatory comments.

"It's so nice not to have to push and shove like an animal. I do so pity those who can't afford decent seats, stuck in the back like livestock."

I knew it was aimed at me, but several other passengers looked at him and I heard angry mutterings in response.

"Fucking smug rich prick."

"He needs a slap."

And my personal favourite came from just behind me.

"I hope I walk past him as we board. I'm gonna fall on him and spill his free drink all over him as I get up." This last comment was especially amusing, as the speaker was a lady who could kindly be described as 'cuddly', or who a harsher person would call morbidly obese. I savoured the image of Ciarán being squashed under her more-than-ample buttocks.

When my own flight was called, I boarded and found my seat easily as the flight was only partially filled. As it was my first time travelling business class, I was pleased to find the little pack with socks, a mask, toothbrush and paste, decent headphones, lip balm, a nicer pillow and blanket —there was no way I was travelling economy ever again after this, and I blessed Angelica for the chance to experience the difference. I knew that first-class would be another jump, but I couldn't justify the extra cost. The plane should arrive at the same time regardless of how much one paid, and while a little extra leg room and a few amenities were nice, paying through the nose for the chance to put your feet up was an unnecessary expenditure. Unless, of course, I got the multi-million pound commission from Angelica's group. Then to hell with it, it would be first-class all the way, baby!

The stewardess looking after me was young and cute, but I still had Angelica's image fresh in my mind so I was pleasant but didn't flirt with her the way I might otherwise have done. I also found that having the image of an attractive woman already in my mind meant I was more comfortable talking to another female. She in turn looked almost relieved not to have yet another businessman hitting on her which, as a result, meant I got my free glass of wine refilled whenever it emptied.

After take-off, we were handed menus for the dinner that would be served later. Wow, in economy you just got asked as the trolley came past, and if they were out of what you wanted it was tough. I chose the chicken rather than the prawn dish as I worried about the freshness. I was offered wine with the meal and when I chose white, I was offered the choice between a Chablis and a Sancerre. I took a moment to think, and the stewardess smiled.

"Why not try both?" she suggested, then handed me both small bottles along with a glass, smiled at me again and moved on. Man, this was definitely the way to travel!

The flight passed smoothly with only a little turbulence. I managed to get at least five hours sleep which was something I'd never managed to do in economy. In the morning, I got a breakfast of cheesy scrambled eggs on bruschetta, while I saw pre-packaged croissants being handed out in economy. I finished my food and used the toothbrush from my pack to freshen up. I had plugged my phone into the charging port in the seat, so it was fully charged now. I packed my charging wire away and made sure my passport and ticket were readily accessible. I packed the little kit from the airline away as well and got ready to land.

The landing was smooth and on time, and the taxi to the gate mercifully short. As we deplaned, the altitude really struck me. Lhasa Gonggar Airport sits at an elevation of 11,713 feet. Airplane cabins are typically pressurised to six to eight thousand feet, and I was used to England which was basically at sea level. As I started walking through the airport, I felt half a lung short. I knew from my research that it was advised to acclimatize for two to three days at around ten thousand feet before going higher, so I booked into a local hotel that was a little lower than the airport, planning to spend a couple of days there and research. I was hoping that my physical condition, thanks to my martial arts training, running and regular swimming, would help me acclimate quickly and smoothly.

I claimed my bag, panting like I'd been swimming for an hour non-stop, and walked out the front of the airport to get a taxi. The driver spoke a few words of English, enough for me to convey the name of the hotel, and we set off. The journey was somewhat unsettling, as it seemed that any traffic laws that existed were viewed more as a challenge by the local drivers than as rules to be obeyed. Also my driver appeared to harbour aspirations of winning a world rally-driving championship and from what I saw, he had definite potential.

We arrived at the hotel and I paid with my card. Fortunately, modern technology appeared to have made it even to the 'Roof of the World' as Tibet was often known. I checked into the hotel, deliberately requesting a suite on the ground floor, and settled in. I set up my Surface and started researching monasteries in the region. I knew from my research into Madam Blavatsky that one of the monasteries she had frequented was the Tashi Lhunpo Monastery in Shigatse. However there was also reference to another monastery where she had translated a number of ancient books from an equally ancient language called Senzar, although she was apparently never allowed inside the monastery itself.

A quick Google search for monasteries in Tibet gave me a list of eighty-five different monasteries. If I had to search all of them, it could take me months to find the right one. There had to be a way to narrow my search and I needed to figure it out before that asshole Heffernan found out where I'd gone and caught up with me.

I counted up the number of monasteries listed in the same region as the Tashi Lhunpo Monastery, as that was the one place specifically named in the Wikipedia article on Madam Blavatsky. There were twelve, which was certainly an improvement, but still too many to check in a short space of time. I found that Tashi Lhunpo itself was in the city of Shigatse, but the list of monasteries I found online just gave regions and religious affiliations, not specific addresses. I went back into Angelica's email and checked the diary pages for any clues, but no monastery names jumped out at me. As it was now approaching lunchtime, I decided to take a break and refresh myself by trying some of the local cuisine.

I found to my surprise that, unlike much of the rest of the area, Tibetan cuisine was eaten with chopsticks in the Chinese style rather than simply by hand. I blessed the fact that I loved Chinese and Japanese food, so I was well used to manipulating chopsticks. In fact, my father had taught me to use them as a child by getting me to pick up salted peanuts, and then ball bearings of incrementally smaller sizes.

I got an order of sha phaley, which was a traditional dish of the area. They were shaped much like empanadas and were cooked by either deep frying or pan frying. The filling was seasoned ground beef and cabbage similar to pierogis but with different spices. I ate quietly and slowly, as this was apparently the custom in Tibet, according to both what I had gleaned from the internet and what I saw for myself. I also made sure to finish what was on my plate, which was certainly no hardship as it was delicious.

Refreshed, but still feeling short of breath, I went back to the hotel room and took a nap. There wasn't much more I could do until I was acclimated to the altitude, so I decided to spend the rest of the day and the following day getting some gentle exercise to help strengthen my lungs and speed up the acclimatization process, interspersed with resting to build up my reserves. I also developed quite a taste for the local cuisine and made a point to try a different dish for each meal. I didn't find even one I didn't like, although the taste of yak took me by complete surprise, being sweeter and juicier than I had expected. I was definitely going to have to try to find some when I went home to England.

On the third day, I woke up finally feeling like I could breathe normally again. I went out early and managed to run five miles without feeling more out of breath than normal, so I felt ready to get on with my investigation. I returned to the hotel and showered, then had breakfast. I decided to keep the room as a base of operation while I was here, but since I'd be out for the whole day, I locked my Surface in the room safe to prevent anyone snooping while I was away. I put some water and trail mix into a backpack I'd picked up the day before in the local market and headed out. I planned to start at the Tashi Lhunpo Monastery and see if they had ever heard of the Veil of Isis, or if they knew anything regarding its lore.

It was time to get back on the trail and kick things up a notch.

Chapter 8

As I left the hotel, the first thing I realised was that I needed a reliable way of communicating with the monks at the monastery. Simply raising my voice and speaking slowly with wild gesticulations in the traditional 'arrogant Westerner' routine simply wasn't going to cut it. I promptly turned around and headed back to the hotel to see if they could help. There didn't seem to be any pamphlets or adverts for local interpreter services, so I spoke to the concierge.

As was to be expected, she spoke perfect English but would be unable to simply leave her post to follow me around for the duration of my search. Fortunately, she knew of several locals who worked as guides. There were a few whom she could recommend, as she had heard good feedback from their clients. The first two she called were already engaged, but the third was currently between clients and happy to act as translator for me. He informed me that he had another booking in a week, so if the search took longer than that he would help me find a replacement. When he told me his rates, I had to use my phone to convert to pounds and it was actually fairly reasonable. I agreed and he formally introduced himself as Yeshe, which meant 'gifted with heavenly knowledge' or wise. Given the nature of my search, I took this as a good omen. Luckily, he lived only a few minutes from my hotel so soon arrived in reception.

Yeshe looked like the archetypal Nepalese mountain guide —no more than five-foot-four, tanned skin, straight black hair, and wearing a woollen coat dyed blue. It was perfectly clear that my Western appearance would stand out here like a sore thumb, so there would be no chance of inconspicuously sneaking in anywhere. I would have to be up front, open and honest with the monks in the hope that they would reciprocate. That was more my speed anyway.

I asked Yeshe whether he was aware of any local legends of powerful artefacts held at any of the monasteries, or whether he had ever heard of the Veil of Isis, and he looked at me strangely. I couldn't be sure if it was because he knew exactly where it was and wasn't sure enough about me to tell me, or because he just thought I was nuts and on some kind of religious scavenger hunt. Still, I had paid him to be my guide and translator, and he struck me as an honourable man who would live up to our bargain.

I said that I wanted to see the Tashi Lhunpo monastery, along with some of the other monasteries in the area and ask a few questions about the Veil as we went. Yeshe told me that Tashi Lhunpo was on the other side of the city. We could either work our way there by stopping at the monasteries we passed, asking questions as we went. Or we could go straight there, and then work our way back if we didn't find what we were looking for.

I didn't think it made much sense to bypass all the other monasteries just to get to Tashi Lhunpo. Bearing in mind that I had no idea which monastery might have the Veil and taking into account my usual lack of good fortune, if we did that it would turn out that the Veil was in the closest monastery. Then again, knowing my luck or lack thereof, if we left Tashi Lhunpo until the end then that's where the Veil would be.

Regardless, I'd never find it just standing around, so we had to make a start. I just hoped that we would find some information as we went, so we'd be able to leap-frog a few of the monasteries and go straight to the Keepers.

It was sunny and cool, the temperature maybe in the mid-teens, so it was perfect weather for walking now that my body was used to the altitude. I made sure to put on plenty of sunblock to prevent getting burned. With the higher altitude, there was less atmosphere to block the sun's UV rays, which was why so many inexperienced travellers to higher climes ended up with nasty sunburns. In fact, when I had been at school, I'd gone on a student exchange trip to France and the family I was staying with had taken me walking in the Pyrenees. I'd worn shorts with no sunscreen, and by the end of the day I'd had blisters all over my lower legs, some almost two inches across.

There was no way I was risking that again. My travel kit always contained a tube of kids factor fifty sunblock, and I made sure my face, ears, neck and exposed arms were coated. I also wore a wide-brimmed walking hat. Yeshe actually looked on with approval as I got myself set for our trek and remarked on my preparations.

"It's good to see someone take proper care here. Many tourists think it's like walking in the woods at sea level, then wonder why they get burned." I felt like the teacher had just given me a gold star and nodded to him in thanks.

"OK Yeshe, you know where we're eventually headed and you know the area. Lead on, sir." I smiled at him, and we set off. Having struck up a reasonable rapport at the hotel, I was a little surprised when we ended up walking in silence. Yeshe was happy to answer questions but fell silent again after answering.

I thought he was somewhat dubious about me at first, but soon realised that I was being somewhat dense. Yeshe was a mountain guide, not a tour guide. His job was to get people safely to their destination and back again, with occasional translation services if required. Most of his clients would be mountain climbers who would be saving their breath for climbing, not chattering like a troop of monkeys.

I fell into quiet reflection as we walked, simply enjoying the day. The atmosphere of Tibet seemed to slowly creep into my mind. I found myself reflecting on some of the religious beliefs of the region, the impact finding a genuine Veil might have on world religions, and what it might mean to me personally.

This led me past the obvious financial independence I would gain into the magickal possibilities it might open up. Isis was the goddess of life and magick to the Egyptians, and she had been powerful enough to even resurrect Osiris, although only for one night. If her Veil was indeed a caul then it would consist of her tissue, which would mean touching it would be like touching a goddess. That alone might be enough to unlock untold powers in even the most mundane person.

The search for the Veil began to take on a whole new perspective, both for myself and for what it might mean if it were handed over to a group already powerful in financial and magickal ways. Even more so if it were found by someone like Heffernan who already had magick and was happy to use it against others to get what he wanted.

The excitement of the initial commission and the promise of the financial rewards, plus the time factor with Ciarán already on the trail, had prevented me from reflecting on all of this initially. Now, however, the simple act of walking, combined with Yeshe's companionable silence, along with the location I was in, was setting my mind free to race down paths I had previously been ignoring.

Could I really turn such an artefact over to a group I knew nothing about? Would it not be better kept locked away and secret, known only to those who would protect and keep it for future generations, but not use it? I started thinking of Chow Yun Fat in the film Bulletproof Monk, protecting a scroll of power but not using it himself. Maybe that was the right way to go.

I still wanted to know if the Veil was real, to see it and even touch it if I could, just to find out if it could unlock that part of me I had tapped into as a child that singular time. I was, however, no longer thinking that handing it over to Angelica's group was the right thing to do. I was certain that Heffernan should never get his hands on it so if it was real, the Keepers had to be warned about him.

I looked up from my introspection to find we had arrived at the first monastery on our trek. I had taken the time to check on local etiquette regarding visiting temples and monasteries while I was waiting around for my body to adjust, so I made sure to adhere to as much as I could remember. I removed my shoes before entering and took off my hat, already having taken the precaution of wearing jeans and a t-shirt with elbow-length sleeves for modesty. I bowed politely to the monk at the door, more in the Japanese style than anything else, as a gesture of respect.

The monk in turn bowed back to me with a beaming smile on his face and waited patiently as I asked Yeshe to enquire about the Veil. The monk looked puzzled and replied that there were many unusual artefacts in different monasteries around the area but that the Veil wasn't one he was familiar with.

I took the time to admire some of the monastery and made a small donation before leaving, earning thanks and a blessing for good fortune for my trouble. Yeshe and I resumed our walk and I was almost pleased not to have had success at the first place we visited, as it would give me a chance to see more of the region and visit more monasteries. They were peaceful places, the monks open and friendly, as long as you showed some respect for their beliefs and customs. Any visit could be either simply pleasant or immensely profound, depending on how deeply you allowed it to affect you.

The next two monastery visits followed the same pattern as the first and I made a small donation at each, earning me the same blessing each time. If they all stacked up like power boosts in a computer game, a few more and I'd find the Veil by dinner! Yeshe and I stopped for something to eat as it was approaching lunch and we had started early. We shared what we had both brought and had a congenial little picnic by the side of the road.

Yeshe was looking at me almost approvingly for the way I had been behaving in the monasteries and I sensed that he seemed to be warming up to my search in view of the way I was approaching it. If he did have any knowledge of the Veil, I was hoping that this might signify a possibility that he would share it with me.

We visited two more monasteries that afternoon, each time with no luck finding any hints regarding the Veil but following the same pattern as the morning visits. Yeshe then said it was time to head back as we had walked quite a way over the course of our search, and it would take some time to get back. We walked back peacefully, until Yeshe startled me by asking a question. It was the first time he had initiated a conversation since we had met.

"This thing you seek, the Veil. Why do you seek it?" he asked. I could tell this was more than just a casual enquiry to fill the silence, so I thought carefully about my answer.

"At first, it was a job. I was hired to find it for others who seek it," I replied, deciding once again that honesty was the best policy. "They had sent others before from their group but none found it. They tried to get other people to search on their behalf but most do not even believe it exists. They offered me a lot of money if I obtained it for them, however

I am now not so sure that it would be a wise course for them to have possession of it. I don't know enough about them to be sure, but any large group has the capacity for some members to use their resources for selfish or destructive ends."

Once I started talking I found it hard to stop, and my reflections of the day seemed to pour out into Yeshe's waiting ear. As I talked, his face went from disappointment at my admission of this being a simple job, to approval of my concern regarding the group and their motives along with my increased respect for the more mystical potential of the Veil. We were walking as I talked, and the sun was dipping as we arrived back at the hotel.

"I know which place we should go to next, so be ready at six tomorrow," Yeshe said as we parted. I nodded at him and thanked him for his help so far.

As I turned to go inside, a taxi came past and my blood ran cold at the sight of the face in the back seat. I would know that oily head and those sharp, scowling, ferret-like features anywhere. I watched as the taxi went further along the street, turning in to one of the more upmarket hotels in the area as I had known it would. I knew my lead had almost run out and I needed to find the Veil tomorrow, or I might never get another chance.

Dr Ciarán Heffernan had arrived in Tibet.

Chapter 9

How the hell had he tracked me down? My mind started racing with questions and scenarios, but unfortunately it didn't have far to run. I knew he would have realised what I was doing when he saw I was heading to Tbilisi —a quick Google search would have shown that I was following the trail of Madam Blavatsky and her link to the Veil of Isis. He no doubt went nuts when he found out I'd managed to ditch him, and then spent the last three days flying from country to country on the list. Or, more probably, ringing around every contact he had to try and track me down. Eventually he had no doubt bribed his way past some poor underpaid airline employee to find out which flight I had taken from Heathrow, thus locating my destination.

My only remaining advantage was that he still had to acclimatize to the Tibetan altitude or risk serious health complications. I might have tomorrow and one more day, but that was it. After that, he'd be right on my heels the whole way. As it was, I knew his first play would be to ring around all the local hotels to find where I was staying.

As soon as I reached that point in my deductions, I ran in to reception, and left word that under no circumstances was anyone to confirm that I was staying here. I told them that there was a wealthy man who wanted what I was searching for and was known to hurt people who got in his way. As I was talking to the receptionist the phone rang, and I overheard a familiar voice asking to be put through to my room. The young lady looked across the desk, smiled at me and said she was sorry but there was no one by that name registered.

I thanked her profusely for my momentary reprieve and headed up to my room. I got my Surface out of the safe and proceeded to further encrypt it with the new facial recognition lockout, determined to prevent that son-of-a-bitch from hacking my tech. I could do nothing about his magickal means, but I would be damned if I was going to make this easy for him. He was unlikely to ever get his hands on my things, but why take the chance?

That done, I fired off an email to Summer, explaining that Heffernan had followed me this far, so she and Emily could relax and stop living above the shop. I knew they'd be glad to get back to their own home, plus I wanted to let them know they were safe and could stop worrying. I also sent Angelica a text to let her know of my progress thus far (or lack thereof) and inform her of the Heffernan development.

Next I took a shower to wash off the dust and sweat of the day, then went to bed. I set my phone to wake me up at half past four so that I could shower and get breakfast before meeting Yeshe at six. I was glad we were starting so early as Ciarán would hopefully be exhausted by the altitude and would therefore likely be asleep, so missing any sign of our departure.

I slept fitfully, plagued by increasingly odd dreams. Heffernan had got the Veil and was suddenly twelve feet tall, holding it up above his head and I was jumping for it like a Chihuahua trying to reach a treat. Then I was back home, watching Angelica wind herself around him as he sneered at me and told me I'd never be good or magickal enough for a woman like her. Damn my stupid subconscious mind!

I woke to my alarm with a sense of gratitude that I'd been pulled out of my own subconscious torment. I showered and shaved, dressed in fresh clothes, then headed down for breakfast. I ate lightly but made sure to take something for lunch and to restock my bag of trail mix, along with getting several fresh bottles of water for my backpack. I was in the lobby waiting for Yeshe by ten to six, and he arrived a couple of minutes later, clearly also a believer in being early for an appointment.

We headed outside and strangely, he had brought an ancient jeep and motioned me to get in. My surprise disappeared instantly as I realised that we would need this to get any further afield than we had gone yesterday. I blessed Yeshe's foresight and common sense, as mine had apparently failed to acclimatize along with the rest of me.

We set off in the direction we had headed yesterday, quickly passing the first few monasteries we had visited. Once we passed the last of the sites from our previous explorations, I expected Yeshe to slow down as we came to the next monastery. He, however, apparently had other ideas and simply kept on going, not slowing down until we reached Tashi Lhunpo. I looked over at him in surprise and he simply smiled at me and motioned me to get out. As we approached the gate, I asked him why we had changed tactics by going to the end of our planned route even though we'd had no reason to do so based on our lack of success the day before.

"I saw your respect yesterday with the monks," he replied, "also, when I questioned you, you didn't lie to me. You admitted that you were being paid to find the Veil for others. You also told me you had realised the issues that could arise if you just handed it over to those you didn't know enough about. For all these reasons, I have seen enough to know you are a good man inside. I think the time has come for you to know more."

He turned and led the way through the gate, stopping at the doorway to remove his shoes. I hurried to catch up, removing my shoes and hat as I had done before, and bowing to the monk at the doorway. This time Yeshe continued on into the monastery, carrying his shoes with him, and the monk simply nodded at him in a gesture of familiarity that he returned so I quickly picked up my own shoes from the rack. Motioning me to follow, Yeshe led the way through a maze of corridors, nodding to any monks we passed who all smiled to see us.

We soon progressed right through the monastery main building and headed out into the gardens. These were beautiful and calming, a mixture of plants, stone and sand displays that seemed to invite quiet appreciation and reflection. Yeshe didn't slow down but simply kept walking out of the gardens, passing through a rear gateway of the monastery. We replaced our shoes, walking on down a well-worn path until we came to an unassuming little hut that could have belonged to a local yak or goat herder.

The surrounding countryside supported that image as it was on a mountainside, with grass dotted by multitudes of pink and white flowers interspersed with an occasional scraggly bush. There was even a fenced off enclosure attached to the hut and the scent of animals was strong. Looking a little way up the slope, I could see a wall that Yeshe told me was called the Thanka wall. Thankas are apparently depictions of a god, scene or mandala, most often used to instruct students at the monasteries.

Higher up the slope I could see yaks grazing, further reinforcing my impression that this was a simple herder's hut. Yeshe walked up to the door, knocked and then stepped back respectfully to wait. After a few minutes, I started to think that the owner might not be in but might instead be out tending to his herd. Yeshe didn't seem discouraged, nor did he knock again, instead choosing to simply wait patiently. I decided to follow his example, given his cryptic but indicative statement of it being "time for me to know more". My instinct from the day before seemed to have been spot-on –he had known more that he had let on, he was just trying to get a feel for me before he opened up.

I couldn't really blame him for that caution, especially in view of who I was up against. For all Yeshe had known, I could have been the two-faced sneaky bastard after the Veil for my own profit and glory – which, despite my not being as bad as Heffernan, wouldn't have been massively off the mark at the start of my quest. Well, except for the 'two-faced' and 'sneaky' bits I hoped.

The sun was starting to warm up, so I made sure to reapply my sunscreen. I got out some trail mix and water, offering some to Yeshe as well. He took a bottle but refused the trail mix, so I put it away again, setting my bag on the ground at my feet to save wearing it while we weren't moving. I fell to simply contemplating the morning, appreciating the beauty of the scenery and the fact that the monastery blocked the city sounds from disturbing the peace.

At last there were sounds of movement from inside the hut, and the door opened to reveal quite the oldest, most wizened monk I had yet seen. His age did not seem to affect his smile when he saw Yeshe. They exchanged a quick flurry of Tibetan including a mention of my name, and Yeshe motioned me to step forward. The monk looked me slowly up and down. I put my bag down again to give him a bow right down to waist level as a mark of respect for his obvious age and (I hoped and assumed) wisdom.

His smile widened further and Yeshe also smiled at my clear mark of respect, then introduced the monk to me.

"This is my mother's great uncle, Bhikkhu Gonpo. Bhikkhu means 'monk' in Tibetan," he said. I bowed again and greeted him.

"It is an honour and pleasure to meet you." Not knowing whether he understood English, I still felt it appropriate to introduce myself. "My name is Gavan Maddox." I looked at Yeshe waiting for him to translate, but to my delight, Gonpo answered me in flawless English though his voice cracked and wavered slightly, no doubt due to his advanced years

"The honour is mine, Mr Maddox. Yeshe must have been impressed by you and have faith in your character, or he would not have brought you to me. I have been waiting my whole life for the one who completes the prophecy and as you can see, I was starting to think I might not live to see it fulfilled. Please, be welcome in my home." He stepped aside and motioned us into the hut.

We removed our shoes again and when we entered, I looked around in surprise. The furnishings were humble but solid and well-made and the overall effect was of a small holiday cabin any couple might stay in in the countryside.

"Please call me Gavan," I said to Gonpo, "whenever someone calls me Mr Maddox, I either look over my shoulder for my father or think a teacher is about to tell me off for misbehaving." Both Gonpo and Yeshe laughed at the cliché, and Gonpo looked at his relative with approval.

"Of course. Please, be seated. I have just made some tea." He turned and walked to the stove, carefully poured three cups of butter tea and handed the first to me. I took a careful sip, not wanting to scald myself but wanting to show respect and appreciation for the gesture. I found the tea was already at a drinkable temperature. No wonder we had been waiting outside —Gonpo must have heard the knock, put the water on, boiled it, made the tea and then given it a chance to cool before answering the door. It had definitely been worth the wait though —it was delicious.

Gonpo and Yeshe seated themselves and we drank in companionable silence. Yeshe had clearly explained to his great-great uncle why I was here as evidenced by Gonpo's earlier comments, but I didn't want to appear rude or demanding by asking questions before I should. My mind however had no such restraint and whirled with questions. There was a Prophecy? What did it say? Who was supposed to come? What were they supposed to do or say? How could they know who the right person was?

I ignored my rapid-fire questions and focused instead on appreciating the tea and enjoying the company. When we finished, Gonpo motioned for Yeshe to clear the cups and then looked at me carefully, almost like a doctor assessing a patient, or a breeder inspecting an animal looking for flaws. I got the sense it wasn't my physical appearance he was inspecting, however, but that a deeper, more spiritual analysis was going on. Was he looking at my aura? My chakras? I wasn't sure how well I'd measure up to that sort of scrutiny, and wished I'd known of a Chakra and Auras shampoo to use that morning, instead of my regular Head & Shoulders.

As I thought that, Gonpo actually laughed out loud, immediately making me think he had some psychic gifts himself. There was no way I was going to do to him what I had done with Angelica, as I knew that would certainly indicate deception and terminate any chance I had of learning more. Instead, I deliberately brought to mind a recap of everything that had happened since Angelica had entered my little shop (had it really only been four days ago?), especially my musings from the day before. Gonpo nodded at me and sat back in his chair.

"Yeshe was right about you," he said, much to my relief, "you are as honest a man as I think I have met in my life. You know your failings, which is rare, and you try to overcome them. You try to act honourably and fairly, your code is simple but decent and you stick to it even when it makes things more difficult for you. You understand the concept of Karma and try to keep the scales leaning the right way. I never thought I would meet a Westerner like you." I think I genuinely blushed a little at his sincere praise, not certain that I truly deserved it.

"You honour me with too much credit," I demurred, falling slightly into his way of speaking without realising I was doing so. "I am a simple shop owner. I am not even a good student of the mystical side of life, I just try to be a good man." I lowered my eyes, almost feeling guilty for not living up to his assessment of me, and not wanting him to see my eyes water as a result of his almost fatherly pride in my character (I wasn't crying. It was dusty, and I have hay fever –leave me alone).

"Your self-assessment only confirms what I said," responded Gonpo kindly. "It is time to tell you of the prophecy, so that together we can see if you might be the one of whom it speaks."

Chapter 10

Gonpo took on the air of a storyteller as he sat back again in his chair. Yeshe quickly finished with the cups and resumed his seat with the anticipation of someone who has heard a story before but still enjoys hearing it again. I sat forward with the eagerness of a child on Christmas morning, waiting for the presents to be handed out, hoping that what they wanted was under the paper.

"Millennia ago, powerful beings walked the earth and were worshipped as gods." Gonpo began. "Many view the stories of these beings as mere tales now, made up to explain things that the people of the time did not understand. The so-called 'modern world' is so wrapped up in science and the technology that comes from it that they have forgotten the old tales and truths, pushing them aside into the realm of folk tales and legends.

"Many relics and artefacts have suffered the same fate. Look at the Ark of the Covenant. Once carried by the faithful, both worshipped and seen as a source of strength and power in battle, now relegated to almost a joke in a movie, according to what Yeshe has told me. Some people however have never forgotten those early truths and strive to keep them to this day.

"Tibet has always been known for its spiritual heritage, so many artefacts have gravitated here over time to be preserved and kept until needed. The Veil you seek, widely regarded as not existing at all now and considered simply a metaphor, is one such item.

"It was entrusted to us centuries ago by a travelling Buddhist on whom it had first been bestowed. He had been to Egypt and apparently met one of these ancient beings. She was growing tired and old as her followers were dying out and the people no longer worshipped as they once had. There is magick in the act of worship, as I am sure you know, and that was what sustained her on this plane. The less she was worshipped the weaker and older she became, and she knew her time here was drawing to a close.

"She entrusted to the monk a wooden box with the symbol 'Tyet' engraved on the lid and told him that one day an honest man would come from the West seeking knowledge of her and seeking her Veil. He would not be seeking it for glory but to protect it from those who might use it for their own ends. That man would be the only one whose touch could unlock the box, and to whom the Veil should be given. Until then he was to vouchsafe it to his order to care for and keep secret.

"That was our order and we have kept faith in the trust shown to us down the years. Over the last few decades people have turned away from many of the more organised religions, going back to some of the earlier teachings. The belief in Isis is once again prevalent in many places, including the West. The Wiccans especially have a strong belief in her.

"The members of our order have handed the box down to the oldest monk among their ranks, to care for in their turn. The honour is currently mine for as long as I am capable, and I had truly thought I would be passing it to the next when I was no longer able to fulfil my duties. I may still if you are not the man I thought, and the box does not open for you."

Gonpo finished his tale with a sigh and seemed to withdraw. I wasn't sure if he was hoping that I was the prophesied owner of the Veil so he could be relieved of the responsibility, or that I wasn't the guy so that he would still have purpose in his life beside the yaks. I couldn't imagine spending a life caring for such an important artefact –although if the box did open for me, I might be about to experience it for myself.

"You are not the first to come seeking the Veil," Gonpo said. "Many have come before you. They have offered riches for the location, threatened destruction of our monastery if they were not told, even tried to break into our library to seek details for themselves. Some have even

71

come over the years who have impressed previous keepers as you have impressed me and so were told of the prophecy. None have ever been able to open the box."

"If I cannot, I swear to you no one will find its location from me. I will tell the group that sent me that I found rumours but no more. I will not lead them to your door." I wanted Gonpo and Yeshe to know just how much their faith and trust in me meant, and they both smiled at my avowal.

"We know," was Gonpo's smiling response, and he pushed himself up from his chair. "However, coming to my door would not get them the Veil. I may be old but I'm not senile quite yet, nor were my predecessors. The Veil is not kept here. We need to take a walk."

As I stood up, my necklace scraped across my chest and I was reminded of the pendant that Angelica had given me. It had stopped Ciarán from casting his tracking spell on me, so how had Gonpo been able to read my mind? I pulled it out of my shirt and looked at it, which drew Gonpo's attention. He smiled at me when he saw what I was looking at.

"Don't worry," he told me. "Your protection spell is working fine. I had no aggressive intentions, so it wasn't triggered. Also, I was just looking, not trying to affect you in any way." I felt reassured to know that I still had my protection.

Gonpo went to a corner of the hut and got a walking stick that was carved with what appeared to be various arcane symbols, the top worn smooth by years of use. I admired it and he told me it was passed down along with the responsibility for the Veil.

We went out, slipping our shoes back on, and Gonpo led the way up the mountain. To begin with, I simply admired the scenery and enjoyed the fresh air. As we kept going however, the fact that we had started our walk eleven thousand feet up and were going even higher soon became apparent. Yeshe and Gonpo were fine, having spent their whole lives at this elevation. I had only been here for three days and, fit or not, I was beginning to notice the thinning air.

"How much... farther do we... have to go?" I asked in between gasps. Gonpo and Yeshe turned around and looked stricken at my plight.

"I am so sorry!" said Gonpo "My nephew and I were catching up on family and I completely forgot that you would struggle as we went higher. Please, take a rest. We still have a way to go, but not much higher to climb."

I was immensely relieved to hear those words and immediately sat down, my chest heaving like a blacksmith's bellows. Yeshe took off his pack and came over to check on me but Gonpo waved him off. He came over, reaching under his top robe for something at his waist. He handed me a piece of some kind of wood and told me to chew on it.

"It will help, I promise. Again, my sincere apologies for forgetting you were not born to this altitude. I must say, you have done very well to not ask us to stop earlier."

This time I was panting too hard to enjoy the praise, but I acknowledged it with thanks and immediately started to chew on the piece of wood. Within a few minutes I could feel my chest loosening and my breathing eased. I looked in wonder at Gonpo.

"What is this?" I asked. "It's incredible! This could help all sorts of people with breathing problems, not just climbers. Is it hard to find?" Gonpo smiled at me.

"I'm glad you're feeling better. Unfortunately that is not just wood. That is a piece of an herb that has been soaked for many weeks in an infusion of other things that itself takes a whole year to make and mature. I keep some on hand as my lungs are not as young as they once were, and it allows me to keep up with the yaks."

I thanked him profusely for his help and got up to restart our trek. Yeshe and I picked up our packs and we started back up the slope. After another couple of hundred yards, Gonpo turned parallel to the slope and headed off to the right. We started walking around the mountain instead of up it, and I noticed that there was a faint path that we were following. It looked to be more of a goat path than anything made for or by men.

I remembered Gonpo had said we still had a way to go, so I allowed my thoughts to drift now that I wasn't fighting for breath. My excitement over the possible culmination of my search coloured my musings and I started thinking about what might happen if I was able to unlock the box and touch the Veil.

I decided to take off my necklace and hand it to Gonpo to hold when I tried to touch the box. I didn't want any magickal interference affecting my chance to fulfil the prophecy. Also, if the Veil could unlock my magick, I didn't want the pendant to block it as some sort of attack. Or worse, shatter under the Veil's power and end up sticking shards of quartz through my chest!

Gonpo and Yeshe were periodically checking on me after their faux pas earlier. I would nod and smile at them when they turned to look. I marvelled at Gonpo's stamina given his age, realising that herding the yaks must be no easy task and probably kept him more active than most Westerners. I also wondered whether he made this journey to check on the box periodically. That brought to mind a possibility, so I took a few quicker steps to catch up.

"Excuse me for asking, Gonpo, but when did you last check on the box? Is there any chance it could have been buried by an avalanche, or found by some hiker wandering off the beaten path?" Gonpo looked amused at my concern.

"Don't worry about that. The box has not been simply placed on a shelf in a cave. It has been protected by powerful enchantments against discovery and damage. You admired my staff when we left —it is no simple walking stick. I told you it was handed down from keeper to keeper, and that is because it is part of the method for unlocking the box's hiding place."

I was reassured at Gonpo's statement and felt all kinds of a fool for not considering that. Of course an artefact like the Veil would have been protected magickally! The monks were good people, but they weren't naïve. They knew that it was a desirable item and that people would seek it over the years. They wouldn't take the chance that distance alone would dissuade those bent on obtaining it, so of course more arcane methods would be employed. Having experienced some of Gonpo's abilities first-hand, I had no doubt there were other magick users within his order. I apologised for my stupidity and Gonpo shook his head.

"When one is a good person, a trusting nature can be the downside, so you do not instinctively think of the evil side of human nature. There is no shame in that."

"Thank you," I replied, "but even I have some arcane defences in my shop, courtesy of a friend. I should have known you would have taken precautions with the box. How many members of your order can use magick?"

"Most have at least a degree of psychic awareness," he replied. "Unlike in the West, if someone here accomplishes a feat as a child it is celebrated rather than investigated, so the child does not have that moment of disbelief that you experienced. I saw your flash of magick when I looked into your mind. To a magick user, it is like a beacon in your memories. You are correct in that your reaction of disbelief is what shut down your developing ability. It is possible the Veil may be able to help you."

I felt my heart accelerate at Gonpo's words. So I wasn't being ridiculous, I had used magick as a child! If the Veil really could unlock my power, I would have more than financial independence to be grateful to Angelica's group for. I would owe them a debt I might find it difficult to repay. I would, however, still refuse to compromise my beliefs and code to do so.

We had been walking for almost an hour and a half from our first stop when Gonpo finally stopped again. I looked around and saw the opening of a cave just a few feet up the slope. From the way the vegetation grew around the opening, it was clear that unless you knew it was there, and stopped in the right place to see it, you could walk right past it and never know. Gonpo turned to me with the most serious look I had seen on any monk's face.

"We are here."

Chapter 11

"Before we go any further, you must know —if you are the one from the prophecy, the box and its contents will be yours to do with as you will. If you are not, I will erase your memories of everything since you arrived at Tashi Lhunpo. You will be left with only the knowledge of a rumour of the Veil, and a feeling that you have spoken to those calling themselves its keeper, but no clear recollection of where that may have been."

My mind flashed to the description in the diary. I realised that the writer must have made the same journey as me, yet been unable to unlock the box. Gonpo must have been aware of my realisation and read my thoughts because he nodded to me.

"Precisely. The one who wrote this diary you think of must have been here but been found wanting by the box." Oh, wonderful, so I had to measure up to some unknown standard? Cue the stomach snakes!

I thought back to the hut, when I had been wondering whether Gonpo wanted me to succeed or not. I looked at him questioningly, my mind open to him and my question prevalent in my thoughts. My sympathy for his position suddenly overwhelmed me, and I suddenly wasn't even sure I wanted to succeed if it meant robbing Gonpo of the honour of being the guardian. He smiled at me kindly.

"It is funny you should think of me as the guardian," he smiled, "as my name, Gonpo, means 'protector' in Tibetan. My order has been protecting the box for centuries but we aware that we are only temporary custodians. Our main purpose has been to protect it while we waited for the prophesied owner to come forth. If you are that one, my life's greatest joy and honour will be to transfer that ownership to you. I will then retire in honoured old age, tending my yaks without another care in this world."

My eyes again filled with tears as he spoke (damn these allergies!) as I thought of the gratitude I felt towards him at his trust, and the joy I would feel to help him achieve that sense of completion and honour. I was suddenly determined –I was going to open that box, insecurities and psychiatrists be damned! I would find out what was inside and see if it was a caul, a woven veil, or simply dust after all these centuries of waiting. Regardless, I wanted this to be the last time Gonpo would have to make this climb.

He smiled at me and motioned upwards towards the opening and this time I took the lead. When I got there I stretched out my hand to see if there was some kind of magickal barrier blocking the entrance. There was nothing, so I went in. I cursed myself for not having a torch, then again for being an idiot. I got out my phone and turned it on, having shut it off when we arrived at the monastery as a mark of respect, as I had done each time the day before. I activated the torch function and looked around.

The air in the cave felt richer than outside, as if the plants around the entrance were keeping extra oxygen in the atmosphere inside the cave. There was a pool at the back covering maybe a third of the floor of the cave. I walked to the edge and saw that it was being fed by a stream emerging from the back wall. There must have been an underground outlet leading away, or it would soon have overflowed its basin to cover the entire cave. The rest of the floor was bare rock, looking as though it had been deliberately kept clear of pebbles and sand. I turned towards the entrance and saw a simple wooden-handled broom against the wall. Clearly this was something that Gonpo did when he came up.

I looked around for any signs of the box or a way deeper into a cave system, but the walls appeared to be solid rock. I walked over to the pool again and knelt at the edge. I tried to shine the light from my phone into the water to see the bottom but, although the water was crystal clear, the bottom was lost in darkness. Being this close to the water I could feel the chill radiating from it, and I knew it must be fed by glacial melt. Falling in would cause hypothermia and shock in seconds.

I stood up and turned to Gonpo who had been watching with amusement, Yeshe by his side. I smiled in defeat, happy that I couldn't identify the secrets of the box's hiding place. Clearly the monks had known what they were doing.

"OK, I give up." I laughed. I walked over to Gonpo, bowed and made a sweeping gesture into the cave. "Please could you light the way?" Gonpo smiled in return and walked over to the right side of the cave. He ran his hand along the wall at shoulder height (on him, at least —on me, probably mid-chest). He appeared to be feeling for something. He stopped after a couple of seconds, having done this before so already knowing where to start. He took the staff and placed the top carefully into an almost imperceptible indentation in the rock. He closed his eyes and started murmuring under his breath.

Within a few moments the symbols carved into the staff began to glow green and blue, then the water in the pool began to match them, as if lit from deep below. Gonpo continued his whispered recitation for almost a full minute, gradually getting faster and faster, finally culminating in a twist of the staff. The symbols flared, the light seeming to travel down the staff into the wall, and the water shone brighter in response. Gonpo set the bottom of the staff back on the ground, leant on it as if it were a common cane and looked at the pool. The light continued to build, losing some of its colour as it did so, until it looked like a miniature sun was rising through the water.

The source of the light slid up through the water, breaching the surface without a ripple. Once up in the air, the light diminished until it was possible to look directly at it. The source was a stone pedestal in the centre of the pool with a wooden box on top. Despite having come through the water, the plinth and box were as dry as if they had been in this raised position for hundreds of years.

The box was no cheap tourist souvenir. It was a middling brown, not appearing to be either teak or mahogany, with the edges and corners still sharp and clean but having a slightly rounded contour. I could see no latch or keyhole anywhere on the front. Indeed, I couldn't even see a seam where the lid met the base. It looked for all the world like a single block of polished wood. There on the top, exactly as Gonpo had said, was the Tyet symbol of Isis. As I leant towards the box I could smell sandalwood. We carry cedar incense in the shop, and they have a similar aroma. Sandalwood oil was used by the Egyptians during mummification, so it stood to reason that Isis might have had her storage box made from such a precious wood.

The pedestal of rock was out of my reach in the centre of the pool and I had no intention of jumping in for a quick swim to get to it, so I looked over at Gonpo again. This time he simply looked back at me and said nothing but motioned me towards the box. Clearly this last step was mine to figure out. Maybe that was part of testing those who came seeking the box?

I thought about the attributes that Gonpo had spoken of back in his hut. Not a single one of them gave me ability to walk on water! That started me down a train of thought that I hadn't expected. Isis was a goddess, and those beings drew their power from faith and worship. From belief. Maybe this was a leap of faith? This started yet another thought process in my head, and I heard the voice of Sean Connery in my mind, saying, "Only in the leap from the lion's head will he prove his worth!"

I asked Gonpo for the loan of his staff, and he smiled and handed it to me. First I tried to reach the box and move it off the rock spire. Maybe I could float it to me? As expected, it stayed resolutely put. I then used the staff to test the water in front of the spire to see if I could detect a hidden bridge (I had no gravel to throw, Gonpo had swept the floor too clean). As the staff touched the water, there was a glow from the pedestal in one section. The staff passed through the lit section of water, but in its wake the ripples disappeared with unusual rapidity and the light itself looked like a path.

I decided it was all or nothing at this point. I handed the staff back to Gonpo with my thanks and took my necklace off. I handed it to Gonpo and asked him to hold it for me. He smiled again and actually put it on himself. I had to smile at the image of a Tibetan Buddhist monk wearing a Mjolnir pendant necklace. Then I turned towards the box, closed my eyes and took a deep breath. As I exhaled, I opened my eyes and strode towards the box. Before I could take more than two steps, I heard the one thing I had been dreading all day.

"Don't even think about it, Maddox." The clipped delivery spun me around to see Heffernan standing in the mouth of the cave, his right hand holding a ball of electricity, the left wrapped around Yeshe's upper arm. "That bitch may have given you protection, but I doubt she gave you enough to share with the rest of the class."

My eyes flicked to Gonpo quickly, then back to Heffernan. He clearly had no idea that Gonpo had my protective charm now, nor did he know that Gonpo could use magick or he would have been watching him more closely. I stepped away from Gonpo, increasing the space between us in the hope that Ciarán would keep looking at me allowing Gonpo to approach him unseen.

Thankfully Ciarán seemed more interested in me than some random monk and kept watching me, just as I hoped. He clearly thought I was moving away from the box in order to prevent him from zapping poor Yeshe. I stopped when I reached the wall opposite Gonpo, hoping that he would take the hint while Ciarán was looking at me to make his move. I knew he wouldn't kill him, being a Buddhist (more's the pity) but he should at least be able to protect his nephew. I decided to try to engage Heffernan to distract him further.

"How the hell did you find us?" I asked him. "Plus, you only arrived yesterday —why aren't you gasping for breath and drowning in your own lung fluids?" I knew showing off his cleverness would be irresistible to him and would, therefore, be the best distraction I could come up with. Plus, I actually wanted to know how the slimy shit had managed it.

"Following you was easy. I noticed you when I drove past your flea-bag hotel last night, so I got a room overlooking the street. The simple expedient of a pair of binoculars allowed me to watch the entrance, so as soon as I saw this local turn up in his rust-bucket I arranged for a taxi. We followed you to Tashi Lhunpo and I waited to see you come out. I sat in a café near the entrance to keep an eye on things and waited for hours. Finally I saw you appear, walking up the mountain from behind the monastery. I was able to catch up when you had your pathetic struggle with the altitude, and a simple invisibility spell kept me unnoticed. As to the altitude, another simple spell keeps the air more concentrated in front of my face allowing me to breathe without any problems, while a final healing spell put my lungs into perfect working order again." OK, I admit it, I was impressed with his ingenuity. Didn't mean I had to like it though.

"Too bad your mundane mind can't handle magick, or you might have got here two days earlier and actually beaten me, instead of taking that time to get used to the altitude and allowing me time to catch up." Heffernan couldn't resist twisting the knife even further and that shot hit too close for comfort, causing me to feel a rush of inadequacy.

While he was showing off, Gonpo was edging around the wall towards him. When he was close enough, he grabbed Heffernan's hand and shoved it against his own face. The electric orb flared against his head and threw sparks around like a halo. Ciarán was thrown back away from Yeshe, bouncing off the wall and crumpling to the floor. Gonpo went and checked on him, then stood up and turned to me.

"He will be unconscious for a few minutes. I suggest you obtain the box before he wakes. I acted to protect Yeshe, but I will not get into a fight on your behalf."

I nodded to him, expecting no less. I closed my eyes again, took a deep breath and focused on Gonpo and Yeshe's faith in me. I opened my eyes and once again strode towards my destiny in the shape of a small wooden box. This time there was no shout to stop me. I simply kept my eyes fixed on the box, forcing myself to believe in my soul that it was meant for me. I walked towards it, never stopping to think what might be underfoot.

I reached the box, picked it up and turned around, quickly walking back to the rock floor, uncertain of how long the support enchantment might last now that I had removed the box from its stone pedestal. Gonpo's eyes lit up when he saw that I had the box in my hands, and Yeshe's face broke into a wide smile as he turned to his uncle.

"I knew it!" he whispered.

I set the box on the palm of my left hand, gripped the top with my right and lifted, confident that the lid would rise off rather than being hinged. It slid up as smooth as warm oil on a polished glass pane, and I looked inside. There was a piece of silk folded in the box, but it was not thin enough to see through, so I didn't think it could be the Veil. It must be wrapping the Veil itself.

I lifted it out and set the box on the ground to free up both hands. I transferred the precious wrapper to my left hand so that I could use my right to unfold it. As I did so, I could see what looked like a cap designed to cover a baby's head, but consisting of a thin membrane with a fine network of blood vessels. It was a caul, and instead of being stuck to paper like a poorer person might have done in later years to keep it safe, the goddess had hers on pure silk. For a split second I even wondered if this was where the tradition of keeping a caul for luck had originated, but immediately focused again.

I admired the perfection of the Veil. After all these years, it had not deteriorated at all. There were no tears or holes where it had been snagged as it was removed. It barely even looked to have fully dried. That in itself convinced me that this was no sham, but a genuine relic from a being who had been venerated as a deity. At that realisation, my hand began to shake at the enormity of what I was doing and what I was holding.

Before I could lose my nerve −or worse, drop such a precious relic −I did what I knew I had to. I raised my right hand and held the caul vertically in my left, using the silk trapped by my thumb to stop it slipping. Then gently put my hands together. As my bare skin touched the caul, I went rigid. It felt as though electricity was crawling over my entire body, but not in a painful way. The sensation built in seconds, and my vision went white. Then everything went black.

Chapter 12

I don't know how long I was unconscious for, but the first thing I noticed was that I was lying on grass and feeling the sun on my face. At first, I thought Gonpo and Yeshe had pulled me out of the cave when I collapsed, but then I thought that the air in the cave was richer so they would have left me there. Also, my body didn't ache the way I had expected it to after the power that had run through me when I touched the caul. In fact, I felt amazing!

The memory of touching the caul also brought back the memory of Heffernan threatening Yeshe, and my eyes flew open to check that he was still out cold. Instead, I was the one who froze.

I was definitely not in Tibet anymore. In fact, I wasn't even on Earth —unless someone had put an extra sun in the sky and turned the grass purple while I was out!

"OK… well that's different!" I thought as I sat up and looked around. In the distance I could see a hill with a city around and on it, with what I can only describe as a palace on the top. It wasn't fortified enough to be a castle, but it was far too big, rich and imposing to even be a mansion. Yup, I was going with palace on this one. I attempted to stand up and immediately crashed back to the ground, clutching my head in pain.

"BASTARDFUCKINGMONKEYSHIT!" I yelled, looking up to see a previously unnoticed tree branch above me. The noise I made apparently disturbed something in the nearby bushes, as there was a rustling and movement of the leaves. I jumped up more carefully and broke off the branch that had assaulted me to use as a weapon against whatever wild animal might be about to try fresh human for lunch.

As I took my stance, something prompted me to think of Gonpo's actions in the cave. He had only acted when it was absolutely necessary, and only to turn Ciarán's energy against him. Gonpo had been chosen as the best person in his entire respected order to protect the Veil –maybe I should learn something from that?

I lowered the makeshift club and watched the bush, only to see a wolf-like creature emerge and sniff in my direction. I lowered my gaze while still keeping it in my peripheral vision and knelt down to present less of a threat. It approached and sniffed me, then snorted and turned to walk back into the bush. If I had tried to hit that thing, I would have almost certainly ended up with its teeth in my flesh. May be there was something to this peaceful stuff, after all.

With no better idea at the moment, I decided to start walking towards the city, only then realising that I still had my backpack on. The Veil was on the ground nearby, and I looked over at where I had woken up to see that the box had also come with me. I folded the Veil up again, deciding to put it back in the box and put it into my pack for safe-keeping. While I was at it, I got out some water and took a long pull. Then I swung my bag back onto my shoulders and set off towards the city.

As I walked, I looked around for any more signs of animal life. Who knew what else might be lurking out here, just waiting for some dumb lost traveller to stroll by? I saw what looked like butterflies on some of the flowers and bushes I passed, but they were much bigger than any I had ever seen back home, and the colours were so much more vivid. Their wings seemed to gleam like gems. The flowers were also totally unfamiliar to me, and in sizes and colours I had never seen. I don't think I even had names for half of the hues I saw.

Other creatures were around, all seeming to be corollaries of animals, birds or insects I was familiar with but all more vivid, bigger, seemingly healthier than their Earth counterparts. The plants showed the same familiar strangeness. There was the rich lushness of a rainforest but the open spaces of the British countryside, and the colours of a cartoon acid trip from a bad batch of LSD (or a really good one). It reminded me of an antipsychotic that I'd been prescribed once when I was younger —thank the gods the doctor had realised how badly I was affected after I sat watching my fingers move for an entire afternoon.

None of the animals seemed afraid of me and even approached to sniff at me as I passed. I stopped to stroke what looked like an oversized meerkat at one point, and it reacted like a dog to a beloved family member, then simply went back to what it was doing.

I kept walking but the city on the hill seemed to get no closer. Just how clean was the air here if I could see the city in such detail from so far away? I had thought initially that I'd be at the city within a couple of hours, but I'd been walking for nearly that already and it seemed no closer. At this rate, I could be walking for days before I made it to the city limits.

Hopefully I'd either find some identifiable fruits to eat or find some signs of habitation where I could get a meal. As friendly and as trusting as the animals were, I didn't really fancy grabbing one and wringing its neck to shove on a spit over a fire. Yes, OK, I'm a giant softie —so sue me.

I stopped for a rest and got my bag of trail mix out. I decided to ration it in case I couldn't find anything edible. I ate a couple of nuts and had some water, realising that despite having walked as far as I had, I felt no sense of fatigue or soreness. Maybe being at high altitude had made my body more efficient, or maybe it had been Gonpo's herb. Regardless of the reason, my stamina definitely seemed to have improved. Another possibility struck me —what if it had been the power surge from the Veil?

I got up and kept going. I looked around as I went, trying to see as much as possible to take in this new environment. I came across a small fox-like animal that had become entangled in some kind of plant which seemed to have a sticky quality to it, possibly to get either pollen or seeds onto passing animals to drop off later. This poor creature looked to have walked plum into the middle of a bunch of fibres, then become hopelessly ensnared as it rolled around trying to get unstuck.

I carefully removed one strand at a time, and the little guy looked at me as if it knew I was trying to help, so held still. I used up some of my precious water supply to help get rid of some of the gunk. When I had finished, I poured some more into my hand for the animal to drink as it was panting from its exertions. It gratefully lapped it up, then rubbed its head on my hand in thanks before scampering off.

I walked on and came to a stream. The water looked as clear as that in the pool in the cave, so I cautiously put my hand in and took a sip. It was clean and sweet, so I refilled my depleted water bottles. At least I wouldn't go thirsty on my walk. I kept going, but no matter how far I walked, the hill seemed to get no closer.

I glanced at my watch and saw that it was approaching evening back in Tibet but with the two suns here, I had no idea how long the day would last. I decided to take my watch off and put it into my bag since there was no point in trying to equate Earth with wherever I was. Instead, I would simply try to enjoy my exertions and keep going.

After an indeterminate amount of time spent walking, I saw my first sign that there were people living outside the city. What looked like a cross between a house and a British country cottage came into view. It was two stories high but thatched like a cottage. There were exposed wooden beams with the panels between them painted bright white. Every window was open, and the entire front was lined with a flower bed filled with beautiful blooms. The only break was where the door stood open, seeming to welcome visitors.

Despite the obvious signs of habitation and care, I saw no one around. I knocked on the open door and poked my head in but didn't want to intrude without an invitation. This was someone's home after all. I walked around the house and found that there was a small barn with a few stalls in it, but they were empty. Behind the house was what could have been called an allotment back home, or simply a vegetable garden. Someone was obviously caring for it, as there were a couple of hand tools and a basket near one of the beds. The basket was half full of plants that the freshly turned earth indicated had been pulled out from the bed. Clearly someone had been weeding the garden but had been interrupted by some unknown event. I considered picking a few vegetables but didn't want to steal. Plus, I still wasn't hungry enough be driven to such lengths.

I decided to help out by continuing for them. Maybe they would let me stay the night (if there was such a thing here) and give me some food in exchange for my helping out with chores. I blessed the memory of helping my mother in her garden, took my pack off and set to work. I moved steadily down the rows, easily able to differentiate the weeds as they were much smaller than the established plants. When the basket was full I looked around and spotted what looked like a compost bin behind the barn, so I took the weeds over and looked. Sure enough the bin held a pile of old plant trimmings and weeds, so I dumped the basket out and headed back to keep going.

I lost track of time in the simple pleasure of gardening and realised with a start that I had finished weeding. I dumped the basket out for the last time and laid the tools in the now empty container. I carried it into the barn, spotting a rack of tools with a couple of empty pegs on which I hung the implements I had used.

As I still hadn't seen anyone, I grabbed a shovel and broom and decided to muck out the stalls. If I was hoping for room and board, I may as well show my worth. I shovelled and swept out the dirty straw, transferring the waste behind the barn where I could see previous sweepings had been left. There were bales of straw piled on one side of the barn, so I pulled one down and loosened it. I placed a healthy layer in each stall, opening up a second bale when I ran low. The remains I piled neatly near the door for use next time.

As I rehung the broom and shovel, I turned to see a bowl of steaming broth and a glass of milk had been placed by the door. I looked outside but still saw no one. Someone must have put it here, but I had no idea who. Still, they were clearly grateful for my work, and I in turn was grateful for the food. I tried the broth and it was thick, rich and savoury. The milk was mild and creamy, halfway between mild goats' milk and cows' milk. I finished both with a sigh of satisfaction and took the empty dishes to the house.

I went to the back door and looked in but still saw no one, so I took my shoes off and went to the sink. I washed my dishes and set them on the board to drain. I didn't feel comfortable being in someone's house without knowing they were OK with it, so I went back out and decided to sleep in the barn. It was warm and dry, so I wasn't concerned. I had slept rougher than this when camping as a kid. I found the lack of interpersonal contact a pleasant relief, as I didn't have to worry about saying something stupid. As long as I kept trying to be helpful, I could also stave off any feelings of possible rejection. My dinner served to prove the truth in my supposition.

I borrowed a blanket from a shelf near the tool rack and laid it on top of my recently created straw pile, forming a soft bed. I lay down happily and closed my eyes. Despite my exertions I slept fitfully, as I didn't feel as tired as I would have expected after several hours of gardening. When my body decided I was ready, I got up to find a steaming bowl of water and a towel which I gratefully used to wash myself. I debated taking the blanket in case the weather turned colder, but I had no way to ask for permission and I was certainly no thief. I returned the bowl to the kitchen and called out my thanks to my invisible hosts, then set off on my way to the city once again.

As I looked towards my destination, I could have sworn it looked closer than before my gardening stopover. It was strange, almost as if physically walking towards the city got me nowhere but yet it crept closer while I slept. I decided to test the theory and found a secluded spot against a tree and took a nap. Once again, I was unable to fall into a deep sleep as my body didn't seem to need it.

I rested with my eyes closed and instead tried to meditate. My mind, unfortunately, was still filled with the need to know where I was, how I got here, whether I had unlocked any magick, how to learn to use it, how I was going to get home, what was happening to Gonpo and Yeshe, what Ciarán had done when he'd woken up, how I could prove myself worthy of being here, did Angelica like me... nope, this just wasn't happening.

I opened my eyes and looked, but the city was no closer. So sleep wasn't the answer. Fine, I would just continue on my journey and take it as it came. It wasn't like I had much of a choice, after all. I stood up and put my bag back on my shoulders and set off.

I walked until both suns were high in the sky, only realising after several hours that I hadn't put on any sunblock after washing in the barn. I felt my arms and my ears to find they weren't even hot. I put my hat on just in case but decided to leave off the cream and see what happened. Perhaps the suns here didn't burn the way the one on Earth did.

I took an occasional sip of water as I went but decided not to stop unless I felt tired, I felt hungry, or the suns started to go down. I wanted to see just how good my stamina was now. The broth from last night seemed to be sustaining me admirably so I just kept striding right along. As I walked, I started reflecting on the prophecy that Gonpo had told me about. Surely, if I was this 'Chosen of Isis' that the Veil had been intended for, they should make it a little easier for me to get where they wanted me? Maybe a few signposts along the way?

I even started to feel a little arrogantly insulted that they were making it so difficult for me. Then I realised what I was doing and mentally kicked myself. It wasn't like I'd been on a life's quest to find the Veil based on information handed down to me through generations of my family. I'd been well paid, and It had taken a whopping four and a half days to track down. I hadn't even been that skilful –I'd made a couple of lucky guesses based on someone else's information, then been fortunate in getting a guide who knew where to take me. Maybe a bit of humility and appreciation wouldn't go amiss. My emotions continued to rollercoaster between overconfidence and insecurity as I walked the miles away.

After several more hours I finally came across a track that seemed to head towards the city, so I decided to follow it. Tracks meant people, so maybe I'd run across another house or even a pub or inn. I'd have to barter work for room and board again as I had no idea what people here used for money, but I'd done it before. I had never been afraid of hard work and I enjoyed helping people. Might even be good for the old ego, stop me getting too big for my britches and still bolster my feelings of self-worth.

I kept to the track, but no buildings came along. I rounded a bend and came across a wagon at the side of the road. It was fully laden, but the harness hung empty. It looked like there was a problem as the wagon was listing to one side. I walked around it and saw that one of the back wheels had come off. It looked like the cotter pin holding the wheel had snapped.

I saw that there was a replacement set on the side of the load area, so I couldn't understand why the owner hadn't simply replaced it and continued their journey. Then I thought that maybe he or she was an older person without the strength to do the job alone. I took my pack off and set to work.

I unloaded the wagon first to lighten it and found that it was full of metalwork. This must belong to a blacksmith of some kind, perhaps bringing items to market or maybe a completed commission. They must have unharnessed the horse —if they had horses here —and headed on to get help. The items certainly felt solid and weighty, so I could understand an older person struggling with the wagon problem.

Once I had the load off, I thought about how to get the wheel back on. I looked around and spotted a large rock that would work as a fulcrum; now I just need a good-sized lever —gods bless Archimedes and my school physics lessons! I remembered some metal bars in the load that looked strong enough. I retrieved one, plus one of the heavy sacks.

I set the rock under the wagon, slid the bar over it and reached up to pull down on the end. The wagon lifted easily, then I grabbed the drawstring of the sack and looped it over the end of the bar to keep it down. I ensured it wasn't going to slip off, and then moved to the wheel. I lifted it up and slid it onto the end of the axle. I grabbed the new cotter pin and slid it into the hole.

I made sure it was secure and moved back to the bar. I unhooked the bag, then eased the wagon back onto the ground. I reloaded the wagon as close to the original layout as I could remember, trying to make sure the load was secure and evenly spread. Then I continued on my way.

Chapter 13

I walked on until the second sun started setting. Despite my exertions of the day, I felt no fatigue. I hadn't stopped to eat, but I didn't feel hungry. I'd had less than half a bottle of water, but I wasn't thirsty. This wasn't simply improved stamina, this was magick in some form. Either the Veil really had unlocked my magick —although I hadn't noticed any burgeoning powers or abilities —or the magick of this place was sustaining me in ways I'd never expected.

I looked towards the city, but it was no closer than it had been that morning. As I hadn't come across any homes, pubs or way-houses, I simply found a secluded spot off the track and lay down under a tree. I used my bag as a pillow and closed my eyes. As before, my lack of fatigue meant that I didn't fall into my customary deep sleep but lay there listening to the sounds of nature all around.

When the first sun started peeking above the horizon, I got up. I had heard water flowing while I lay with my eyes shut, so I followed the sounds to find a stream nearby. From the direction it was flowing, it might even have been the same stream I had found before. I washed my face and used a corner of a spare handkerchief to clean my teeth as best I could, not having my toiletries bag with me.

I looked towards the city as I had the night before, realising with a start that it was definitely closer now. Maybe it was only during the night that it approached? I hoped that meant that it would continue to approach in the same way. I set off walking once again, not with the expectation of getting closer to my destination, but simply as something to do.

I walked the entire day without seeing any signs of people, simple enjoying stretching my legs. The lack of distractions actually made me feel morose, as opposed to my ego surge from the day before, and I started thinking again that maybe I wasn't worthy of being anyone's prophesied "chosen one". It wasn't like I'd ever really done anything to prove myself. No wonder they didn't want me in their city.

I also wondered once more what had happened once Ciarán had woken up in the cave to find me gone. Had he hurt Gonpo or Yeshe? If he had, I'd track him down and kick his ass, magick or no; Angelica's crystal would take his powers out of the equation. The thought of Angelica brought another issue to mind. Should I really turn over an artefact like the Veil to a group I knew nothing about? I would have to think carefully about that while I tried to get home.

As the second sun started heading down, I realised I had been carrying my bag all day without a break. Although I wasn't tired, my shoulders felt a little tight, so I found a rest site for the night and set my bag down. I could hear the stream again, although the sound had developed into a deeper note as if the stream were becoming a river.

I took the opportunity to run through a few of my karate katas, both to keep current and to stretch out my joints and muscles. I also often found that a bit of exercise was a good antidote to a low mood, and I certainly was feeling a bit down on myself after my reflections earlier. I went to the river and washed up again, then set myself up for the night as I had before and closed my eyes in the hope of seeing the city even closer in the morning.

As soon as it got light I jumped up and looked towards the hill, excited to see how much closer I was. I saw to my dismay that I was no closer than yesterday morning. This reinforced my despondency from the day before, so I sat down in disappointment to try to figure out what was different about yesterday that meant I hadn't deserved to get closer to the city.

Once I phrased it like that to myself, I realised what was happening and rolled my eyes at my own short-sighted naivety. The previous two days, I had done good deeds. I had helped the little animal and done the

Boba Job weck.

yard work the first day, then repaired the wagon the day after. Yesterday I had seen no one who needed my help, neither people nor animals, so I had not earned the next increment in my approach. Good deeds, then, were the steps on my journey, not just the lack of confrontation I had shown with the wolf in emulation of Gonpo's philosophy. I mentally kicked myself for not figuring that out earlier —again the behaviour of the monks should have been my guide. I would have to keep my eyes peeled for even the smallest of helpful tasks I could perform.

I stood up with a renewed determination to be as kind as I could to any and all I saw. I picked up my bag and set off with renewed vigour. I looked around as I walked for anything I could possibly do that might be considered beneficial. I cleared a couple of fallen branches off of the track, got rid of a few rocks that might damage wheels, and filled in some potholes that I saw. To the side of the track I saw a chick that had fallen out of its nest so I used a leaf to pick it up and put it back, not wanting the parents to be distressed by an unfamiliar smell on their baby.

Later in the day I came across someone in true need of my assistance. What looked like a hawk of some kind with snowy white plumage was on the ground crying piteously. Its left wing was held out from its body at an awkward angle, clearly injured. I hurried over and saw that the feathers on the injured wing were sticking up at odd angles and a couple had broken shafts. It looked like the poor creature had flown into a high-tension wire back home. Here, I had no idea what it might have hit, although it did have the somewhat slim and gangly look of an adolescent. It looked like inexperience had been its downfall.

I started by offering the poor creature some water as I wasn't sure how long it had been there. By the eager way it drank, it must have been there a while. I thought it was lucky some larger animal hadn't come along and eaten it. I found some small twigs from a nearby bush and tore one of my handkerchiefs into thin strips. This was the first time I was glad I had hay fever —at least I had some kind of supplies. I gently straightened the wing and bound some twigs to it as a splint. I smoothed as many feathers as I could, but the two with broken shafts had me stumped.

I had once read about a professional cutting a feather, gluing a wooden pin into the shaft and then binding it as a temporary fix until the bird moulted. I didn't have any of those kinds of supplies or anything approaching that level of expertise, so the best I could do was splinting again. I found the smallest twigs I could and pulled some threads from the torn cloth, then straightened the feathers and bound the twigs to them.

There was no way the bird would be able to fly until the wing healed, so I decided to keep it with me and care for it. Besides, it would be company —something that had been severely lacking the last few days. If I was going to be looking after the hawk for a while, I needed to come up with a name. One problem I immediately had was that it was impossible to tell if some birds were male or female without a blood test, something I had learnt when my mother raised a parrot. I therefore made the executive decision to refer to it as a 'he'.

I went to look up a list of names on my phone, then laughed at my stupidity. I realised that I was seriously beyond my coverage, despite my normally comprehensive roaming package, plus I somehow doubted the trees supported 4G! Damn my reliance on modern technology. The hawk cocked his head at me and shuffled a bit as I giggled inanely, so I settled down as I didn't want to stress him more than he already was. I knew the stress of injuries could kill birds.

I sat down next to him, and he looked at me cautiously. I got my trail mix out and ate some seeds, quickly realising that a bird of prey would need meat. As I sat thinking how to get something for him, he stepped over to my bag and pecked at one of the pockets. It was a small pocket on the front that I didn't use, but I opened it to see what he was after.

I found two bags of yak jerky that I had bought to try from the same market I had got the backpack from, and then completely forgotten about. I opened one and offered a couple of pieces to the hawk. He snapped them up eagerly, cementing our tenuous friendship. Now that I had taken care of the urgent issues, I went back to choosing a name for my new friend.

I thought of and discarded name after name. There were the obvious trite options of Snowy, Cloud and Ghost. Yes, he was white —I didn't need to dogpile it. Then there was Phoenix, as he had come back from an injury. Raptor, Blade, Flash, Lightening, Frost, Thunder —none of them fit. Then I thought of my own name. Gavan actually meant white hawk in Welsh, so why not a variation on that —at least we'd fit together.

I had looked up variations on my own name a few years ago one weekend –I was bored, OK, we've all been there. One that I had loved was Gauvain, which meant white hawk of battle. It fit on multiple levels, and when I looked at him and said it aloud, he cocked his head at me and gave a soft skree. I decided that was approval and sealed the deal with another piece of jerky. I tried a piece too, as I had bought it to try myself after all. It was delicious, but I chose to keep it for Gauvain. I wasn't getting hungry anyway, and I had my trail mix to keep me going.

I held my hand out and Gauvain stepped cautiously onto it. I then realised I needed to pick my bag up and put it on, so I set him down again and stood up to get ready to set off. Gauvain cried plaintively, clearly thinking I was going to leave him, so I quickly knelt down and picked him up again. As he clung to my wrist I stroked his head and back, being careful of his injured wing, and softly promised him I would never abandon him.

He skree'd softly again and I was sure he actually understood me. I set him on my shoulder, and he dug his claws into the padded strap of my pack. I set off again, walking more carefully to begin with until I knew Gauvain was secure. There was clearly nothing wrong with his grip, as he didn't shift at all when I stepped over a branch on my way back to the track.

I resumed my accustomed pace and chatted to Gauvain amiably as we went, describing what I saw and telling him about my shop, Summer, my childhood including my various personal struggles –anything and everything to let him hear my voice and get accustomed to me. He shifted around occasionally, and even walked across the top of my bag to the other shoulder at one point. He nibbled my ear after a few hours, so I stopped and we had light snack.

As the day drew to a close I found a new spot to spend the night, choosing the same side of the track as before to be near the river. I fed Gauvain some more jerky, hoping that it wouldn't take too much longer to get to the city or else I might have no option but to kill some small animal to feed him. We settled in for the night, Gauvain snuggling up against the side of my face and tucking his head under his good wing.

That night was the first time I actually slept since I had arrived. I chose to think it was the contentment I felt at having a friend, as I had worked physically harder before but not slept. It was amazing what a difference a full heart could make.

I was woken in the morning by Gauvain shrieking at the sun and I stood up to stretch. I felt refreshed and content, so I took Gauvain to the river and we freshened up for the day. I found a small rock just under the surface of the water and stood Gauvain on it to flick some water over him as I didn't typically carry a spray bottle with me to give him a shower. He was a little tentative with his left wing but at least he was moving it.

Once we were clean, I carried Gauvain back to the camp and we got set for the day. I looked along the track and got a clear sightline to the city for the first time that morning. I stopped in shock. We would be there in under an hour and I knew it wasn't an illusion. I could see the ground all the way up to the city gates. Now maybe I could get some answers.

Chapter 14

I set off at a brisk pace along the track, wanting to reach the city as soon as I could. I thought it strange that I had seen no one, even this close to the city, but remembered my invisible hosts at the thatched house. I decided to simply continue on enjoying the lack of necessity for personal interaction. The track ended where it joined a more established road, which looked to be paved in a similar way to Roman roads that I had seen in England at historical sites. Clearly someone was maintaining them, and there had to be people around if there was a city.

So were they shy? Hiding from me? Scared of me? I was, after all, a stranger. Though why an entire city of people should be scared of one stranger was a puzzle. Perhaps they'd had problems with strangers being hostile before. Maybe, like the American Indians, they had known strangers to bring diseases. Whatever the case, I could sense that I was going to have my work cut out for me to make friends.

I arrived at the gates of the city after about forty-five minutes of walking, my pace increased by the excitement of imminent arrival. The gates were standing wide open, and there were market stalls set up in front of them, so they obviously weren't anticipating a need to close them in a hurry. There was no sentry box at the gate, and I wasn't challenged, so I walked through the arched opening and into the city.

The area just inside was definitely a market, and there were booths selling goods of all kinds set up. The ones to the right seemed to be food stalls, with baked goods perfuming the air. Just beyond those were fruit and vegetable sellers, and behind were the butcher stands. At least meat was eaten here, so feeding Gauvain wouldn't be a problem, if I could just find someone and figure out a way to buy some.

To the left were clothing stalls, with cloth and leatherworking vendors beyond those. At the back on the left side were booths filled with metalwork, and I saw one that may have held the contents of the wagon I had repaired.

I still saw no one as I walked around, although I occasionally thought I saw items that had shifted position while I was turned away. I admired some of the goods, but having no way to ask prices, and no idea of what they used for currency, I couldn't buy anything. I was not hungry or thirsty, as I had become accustomed to, so I had no need of anything, and I absolutely wasn't going to just walk around and start helping myself.

I wandered through the market for hours, even coming across some jewellery stalls further in from the gates. Some of the pieces were truly exquisite, and I admired them out loud in the hopes that whoever might be there would see that I appreciated the workmanship. I wished I had some way of buying things, as a couple of the pieces would have made wonderful souvenirs for Summer and Emily. I would have to come back if I could, once I had figured out who and where these people were, how to communicate and what to use for money.

I walked away from the last jewellery stall with regret, and looked back several times, hoping that the twin pendants I had seen for Summer and Emily would still be there when I was in a position to buy them. The market ended at a large fountain, decorated with carved plants and wild animals, something that would not have looked out if place in an Italian piazza. I sat on the edge and enjoyed the cooling spray of the water. Gauvain, who had been somewhat subdued on my shoulder in the market, shook his feathers, stretched out his wings and skree'd happily. His wing seemed to be moving better already. Did animals heal faster here? Was it the result of magick? I wasn't sure, but I was glad to see he was feeling better.

I gave him some jerky, noting that he was already halfway through the first bag. Hopefully I'd be able to figure the shopping thing out before the second bag ran out. Then I realised that as he was healing so quickly, his wing could be fully recovered before then and he might just fly away back to the wild.

The thought of losing my new friend put a dampener on my excitement but I consoled myself that I had helped him out of kindness, not to obligate him, and if he chose to leave then he was free to do so. I would miss him but be happy to see him healed and flying free.

I saw what looked like a drinking fountain to one side and when I went over, I saw that the bowl was wet so it had apparently been used recently. I didn't see any stalls nearby, and there was nowhere to put any money, so I thought it must be like the free fountains in some markets back home. I took the opportunity to have a drink, and the water was pure and sweet like the river I had drunk from. I refilled my bottles, just in case, then said thank you to whoever might be listening.

As I continued to wander around the city, I saw many signs of active habitation —washing hung to dry, smells of cooking and baking wafting out of an open window, a child's ball in a garden waiting to be played with. I still saw no one, so I started to think that maybe I wasn't able to see them, either because of a lack of magickal ability or because they simply chose not to be seen. My apprehension rose once again, rearing its ugly head to suggest that maybe I wasn't worthy of being allowed to see them.

I went back to the market area and saw that several of the stalls had sold their goods and were packed up, but again no one doing the work. I sat down on the fountain lip again, smiling as Gauvain preened in the gentle spray. As he did so, I heard a child's carefree laugh and I went still. It was the first active sign of life I had positively witnessed, as opposed to things simply being left for me or seeing things in a different position. I looked down at my feet and saw a drawing of a bird in the dust. I pointed to it and spoke out loud.

"Bird. What a pretty picture. This bird is my friend. His name is Gauvain." I heard another delighted laugh, and then footsteps as the child ran off. After only a few steps, I heard what sounded like a stumble followed by a thump, and then heard a shrill cry. I looked towards the source of the cry and stopped short in shock.

There on the floor was a young boy, dressed in what looked like a home-spun t-shirt and shorts, sitting on the ground crying and clutching his knee. I hurried over to him and knelt near him. He looked at me without fear, more concerned with his knee which, from what I could see, he had skinned quite nicely when he had fallen.

I got out a fresh handkerchief –I was running out, I only had one unused one left –and poured some of my water on it. I came nearer and spoke calmly and reassuringly to the boy, unsure if he could understand me, and explained what I was going to do. His cries lessened and he moved his hands away. I poured some water over his knee to wash away the traces of dirt and grit, then removed a couple of stubborn pieces with gentle wipes of the cloth.

A small flap of skin was still attached to one side of the graze. I carefully flattened it out using more water to stop it sticking to itself, then placed it over the skinned area where it came from. I then wrapped the handkerchief over the area and tied it behind his knee. Gauvain had watched the proceedings with a critically cocked head, skreeing softly in what I took for approval as I finished. The boy laughed at this and put his hand out towards my friend. I coaxed Gauvain onto my wrist so the boy could touch him.

"Just stroke his head gently. Not too hard, you don't want to hurt him," I said kindly.

"Oh no, I wouldn't want that," said the child cautiously. I stilled, ecstatic at this indication that the people here apparently could understand and speak English. If I could just make contact, I'd be able to communicate!

While my mind whirred, the youngster stroked Gauvain who closed his eyes under the gentle touch. I thought to try to get a little more information from my new acquaintance, so decided to try asking a question.

"Where are your parents?" He stopped stroking Gauvain and looked at me directly.

"Oh, we just finished shopping so we're going home now. They're right there." So saying, he gestured behind me. I spun quickly enough that Gauvain flapped his wings to keep his balance, and then I froze for the third time in quick succession.

In a semicircle around me, all smiling in approval at my help and attitude towards the young boy, were dozens of people. I guess they could decide whether to let me see them or not. I looked around in surprise to see so many people, especially after seeing no one for so long. I had no idea what to do or say.

"Hi!" I said cautiously, raising my hand to wave. I quickly lowered it, feeling like an idiot.

The young boy laughed at my innocent salutation, then got up and ran to a couple who smiled and hugged him, the man ruffling his hair in the way fathers often do to their sons. It didn't take a rocket scientist to figure out that these were his parents, so I walked over to them.

"He just skinned his knee. It didn't look too bad and I cleaned it up, but you might want to keep an eye on it to make sure it doesn't get infected." They smiled at me, and the boy's mother laid her hand on the back of mine.

"We saw what you did, and we're grateful for the care you showed our son. It was very kind of you," she said sincerely.

"I was glad I could help. If you don't mind, could I ask you a few questions? It would really help me out." I wanted to find out as much as I could about this world, the city, the people... everything, really. I just didn't want to overload them or seem too pushy.

"Actually, tonight is a celebration dinner for the whole city. There will be food, entertainment and games in the market square, with most of the city in attendance," the boy's father replied. "Please, join us, then we can talk in a more relaxed way."

"That would be wonderful, thank you!" I enthused. At last, a chance to talk to other people and find out where I was, why I had been brought here, how the people were able to hide in plain sight, how they already knew my language, why they looked human when we clearly weren't on Earth... I had so many questions to ask. Maybe even how to get home.

Chapter 15

Having nowhere else to go, I decided to hang around the market square until the festivities began in the evening. Even though I had already reached the city, I still felt as though my actions were being evaluated by someone. Plus I had never been one to just sit back and watch others do all the work, so I set my bag down by the fountain and stood Gauvain on a handy carved branch. I then helped some of the stall holders to pack up their goods and break down the stalls. There was a storage area on one side of the market, behind where the metalwork stalls had been, where the collapsed stalls were placed.

I chatted with some of the market workers as we got everything tidied up –not about any of my burning questions, simply about the day, introducing myself, talking about the goods they had been selling, just general chit-chat. When we had finished, a man who must have been the market master (overseer? coordinator? manager?) came over and thanked me for my help. He was a portly chap with a bald head, wide smile and open, approachable face. He had a large, open, leather pouch on his belt, and he reached into it as he spoke. He handed me a small leather bag containing some coins. I tried to say that I had been happy to help, but he waved off my protestations with a smile.

"You put in honest work and helped us get cleared up in good time. That means we can get set up more easily for tonight, and it's only fair to reward a man for his labour. Besides, although you couldn't see us at the time, we all saw you wandering through the stalls admiring the goods but unable to buy anything. We also saw that you didn't simply take what you wanted, as some might have if they saw stalls with no one around. Then you helped the boy when he fell. I know a good man when I see one."

I stammered my gratitude, pushing down the feeling that I didn't deserve his appraisal and asked if they would like some help setting up for the evening. He thanked me for the offer, and I joined several others putting up tables along one side of the square. Then we stacked up large bricks, similar to breeze blocks back home, piled wood and coals in between, then laid heavy metal grills on top. The fires were lit, and we were done. The cook-fires would need time to set and be ready for use, which was why we had lit them now.

Almost everyone headed home to get ready for the festivities, and I asked if there was somewhere I could wash up. As before I hadn't found that I was sweating even with heavy work. I had still got dusty however, and my hands were covered in coal smears. I retrieved my bag and Gauvain, who seemed happy to see me again, then the market manager showed me his office with a bathroom attached. I almost cried in relief to see that although they clearly had nothing like our level of technology, they did at least have indoor plumbing and toilet paper —no more leaves!

There was even soap by the basin, so I was able to have the best wash I'd had since the thatched house. I even took the opportunity to rinse out some of my handkerchiefs. I would lay them over my bag near one of the fires, and they would soon dry. I went outside and set up my makeshift laundry dryer, then sat down on the ground with my back against the fountain. I put my head back and closed my eyes to simply enjoy the sunshine, with one leg out straight and one knee bent for Gauvain to sit on since my shoulders were obviously against the stone. He sat there briefly, then climbed down my thigh to snuggle up against my stomach. I marvelled at how he had taken to me, when I had only rescued him yesterday.

That again set me wondering just where I was. Everything was so different here, yet so familiar at the same time. The animals were different from those I knew, but close enough to not be strange. They were still wild, but yet unafraid of me. The people looked human, but almost an idealised version. As I had worked alongside them, I had noticed that their facial features became ones that I recognised. One had my nose, another my chin, one little girl had my eyes (and I was absolutely certain I had never known her mother, personally or biblically!). One of the women had Summer's eyes, another had made me spin around to do a double-take as she passed as she had Angelica's hair −colour and style exactly. They seemed to be able to read my mind and access my memories, adapting themselves and their appearances to make me more comfortable.

On one level, I appreciated the gesture, as it indicated a desire to help me relax. On another, I couldn't help but be a little suspicious. What were they seeing in my memories? Why were they so keen for me to feel comfortable? Were they really as benign as they appeared? What would they think of my personality issues?

I was keen to believe the best in people, but having dealt with people like Dr Dickwaffle, as a friend of mine had once referred to Ciarán, I always kept a healthy dose of scepticism. It didn't mean I would stop helping or being nice, as that was who I always tried to be. It just meant I kept my eyes open and was prepared for people to reveal a different side to themselves, usually when one least expected it.

Thinking of Ciarán again set me off thinking about him in the cave with Gonpo and Yeshe. I wondered how long he had been unconscious, then how Gonpo had handled him when he woke. That thought led me to wonder if Gonpo knew what had actually happened to me when I touched the Veil. His order were the guardians but that didn't necessarily mean they knew all the details surrounding it. I'd be interested to discuss it with him, if and when I ever made it back.

After a while, I checked on my handkerchiefs and found them dry, so I folded them up and stowed them away. They had become quite a valuable resource, despite the fact that my hay fever hadn't been an issue since I had been here.

Several people arrived in the square with a cart laden with meat. They quickly spread out the now well-seasoned coals and set the different joints on the grills, the thickest pieces in the hottest areas and the smaller pieces towards the edges. As I had always been a keen cook, I once again set Gauvain on the stone fountain branch and wandered over. I found they were using many of the herbs and spices I recognised from my own kitchen —salt and pepper of course, and also paprika, cumin, rosemary, sage, oregano, chilli, garlic and onion. Some pieces were being done plain, some with a dry rub, some with sauces basted on. They had huge slabs of beef in different cuts, lamb, pork, poultry —it was a barbecue lover's paradise.

After the meat had been cooking a while, others began to turn up with bowls and platters of cold food which were set up on the long tables we had erected earlier. Soon the trestles were laden with delicious dishes, including one whole table of bread, baked to be bowls and flat dishes so that plates would not be needed and there would be less washing up and waste. People were bringing their own drinking vessels, so a wide array of mugs, tankards and goblets were on display, along with a few spares in case any got broken. I got myself a mug from the spares, expressing my thanks to the young man stationed near them.

The aromas of the cooked meats were perfuming the air, and a light evening breeze was wafting them through the city, calling any stragglers with an inaudible but unmistakable insistence. I saw the family with the young boy I had helped earlier arriving, and they waved to me. The young boy ran over to me, wanting to say hello to Gauvain again. He was nestled on my shoulder sleepily, having been plied with scraps by the cooks while they were preparing the meats. He was now in a bit of a food coma. He opened one eye and nibbled the boy's finger gently, then closed his eye again.

The boy was ecstatic at the attention and seemed to be excited at the prospect of all the lovely food. He was also looking for his friends, and soon spotted a group his own age. He quickly told his parents where he was going, then scampered off. His parents smiled indulgently and walked over to me.

"Hello again," I said as they arrived, "I'm glad your son seems none the worse for his little trip earlier. I must apologise, I neglected to introduce myself. My name is Gavan."

"Oh, you have no need to introduce yourself," said the boy's father, "everyone knows who you are. In fact, you're the reason for this celebration. We've all been waiting for the one who would find the Veil since Isis returned from your world. But speaking of introductions, we should introduce ourselves. I'm Liam, this is my wife Alexandra and our son Conor." Liam was a slightly built individual, around five-foot-ten, with fine sandy hair and features that were more delicate than many men I knew, although there was an indefinable air of dependability about him that inspired confidence. His wife was statuesque and almost as tall as him, maybe an inch or two less, with chestnut hair that fell in waves to a few inches past her shoulders. They both had brown eyes. His were a couple of shades lighter than hers, and her skin was almost Mediterranean whilst his was much fairer. Conor was definitely their son, as he had his father's eyes and his mother's hair and skin.

I had been startled and my stomach had knotted at Liam's mention of everyone knowing me, and his casual discussion of the Veil. Clearly it was a well-known prophecy here, if its culmination was cause for celebration. Also, for Liam to mention Isis so freely meant she must also be well-known. I needed more information, and I could see that Liam and Alexandra were standing there with patient smiles on their faces, waiting for me to wrap my head around things.

"So where is here, exactly?" I asked first. "I still don't even know where I am. I have a whole host of questions, so I may as well start at the beginning." They smiled at me and this time it was Alexandra who answered, sounding almost like an instructional podcast.

"Where we are has been debated by humans for thousands of your years. Some have called it the Garden of Eden, some have called it Shangri-La. It has been called the etheric plane and the astral plane. Those who have had what your kind call 'near death experiences' have caught glimpses and called it Heaven. It has been referred to as the Elysian Fields, Arcadia, Paradise and Xanadu. The Gaelic people use Neamh or Nèamhan. The Welsh called it Nefoedd. The Egyptians amongst whom Isis spent her time called it the Field of Reeds, The Fields of Aaru or simply Aaru. We do not have a specific name for it, as to us it is simply home. However, you could pick any of these and we would understand you."

My mind reeled with the implications that some of the names conjured up. I could certainly see how the scenery here would support many of the myths associated with those labels, although to use some of them would carry such weight to me personally that I thought my brain would either implode, explode or simply melt into happy grey mush from the connotations.

Since Isis was known originally as an Egyptian goddess, and it was her Veil that had brought me here, I decided to use Aaru. This was the first time I had encountered that particular variation, so it held less awe for me.

"OK, that was a serious list of major names," I replied with a swallow, my guts now definitely tied up tight and my stomach climbing into my throat, "so I think I'll just stick with Aaru, if that's alright with you. Some of those others are a little too significant for me." Liam smiled back at me in understanding, while his wife laughed lightly at my comment.

"So, am I really here? What I mean is, is this just some psychotic illusion in my head? Was I astral projected here by the Veil? Or did it transport me, 'body and soul' as it were, to this physical location?" At that they both nodded, acknowledging that some of the names would conjure up exactly those ideas –although I hoped they weren't aware of my fear that this was a full-blown psychotic break and I was actually strapped up, gibbering in a rubber room somewhere.

"Oh, you are definitely here physically," replied Liam, smiling at me. "The Veil acted as a gateway, keyed to transport only the one for whom it was destined." I felt quite proud again at that point, that Isis had chosen me across the centuries, then instantly humbled by what that meant in terms of responsibility. To be chosen by a goddess! What did that mean? What would I be expected to do? My self-doubt reared its ugly head again, reminding me that according to the old legends, even gods made mistakes. I'd definitely have to work hard to prove myself worthy of being chosen.

My new friends quickly saw that I was becoming overwhelmed by what was happening to me and rushed to reassure me –although their next statement did anything but:

"Don't worry, Isis will explain everything when you meet her tomorrow. We have to say, you got here faster than we expected. We all thought it would take you a good couple of weeks to figure out how to reach the city."

While flattered by their amazement, the thought of being presented to Isis –an actual goddess –the very next day made me a little light-headed. I thought I'd ground myself with a question on a more innocuous topic –how little I knew!

"So what's the name of this city that I've been trying to reach?" I asked, little imagining the thunderbolt I had just sent hurtling towards me.

"Oh, that's much easier!" Alexandra laughed. She spread her arms wide to indicate the city and called out "Welcome to Dinas Affaraon!"

I promptly sat down on the edge of the fountain in shock.

Chapter 16

Innitus started up in my left ear, I felt a buzzing sensation on top of my head, and I laughed out loud. Gauvain, who had woken up when I had thumped down onto the fountain, screeched and flapped his wings at my outburst. I distractedly thought that I would have to look at his left wing tomorrow, as he seemed almost healed after only the one day so I might be able to remove the splints. My new friends looked at me in concern.

"Are you alright?" Liam asked, his brow furrowed in concern. "You just went as white as snow and your thoughts became strange." At least that confirmed one thing for me –these people could read my mind. Still, I had nothing to hide any more now that I'd found the Veil, so if they wanted to see what was in there, that was up to them. My sarcastic side piped up with a snide comment at that thought.

"If they get disturbed by your twisted brain, that's not your fault!" They actually laughed as I thought that and hurried to reassure me.

"We can read your thoughts, you're right," Alexandra said, "but now that we know you, we wouldn't do it routinely. We respect each other's privacy. We only did now as we were concerned for you. What was it that distressed you? I only told you the city name." The thought of the giant cosmic coincidence almost set me off giggling inanely again.

"That was all it took." I smiled at them both and explained further. "It wasn't distress, just surprise and shock at the unlikelihood of what just happened. You see, back on Earth, I have a small shop that sells crystals, incense, symbolic jewellery and books, both mundane and some genuinely magickal items. The thing that caused the reaction to the name of your city was the fact that, completely without any knowledge of Aaru or any of you, I named my shop Dinas Affaraon."

They both looked at me for a second, then broke out into peals of laughter. Liam managed to finally catch his breath and calmed down enough to reply, while his wife was still holding her sides and gasping.

"Oh, that is priceless! No wonder you were startled; that has got to be the most unlikely coincidence I think I've ever heard of! What made you choose that as the name for your shop?"

I explained that my name was Welsh in origin and that Dinas Affaraon was supposed to have been in Snowdonia back on earth. When I had been planning the shop, I had looked up the names of some cities that were, at least as far as I knew at the time, legendary, and had been taken with the mythology associated with Dinas Affaraon. The idea that it had also been known as "The City of Higher Powers" had appealed to me, and I had thought that anyone in the genuinely magickal community might view it as somewhere to go for information. (It had worked, too, which was why my commission side interests brought in a goodly income on top of the regular turnover. But I digress.)

Liam and Alexandra were still chuckling, and some others had come over to see what was so funny. The story spread from group to group, until soon the whole square was laughing along with us. The noise made Gauvain screech again, but he settled as the laughter eased. It was the first time I could remember where a large group of people were laughing and I was involved that I wasn't concerned that they were laughing at me. Instead, I knew they were laughing with me, which both endeared them to me and helped me relax.

I made sure to try at least a little of most of the dishes, which were mostly recognisable from Earth but coming from all parts of the globe. There were several pasta dishes, couscous, potato salad, green salad, gazpacho, a whole school of fish dishes, antipasti of various kinds, beans, and about a dozen different sauces. To drink there was mead, beer, cider and both red and white wine. For dessert there were fruit pies and cream in every flavour imaginable.

Everyone was much more relaxed after the meal, and a few people got out some instruments and started playing. Some of the songs were old folk tunes that I recognised, some I had never heard before. There were even some modern songs, indicating that the people here were still aware of what was going on in my world. I joined in singing when I knew the words, but quietly as my voice was only mediocre at the best of times and could certainly never compare with what I heard here.

The children were playing catch and chasing after each other, and there were several games going on in small groups of the adults, although I didn't understand how they were played, plus I was enjoying mingling too much to sit down with one group exclusively. Gauvain had picked at some of my meats, but he was still stuffed from earlier, and soon fluffed his feathers up to doze on my shoulder.

The festivities continued well into the evening, but eventually started to wind down. Those with small children were the first to start leaving now that their charges had exhausted themselves with their games and stuffed their little bellies with sweet treats. Then the adults started filtering away. Some of the younger adults started pairing off and I could tell by the smiles that tonight was definitely going to be a good night for them.

Eventually there were only a few people left helping to clear up the leftovers. I pitched in once again, then wondered what I would do for the evening. I collected my bag and looked around for a comfortable spot. Just as I was thinking it might be best for me to head outside the gate to find a soft spot on the grass, Liam came jogging back into the square.

"I just realised I had forgotten to let you know we were getting a bed ready for you for the night. I'm glad I caught you!" said Liam apologetically. "We know you haven't got anywhere set up, so we got our spare bed made up for you. Then we can take you up to the main hall in the morning to see Isis. Everyone will be there; we're all so excited to witness what happens."

"Oh, great. No pressure then!" I laughed. Liam chuckled along with me, understanding at once how it sounded.

"Oh, don't worry, you'll be fine. You've proven your character first by getting here at all, then by making it to the city so quickly, and finally by your behaviour since you got here. Isis will be aware of all that, and I'm sure she'll be as impressed as we all have been." I tried not to let his praise go to my head, but I definitely stood a little straighter after hearing all that. I'd have to be careful that all this positivity didn't push me back into my arrogant frame of mind from a couple of days ago. My emotions had certainly been put through the wringer since I started this little quest.

I thanked Liam for his reassurance and his offer of hospitality, and we headed off to his home. When we arrived, Alexandra looked up from the book she was reading and sighed in relief.

"Oh, good, you caught up with him. I'm so sorry we forgot to invite you earlier, Gavan. We just got so caught up in all the excitement of the celebration. After all, Isis returned almost four thousand Earth years ago, and for us here, that is considerably longer."

Liam suddenly looked across at her, and she caught herself before she said more. I had already caught her slip though and wondered just what the time difference was.

"So, I can be here for a while and it won't be as long on Earth?" I asked. "Do you know what the difference actually is?"

"I think that's something that Isis will want to discuss with you. Just know that when you go back you'll be surprised," Liam said cautiously. "I'm sorry, I'm not trying to be mysterious or obstructive. I just think it's better if we let Isis explain things in her own time and her own way."

"OK, just promise me that this won't be like the legends of people taken to fairyland where they stay there for an evening, but a hundred or a thousand years pass on Earth. Then when they set foot back on their home soil, all those accumulated years rush in at once and they simply crumble to dust." I wanted to at least make sure that I hadn't already abandoned Summer for the rest of her life to wonder what had happened to me. They laughed lightly and rushed to reassure me.

"Oh no, just the opposite!" Alexandra said, smiling openly. At that point, my mind went to the tale of The Lion, the Witch and the Wardrobe where the children go to Narnia, win the war, free the people, grow up and rule for years, only to finally stumble back through the forest and end up walking out of the wardrobe as children again.

That meant if my magick could be unlocked, I might have time to learn how to use it before I had to go home. I nodded in understanding and decided to try to get some sleep. I wanted to be as fresh as possible for my meeting with the goddess in the morning.

Alexandra showed me to my room and pointed out where the bathroom was. I set Gauvain on the headboard of the bed and lay down with a sigh of contentment. This would be my first night in a proper bed for several days, and I couldn't believe how much I'd missed the sensation. I'd been camping before, but I'd always had a mat for the floor and a sleeping bag. I certainly hadn't come out equipped like that when I had met Yeshe that last morning!

As I closed my eyes Gauvain jumped off the headboard and fluttered to the pillow, then walked over to snuggle into the crook of my neck again. It was comforting and gave me a real sense of belonging, so I was once again able to sleep for several hours. When morning dawned, I went to the bathroom and got ready for the day.

I was stuck with the same clothes I had been wearing and I didn't have any deodorant or aftershave, nor a toothbrush or razor, but until this morning I hadn't thought much about it as I'd been away from people. I'd cleaned my teeth with my handkerchief corner, but that was no substitute. It was strange to see that despite my usual brisk stubble growth, I still didn't need to shave. I washed myself well with the soap provided and used the towel that had been left for me on the bed the night before.

I settled Gauvain on my shoulder and went into the kitchen to see that Alexandra was already up preparing breakfast and humming softly to herself, so I offered my help. I set out the cutlery and plates while she toasted some bread and made what smelled like an herbal tea. As we finished, Liam came in with Conor and we all sat down. I wasn't overly hungry after last night's blow-out but sipped my tea and thanked my hosts for their hospitality.

"It was our pleasure," replied Liam, "and the least we could do after you cared for Conor when he fell." I smiled and turned to see Conor tucking into his breakfast with the typical gusto of an active young boy.

"So, how's your knee feeling this morning, Conor?" I asked him. He smiled up at me with his cheeks full of toast and nodded vigorously. He chewed quickly and swallowed a couple of times while we all laughed at the sight of him trying not to choke or spray crumbs across the table.

"It's much better, thank you very much," he said, then reached into his pocket and pulled out the handkerchief that I'd used as his bandage and handed it across to me. "Mum washed it out last night when we got home," he added.

"Oh, thanks very much," I said, both to Conor and his mother who was beaming at him in approval of his manners. We finished our meal quickly and I helped clear the table and wash the dishes. Liam remarked that my meeting with Isis would happen in about an hour, so we should head up to the hall. Conor was almost bouncing with excitement at the thought, whereas my stomach was doing hula-hoops around my throat at the prospect. Alexandra noticed my anxiety and smiled at me.

"Don't worry, she's very nice. Don't forget, she's been waiting for you for a long time, so I'm sure she'll be glad to see you." Her comments had me wondering just how Isis had known, all those centuries ago, that I would be the one to fulfil the prophecy. Or had she simply foreseen that someone would one day be worthy but not known who nor how long it would take?

We all walked together up the main road leading to what I had thought was the palace. When my new friends had mentioned 'the main hall', I had thought that they meant an audience chamber in the palace. When we got there, the doors were open, and I was amazed to see that the entire structure was just one big hall with a few decorated columns around to support the ceiling. This wasn't a palace at all! So where did the goddess live?

Liam noticed my confusion and asked what was wrong. I told him I had seen the building on top of the hill as I was approaching the city, but that I had assumed it was the palace where Isis ruled as a queen. He laughed until tears ran down his face, Alexandra joining in when he told her in gasps what I'd said.

"Isis isn't a queen here!" He finally managed to gasp out. "No wonder you've been so anxious. Oh I'm so sorry, if we'd known we would have explained it all. I completely forgot that in your world Isis was a goddess, so naturally you would think she'd be queen here. If I'm honest, everyone here would have powers if they came to your world, but only a few ever went. Everyone here is generally far more equal to each other than people are on Earth. Isis is important here, but mainly because she acts as a sort of council leader to help organise the running of the city."

This explanation represented a complete paradigm shift in how I understood what was going on, and took some time to sink in. So everyone here was basically a god? Was I just some talented primitive who got lucky by comparison? Rather than reassuring me it actually made me withdraw slightly, although no one seemed to notice as everyone was arriving now, and they were all catching up and chatting about the party last night. I tried to back away to the wall, but more people were arriving so I was trapped at the front where Liam had led me. I had to close my eyes for a moment to centre myself and I started counting my breaths as a coping mechanism in order to try to stifle my sudden urge to run screaming from the room.

Then everyone turned to a door at the other end as several people filed in from what looked like a meeting room off the main hall. I was ushered to the centre of the room as the council members (or so I assumed after Liam's explanation) joined the throng with much shaking of hands, hugging and smiling. One of the women made her way through the throng to stand opposite me and smiled.

"At last," she said, "we've all been waiting for this for a very long time. Hello Gavan, I am Isis. I'm so very pleased to finally meet you."

PART 2

The Awakening

Chapter 17

OK, I'm not proud of this but I'll admit it: I stood there with my mouth open like a big dumb dog. Everything I had expected had just been chucked out the window, stuck in a blender and put on 'smoothie'. What the fuck did I do now? Bow? Kneel? Grovel with my head on the floor? Say "Hiya babe!" and give her a big wet kiss?!

Did I call her your highness? My lady? Your holiness? What the hell did you call a goddess when they were standing right in front of you? Miss Manners never covered that shit, I can promise you! My brain was racing faster than the Flash on speed-laced Cafegeddon, but nothing was making it through to my mouth.

After what felt like an eternity, but was actually about two or three seconds, I swallowed (where the hell had all my saliva gone?) and opened my mouth to speak.

"I'm honoured to meet you, my lady." Everyone smiled, and then she winked at me, leant over and stage whispered her reply.

"Nice recovery!" I laughed along with everyone else, fully aware of how I must have looked, and started to relax.

"I'm sorry, I've just never been presented to a goddess before. Finishing school doesn't exactly prepare one for that —not that I ever even went to a finishing school." I finally found my voice and had to make a huge effort not to let my nervousness send my mouth from freeze-frame into hyper-speed with the adrenaline swilling around my system.

It didn't help that Isis was very attractive. She had a slim face, with cheekbones to make a supermodel weep. Her eyes were almond-shaped and deep green, her hair was that deep rich shade of natural red sometimes called titian, falling in elegant waves to her shoulders. Her chin was slightly pointed but still delicate and with a firm strength to the jaw. There was no trace of the black hair and dark eyes that I would have expected to see on an Egyptian goddess.

She was dressed in a white toga-like dress that left her right shoulder bare and had a gold clasp on the left shoulder. She had a golden rope-belt around her waist, and brown leather sandals with straps that went half way up her calves.

If I had been asked to guess, I would have put her age in her mid to late thirties, as she had a couple of tiny laugh lines, but she would definitely have been what some would term a Yummy Mummy, or the less delicate would call a MILF. As my brain thought that, I once again went into mental lockdown at what I had just considered about a goddess.

She, on the other hand, had clearly read my mind and heard exactly what I'd just thought which sent her into peals of laughter, followed by looking at me through lowered lashes and putting on an exaggerated sexy pout.

"You have no idea!" she joked in a deliberately husky voice. I flushed redder than a traffic light and shifted in some newly-acquired discomfort, then dry swallowed again. My anxiety was sending my fight or flight response into an even higher gear than it had been earlier, so I had to force myself to remain still.

"Don't worry about standing on ceremony here, we're all equals. Just call me Isis," she said, kindly. "I know you're a bit overwhelmed and have lots of questions. We'll get to all those, I promise. However, the first thing is to correct something that went wrong years ago. I know Gonpo told you that your childhood experience shines like a beacon to a magick user, and he was right. It's time to unlock that potential."

This was clearly what everyone had been waiting for, as they all leant forward or craned their necks to see what was about to happen. Fortunately for me, Isis continued loudly enough for everyone to hear.

"I think something this important and personal should be done in a more private setting." I sighed in relief at the fact that I was not to be made a spectacle of, while everyone else in the hall deflated a little. Conor couldn't quite contain his disappointment and let out a loud sigh.

"Aww! I wanted to see!" he whined, and I laughed along with everyone else, then winked at him, thankful for his innocent outburst which eased some of the tension from the situation.

"I'll tell you what I can later." I promised him, and he responded with a beaming grin.

Isis raised her hand and we were suddenly in a totally different place. It was a small room, maybe ten feet square, with no windows or doors that I could see. There was a candle in each corner on a tall stand, and a plinth in the middle of the room about four feet in height. The pedestal was topped by a wide black bowl that appeared to be made of black marble flecked with silver, looking like the night sky with uncountable stars.

Isis motioned me forward to the bowl and I saw that it was full of water. I stared deep into the water but saw nothing except the bottom of the basin.

"You need to open your mind." Isis said from behind me. "Let go of your preconceptions and find your innocence again." I wasn't quite sure what she meant by that, but my thoughts were far too mixed up right now to let go. Plus, my thoughts weren't exactly innocent with Isis standing so close to me. I took a deep breath and shook my hands out, then put them on the sides of the bowl. Isis circled around to stand opposite me, then held out a small oval pebble.

"Try this," she said, dropping the pebble into the centre of the bowl. I focused on it as the ripples spread outward, calming my mind. The pebble drew me in, seeming to fall far deeper than the bowl would have allowed. As I followed it, I relaxed and my memories started to spool through my mind's eye. I trailed back to that moment in the back of my mother's car, and suddenly I could feel the string wrapped around my hands again.

I had that pure certainty of childhood that this was possible and yanked up on the string as I had done before, all those years ago. The string passed through the plastic handle and I stared at it. I felt the joy of success deep in my soul and then saw the memory freeze as I stopped it and changed my next words.

121

"I knew it!" I said reverently, and suddenly I was outside the memory looking at myself. Everything except the picture of my childhood self faded away, then the colour drained out of the image. I was left staring at a glass replica of myself, only it was filled with what I can only describe as light made liquid. I knew that the luminous fluid was my magickal essence, which had been locked away all these years, so I reached out hungrily. As the mental image of my hands touched the crystalline cheek of my face, it shattered into a billion stars, merging with the light of my power which evaporated, turning into a sparkling cloud. I breathed it in deeply, feeling a rush of burning cold deep in my chest, splintering out into the rest of my body until I felt the tingle in the tips of my fingers, toes, and even the top of my ears.

I opened my eyes and looked at Isis. She smiled approvingly at me and I returned the smile with an almost feral glee, causing her smile to falter for a moment although she recovered quickly. I looked back into the bowl and saw that the stone had changed from clear to a deep purplish red. It seemed to have absorbed some of the flecks of light from my mind, and now where the light hit it there was a point of light with six rays emanating from it —a six-pointed asterism star ruby. As I looked deeper into the stone, the lines of the asterism warped and fused to form a pair of wings, making me think of both Gauvain and the legendary protective wings of Isis. She picked it up and handed it to me.

"This is now your heart-stone. Its uses will become clearer to you as you become more accustomed to using your gifts," she told me. I accepted the stone with elation, knowing that I was now a... Wait, what was I now?

"Umm Isis," I said, keen to clarify my definition, "what exactly am I now? Am I a mage? A sorcerer? A wizard? A warlock, a witch or a Wiccan?" (Why do most of the magick users' names start with 'W'? What a wonderfully weird web of words we weave!)

Isis looked at me like a disappointed teacher and replied, "You are Gavan. Why do you need another label? I know humans like to feel they belong, and so like to pigeon-hole themselves, but you are now more than that. Don't limit yourself by attempting to put a name to what you are." I nodded my head in understanding but flinched slightly, in the knowledge that I had fallen short of her expectations after only a minute. I then reached into my bag and got out the box containing the Veil, offering it to her.

"I believe this is yours. I would hate for it to fall into the wrong hands and cause problems." She looked at me pityingly.

"Your education really needs to commence as soon as possible. Stop thinking like a human. We just established that you're more than that now." I could see I was going to have to knuckle down to some serious re-learning if I was going to live up to her expectations for me now. "Take out the Veil." I opened the box and got out the fabric with her caul on it, unfolding it carefully. My hands were shaking with nerves and I nearly dropped the precious artefact, so Isis reached out and steadied me, smiling reassuringly.

"Now peel the Veil off the fabric," she instructed. I did so, and it came away with minimal effort, like taking one of those glass stickers off a new jar.

"Now take it into yourself."

My eyes flew up from looking at the Veil to meet hers. I stopped myself from making a stupid comment and tried to think what she meant.

"I'm thinking you don't mean to eat it, but I'm not sure how to absorb a solid object," I said cautiously.

She shook her head, pinching the bridge of her nose and closing her eyes. She sighed, scrunching up her face in the exact way Summer did whenever I said something particularly idiotic or just plain gross.

"Of course you don't eat it; that's just disgusting! You need to expand your understanding of how things work now. Reach out with your senses towards the Veil; try to feel its essence. Then, pull that essence towards yourself."

I understood on an intellectual level what she was saying from my reading of magickal texts, I just wasn't sure how to go about it. Then I reconsidered something. She had said I was more than merely human now, so I couldn't use purely human senses. I wasn't what she was either, however, so maybe I had to do this my own way. She smiled then, apparently following my thoughts to see how I was doing, then nodded encouragingly.

I remembered how my memory had turned to crystal and been filled with light, so I tried to imagine the Veil in a similar way. I closed my eyes and pictured it in my mind, then reached out to the physical form I felt in my hands. It immediately flared so brightly before me that the light from my memory was like a candle beside a supernova. I flinched so hard in surprise that I dropped the Veil as I clutched the sides of my head.

"It's too much, I'll never be able to absorb it!" I cried, my voice breaking with my anxiety. I opened my eyes to see Isis had caught the Veil and was looking at me almost with relief at my comment.

"I'm glad to see your caution and willingness to hold back," she said. "When you smiled after unlocking your magick, I saw a darkness in your expression; it was like someone ready to use their power over others." I rushed to reassure her, remembering what had passed through my mind.

"I only thought of how I could use my ability to stop others. I had a problem with being bullied as a child, which left me with a longstanding hatred of those who abuse others. It will also mean that I can prove that my belief in magick is not some fanciful delusion, which is a widely held opinion among others that I have wanted to change since my childhood."

"I'm happy to hear your explanation, but you must still be cautious. Such hatred could still become dark if allowed to fester, and righteous anger can become tyranny if left unchecked. Now, have faith in yourself and believe in my choice. Take back the Veil and try again."

So saying, she held the Veil out to me and I took it from her, carefully holding it out in front of me on my upturned palms. I took a deep breath and closed my eyes again, picturing the Veil as I had before, still flinching slightly from its blinding luminescence. I imagined the fragile crystal surrounding the light cracking, rather than shattering as my memory had, allowing the power to leak out gradually instead of all at once. I was still concerned that such a huge rush of power might be dangerous, since this was all so new.

As it shone through the crack, the light became a beam centred on my face, creating a feeling like standing with your face to the sun on a warm, cloudless day. It still felt cold, similar to the rush I had experienced from my memory, although it wasn't the burning freeze of before. This was the refreshing coolness of a cold drink on a summer's day that you felt drop through your chest and spread out into your entire being.

As I grew more confident, I imagined the crack widening more and more. The beam became more intense, like turning up a dimmer switch, until finally the whole shell shattered and I shouted out loud. The final rush of power lifted me up onto my toes and made me fling my head back with my arms spread wide as if I had been electrocuted, then I dropped to one knee as I gasped for breath. After a few seconds I stood up and took one final deep breath to centre myself, and then I opened my eyes to see Isis looking at me approvingly.

"Well done. You managed that better than I expected. You definitely have a knack for this. We just need to get the foundation skills drilled into you, then teach you some of the higher abilities. Liam and Alex have already offered to teach you the basics, so you can head back there. Just be aware, you now have some of me within you, which gives you the potential to be amongst the strongest magick users. Our teaching here will set you on your path, but no one can walk it for you. You will encounter your own unique challenges and obstacles. How you approach, confront and overcome them will determine who and what you will become. We cannot give you a map; that is something you must create and develop for yourself. Remember my warning and keep it close to your heart –do not let the darkness win or it will be far worse than you could ever imagine. Keep to your path, find the balance between the light and the dark that we all must strive to achieve. I must warn you not to abuse my gift or bring dishonour to my name. To do so would have dire consequences, both for you and those close to you."

I placed my closed right fist into my open left hand in front of my face and bowed in the martial arts fashion, then straightened up to look at her again. The familiar action calmed me and balanced my mind.

"I will remember and bring you only honour," I replied ceremonially. I then looked down to see that the silk, now that the Veil had been removed and was no longer sustaining it, had crumbled to dust. The box, however, would make a nice memento; especially if it retained the magick of only opening for me. Then a thought occurred to me.

"If the Veil is within me, does that mean I can return here at will? What about anyone else having the chance to get here, or find the same kind of power you have just given me?"

"It took nearly four thousand years for one person to meet my criteria, and you're already expecting someone else?" She smiled in amusement. "What you have is only the representation of my Veil from your world. It exists, as do we all, in multiple dimensions in multiple forms. And yes, the Veil will allow you to return, as long as we permit it. Now, one final thing before you start your education."

Isis reached across and stroked Gauvain, who had been sitting quietly on my shoulder observing the proceedings. As she did so, the splints and strapping came off of his wing and fell to the floor. He shook himself and stretched his wings out, and then opened his beak. He skree'd, but I suddenly felt a presence in my mind.

"Many thanks, my lady. That is a vast improvement."

Chapter 18

I turned to Gauvain in shock.

"Dude, you can talk?" I was actually quite taken aback. "Why the hell didn't you say anything before?" Gauvain looked at me with ill-concealed contempt.

"My dear Gavan, do use your intellect. Isis clearly enhanced my abilities when she completed the repair of my wing. You really must improve significantly if you wish to not embarrass the both of us." His voice sounded like an upper-class English gentleman, thanks to his word choice and picking up on my native accent, but underneath there was strength and resolve in his tone.

He was right, and I did feel stupid for not catching on. I was really going to have to try a lot harder if I wanted to prove myself worthy of the trust Isis had shown in me, the gift she had given me by unlocking my power, and then enhancing those gifts by helping me absorb the Veil. I let my mind race, and quickly understood what had happened.

"So we're fully linked now, I take it? Gauvain has access to my mind which is how he can speak to me, and knows my language?" I extrapolated quickly, but still had a couple of questions. "Just how far does that go? Can I learn to access his thoughts? Like, would I be able to send him ahead to search terrain and see through his eyes as he did so? How far would the link stretch?"

"Now you're starting to use your mind properly and ask more intelligent questions," said Isis approvingly. "It's about time. Yes, the link goes both ways, but you'll have to learn what you can and can't do by experimentation. You both have access to your memories, which is why Gauvain is able to speak and knows your language skills, but you are distinct from each other. Everyone's link to their spiritual partner, what some on Earth call familiars, is different. Yours should be quite strong, given how you met and the affection you developed before you were linked, but exactly how strong and flexible will depend on how much you use it. It's like any other ability —the more you use it, the more natural it will be, the more refined it will become and the closer your minds will be."

Gauvain and I looked at each other and I could feel our parallel determination to make our bond as strong and multi-faceted as possible. We would practice as many different uses as we could think of. I was also resolved to work as hard as I could to master every aspect of magick I was taught. I refused to shame my partner, or Isis who had honoured me so greatly by bringing me here and showing such faith in me.

"So is the first lesson translocation to get us out of here?" I asked. "Do I just visualise where I want to be and concentrate?"

"NO!" Isis threw her hands out as she shouted, showing the first sign of distress I had seen in her. "Translocation, both on the same plane and especially across planes, is an advanced skill. You won't learn that until you have mastered the basics and I urge you not to try. You could kill yourself, kill someone where you landed. In fact, all sorts of things could go wrong. I'll take us out, the same as I brought us here."

So saying, she raised her hand and we were back in the meeting hall. Everyone had already left to get on with their daily activities while we had been away, so we had the hall to ourselves. I had no words to express the gratitude I felt at that moment for the gift Isis had given me, so I dropped to one knee and bowed my head, feeling a lump in my throat at the upswelling of emotions (damn, my allergies were starting to make my eyes water again —really, it was the allergies!). Gauvain felt the sensation through our link, shuffled up close to my head and nibbled the top of my ear. I cleared my throat a couple of times, then managed to croak out a few words.

"I promise to do my absolute utmost to justify your faith in me, Isis. I will never forget what you've done for me or be able to truly show my gratitude." I looked up, blinking to clear my eyes (man, they really need to find a way to clear the dust out of here) to see her looking down at me fondly.

"Just remember who you are, and don't lose yourself to the power," she said. "I won't be directly involved in your instruction, but I will be kept updated on your progress as well as looking in on things from time to time." That thought alone would be enough to keep me focused and humble. I stood up and looked her straight in the eye. I said nothing, to avoid coming out with something trite or inane, and simply nodded to her.

She smiled kindly, stroked Gauvain and then stepped forward to kiss me lightly on the cheek. She then turned and walked out of the hall as I simply stared after her, already developing a bit of a crush. Unbidden, an image of Angelica surfaced in my mind and stood next to an image of Isis. They merged into each other, leaving me with Angelica's face but Isis' hair (I had a thing for redheads, so sue me). The body was all Angelica, at which point I realised that apart from the hair, everything was Angelica. I knew then that if a real-life goddess couldn't eclipse her, my feelings for Angelica could become very dangerous –mostly to me.

At least the realisation brought me back to reality and cleared the rose tint out of my vision. It was time to get to work, so I squared my shoulders and picked up my bag. At least my link with Gauvain meant he was ready for the strap, so he hopped around to let me settle it then dug his claws in for a firm grip. I headed out of the hall to find Liam and Alex and start my schooling –I heard an echo of Robbie Coltrane saying, "Yer a wizard Harry," as I set off, and chuckled to myself.

As I walked, I tried to feel for the magick within myself. I had no idea what I was supposed to feel, so failed dismally. I tried to create electricity in my hand but although I felt a tingle, I saw nothing. I was unsure if it was just wishful thinking that had caused the tingle rather than magick.

I thought about it, deciding that rather than trying for some flashy trick, I would try something useful and see if I could open my mind to detect other people around me. Not necessarily their thoughts at first, just their presence. I remembered the hint from The Inheritance Cycle, that it was always useful to know who was around you and what intentions they might have towards you.

I tried to imagine the walls around my mind shattering like the shell of the Veil or my memory construct, then decided that wasn't the right image to use as I wouldn't want them gone all the time. I had to be able to close my mind if necessary, so I changed it to pulling back curtains on a rail, allowing me to see the world around me in a way I never had before. My awareness flowed out to flood the area around me, and I immediately felt ripples in my consciousness as I picked up on various forms of life close by. There were strong and weak ripples, so now I had to find a way to tell what each kind of ripple was.

Satisfied that I had made a start, I hurried to Liam and Alex's home to begin my formal training. As I got nearer, I felt three of the strong ripples ahead of me in the house. All three felt different, two stronger than the third. The two stronger ones also had different feels to them. I couldn't tell any more at present, but it was my first day.

I knocked on the door, going in when I heard Alex call. She squealed excitedly when she saw me and dusted her hands clean of the flour she was working with, wiping them on her apron as she walked towards me.

"You're back! How did it go? Did it work? Did your magick get unlocked? How did she do it? What have you managed so far?" She bombarded me with questions in her excitement and eagerness to hear the details.

"Give the poor guy a chance to speak, Alex!" Her husband laughed as he walked in. "Sorry to bombard you like that," he continued, "but we're just so excited by the realisation of the prophecy. Also, if we're going to teach you, we need to know where we're starting from."

"Well, so far Gauvain and I are linked and can hear each other's thoughts. I managed to become aware of other life energies around me, but I can't tell who or what they belong to yet. I certainly haven't heard anyone else's thoughts. I tried to create electricity in my hand but barely felt a tingle." I felt somewhat embarrassed by how pathetically little it sounded when I laid it out like that, but they rushed to reassure me.

"Don't worry, it's not as bad as you think. Even our own children don't unlock their powers until they hit puberty, and it certainly doesn't all come to them at once," said Alex kindly.

"We aren't all gifted to the same degree, either," Liam added. "Some of us struggle with the basics while others –like Isis, for example –have abilities that make the rest of us seem almost like simple humans. Alex and I are considered to be above average in power and ability, so we are often asked to teach children when they come into their powers. There are a few teachers around the city, but we're the closest to the gate you came in through. That was why we volunteered to teach you. We're used to explaining things to someone who has no idea what they're doing. I'm actually impressed that you managed to start perceiving others around you on your own —you must have a good degree of natural ability. I'll be interested to see how far you go."

I had to smile, as Liam started to take on the tone and mannerisms of a school-teacher towards the end of his little speech. Gauvain roused himself and stretched his wings.

"It will be good that they are used to instructing children," he remarked. "I sense you will need all the help you can obtain if we are not to dishonour the trust Isis has placed in us." His precise speech and attitude made me think of a samurai, and I was even more certain that his name reflected his personality. Then I processed what he had said and bristled.

"Hey, I'm not that bad!" I objected, somewhat annoyed at his lack of faith in me. "I made a start just on our way here!" I had enough trouble believing in myself —I didn't need someone permanently linked to me who was going to be putting me down and doubting me.

"I merely stated a fact. I am not trying to be offensive…" he started.

"Well, you are!" I retorted, stung by his attitude.

He shuffled uncomfortably, realising that he wasn't exactly being supportive, and he did owe some allegiance to me for rescuing him, patching him up, and caring for him. Also, now that we were linked, we should be more supportive of each other, not fighting and sniping.

"I simply want you to realise that despite Isis' gift to you, you should be aware that your abilities will not simply flow without effort. You will have to work hard to unlock and master them."

"I know it's not going to be a cakewalk! At least I'm not the one who crashed and burned using the natural gifts I was born with!" I jibed facetiously, still unhappy with his apparent lack of faith in me so looking to embarrass him and sting him in return. It may sound childish, but it was how I often reacted to combative situations. Liam and Alex had been watching me with amusement, but I was unsure if they could hear Gauvain like I could. I looked at them and raised an eyebrow, to which Alex laughed but shook her head.

"We could tell you were talking to Gauvain, but he was only talking to you. Spirit partners can talk to other people if they wish to —magick users most easily but anyone if they truly try, as you will be able to once you've learnt the skills. Usually they talk primarily to their bonded companion. You two are going to be together a long time, so you're going to have to be careful. You won't agree all the time, just like any relationship, but beware of letting a little disagreement or even a well-meaning comment taken the wrong way get blown out of proportion. Now apologise to each other. I'm guessing Gauvain was just trying to keep you grounded and point out how much work you'll have to put into your studies. Gauvain, Gavan is going to need your help and support, not belittling comments that erode his self-confidence."

Gauvain and I looked at each other. He cocked his head and looked out of the eye nearest me, under the ridge above his eye. I reached up to stroke him, and he bent his head to press into my hand. As I touched him, my sense of his emotions strengthened. I could feel his regret at having upset me. I softly held the end of his beak and kissed him between his eyes, and he made a soft rrk almost like a purr. I could feel his love for me washing across our link, so I sent mine back and I could feel it strengthening the bond we shared.

"Good," said Alex, with all the authority of a mother disciplining her wayward children, which made both of us shuffle our feet guiltily, then share another look like we were conspiring to commit more mischief. "Now, it's time to get to work."

Chapter 19

"When your power was unlocked, what did you feel?" asked Alex continuing in the same firm teaching tone, and her husband leant forward in interest. I closed my eyes, thought back to the room with the bowl, and considered what had happened. I remembered thinking back to my childhood memory, the image turning to crystal and shattering, and the liquid light infusing into my body and causing the rush of burning cold. I opened my eyes and described the sensation to Alex.

She smiled at me and said, "That's good, we can work with that. You need to bring that sensation to mind, then direct the 'cold rush' to where you want it to create whatever you're trying to do. After a while, you'll get used to calling up your power without thinking of the cold and it will just be there, but you've spent years without your power, so you need to retrain your mind to access it."

"OK, that actually makes sense. What should I try to do first?" I asked. Liam looked around the kitchen and picked up a cup. He placed it in the centre of the kitchen table and pointed to it.

"Move the cup," he said, moving aside and sitting down again. I looked at it and tried to reach out with my mind. I had about as much success as a goldfish trying to climb a tree.

"Remember the cold. Let it flow down your arm, then direct it out of your hand to push the cup. Don't try to lift and carry it, just slide it at first," he instructed. I sat down, closed my eyes and felt for the cold.

I felt, reached, strained (but stopped before I farted or worse), and got nothing. I opened my eyes and let out my breath in a frustrated rush.

"Don't try to force it," said Alex, "remember the sensation and let it grow."

I nodded at her, then turned back to the cup. I closed my eyes again and thought back to the memory. After a moment, I felt the cold build in the back of my mind. I cajoled it to grow, then directed it down my right arm into my hand. As it got there, I opened my eyes and reached towards the cup, trying to guide the cold energy out of my fingers to push the cup across the surface of the table. It didn't move, but a light layer of frost developed on the rim. I huffed again, but Alex and Liam were pleased.

"Don't expect to be perfect straight away. The first thing you have to do is learn to access and channel your power. Then you can make it do what you want. You just made the first step —you channelled power. OK, it didn't do what you wanted it to, but you did something," she rushed to reassure me, putting her hand on my shoulder.

I didn't let on, but I truly was excited. I had used magick! The power had been there! That knowledge alone would make it easier next time. Now, as Alex had said, I just had to get used to accessing it more naturally and making it do what I wanted. I straightened up in my seat and felt for the cold again. This time I knew with absolute conviction that it was there waiting for me, so felt it much more easily. I sent it down my arm towards the cup again, and this time it froze completely, but still didn't move.

"Excellent! You were much smoother this time. It looked easier and less strained, also more efficient as we can see by the total freezing of the mug," said Liam, applauding. "Maybe now that you know the power is there, stop thinking of it as cold. It's clearly colouring your thinking so the force is coming out as a frigid stream rather than pure energy that you can direct."

Again, it made complete sense. Think of cold and you get cold —it wasn't exactly rocket science or quantum physics. This time, instead of thinking of cold, I would remember the light. Maybe if I pictured my power as a pool of liquid light, I could direct a flow of it down my arm and out of my hand to achieve the desired effect. I closed my eyes and pictured a reservoir of light, then a stream coming from it flowing towards my fingers. I aimed it at the cup, but aside from melting the frost, there was no movement. I tried several more times, getting increasingly frustrated with each attempt. Finally, I grew angry and pictured the store of energy emptying to rush down my arm like a tsunami. I opened my eyes to stare at the cup, shoving my power at it with all the weight of my accumulated irritation behind it. The resulting force hit the cup so hard it shattered into fragments, making my teachers jump slightly at the sudden noise and sit back in their chairs away from the table. They look at each other somewhat startled.

"Um, yeah, OK, so that was… better," stammered Liam. "At least you got away from the cold."

"I'm guessing you weren't expecting me to be able to shatter a mug this early on?" I asked, somewhat proud of the fact that I had unleashed enough power to shock my instructors.

"Not exactly, although we probably should expect that nothing will be routine with you. You're older, for a start, so your mind will be harder to re-train. Your awakening wasn't exactly normal either, so we have no frame of reference for your unique situation," stated Alex, sitting forward again. "Don't be too eager to just use power. Without control, power is almost useless and frankly dangerous. Until you can learn to use just the level of force you want, this is the only exercise you'll do. Also, be careful of your emotions when practicing. Becoming angry may give you a brief boost, as it just did, but it can become a crutch you lean on too much. After a while, it can become the only way you can access your power, then your magick becomes linked to negative emotions and turns dark." She was very firm, tapping the table with her index finger as she made her points.

I definitely understood that control was key, but right now I was just so excited at seeing the results of my power, I was almost bouncing in my chair. Then I suddenly had an image in my head of a certain diminutive green master warning his student about the Dark Side, and I sobered. Liam waved his hand and the fragments from the mug reassembled into a complete piece. At that point I felt something warm trickle over my top lip and wiped at it with my hand. I saw a drop of blood smeared along my finger, evidence of the strain from using such a blast of magick, and they both looked at me tellingly.

"I think until you learn a little more precision, you can use a rock –if only for the sake of our kitchenware!" joked Alex and I laughed along with them, pulled out of my dark thoughts to once again feel the joy of the progress I'd made. Liam went outside and picked up a small stone, maybe an inch across with a flattish base and a domed top. It looked like an egg that had broken in half, and he set it on the flat side.

"Just be sure to have a solid surface behind the pebble wherever you practice," he said. "You don't want to hit it as hard as you just hit the cup, or the stone could fly off and really hurt someone." I calmed myself again at the thought of the potential damage I could cause without meaning to while I was learning. I nodded at him seriously.

"I understand. The last thing I want to do is hurt an innocent bystander," I replied. "I'll make sure to be careful."

I readied for another attempt, this time on the rock, making sure to calm myself first to avoid a repeat of my recent emotional surge. I visualised the light again and this time pictured a valve to allow me to adjust the release. I opened it a little and directed the flow down my arm and sent it flying towards the stone... which barely quivered. I looked at it in annoyance, but Liam almost looked pleased.

"You're going to have to get used to building up the right amount of power, guiding it how you want, and controlling the release. You're not trying to destroy a building, nor are you just moving a single hair." He was encouraging in his tone, but I could sense the undercurrent of relief that my earlier outburst had been tempered by control.

"Until you can move the rock reliably every time," continued Alex, "you need to work at this exercise at least three hours a day. Don't neglect your practice, or you'll never get it. At the same time, I would recommend a break after every hour of training. Otherwise you can end up getting frustrated, which can lead to you trying too hard out of anger, which is when you lose control. You're also more likely to over-strain and cause yourself injury, potentially far more serious than a simple nosebleed." She actually shook her finger at me with her final comment, reminding me of my lapse. I took it on the chin as a well-deserved reprimand and warning.

"How do I know how much power to use?" I asked thoughtfully. "What I mean is, if I'm trying to move something, do I have to work out how much it weighs to know how much power to use? Like, will it take twice as much power to move something twice as heavy?"

They both smiled at me at that. "Now that's exactly the sort of thing all our students ask, because they're all used to doing things the physical way, the same as you. Learn to move the rock the way you want to, no more and no less, then we'll talk about it some more. Don't try to run before you can crawl. You took a big step today, learning to at least access your ability when you want to. Bear in mind, when you woke up this morning you didn't even have magick." Alex sounded exactly like one of my old teachers with that little speech, but I was a lot more receptive than I had been back then —this was magick, not geography, so I was far more motivated to pay attention and do well.

I was noticing that Liam seemed to do more of the encouraging, whilst his wife more naturally assumed the role of stern mother and schoolmistress. Their differing styles complemented each other seamlessly and I could tell that I would learn a lot from them. I had to admit though, I was definitely ready for a break before my next try. The unfamiliar exertions had given me a slight headache to go with my minor nosebleed. Something more routine also sprang to mind.

"Speaking of not having magick, something occurred to me yesterday when I was walking through the market. I know you guys do actually use coins here —the market manager gave me some for helping break down all the stalls after the market. But how can I actually earn some money to pay for my room and board? I don't want to be anyone's charity case, plus I'd like to be able to buy some souvenirs for a couple of friends back home." My erstwhile tutors actually looked a little proud of me at my enquiry.

"You know, with all you have going on I would not have expected you to think about such a mundane thing," said Liam. "Isis had already spoken to us about supporting you while you were here, seeing as she was the one who brought you. She offered to give us a stipend so you could focus on your studies."

"I appreciate that, really I do," I replied, "but I think having some contact with other people and being a useful member of society is more me. Also, I might see other people using magick in their professions and pick up some tips."

"Picking up advice and tips is one thing," said Alex firmly, jumping on my suggestion and raising her finger to back up her tone, "but you are absolutely not to try anything other than your exercises. I don't care if you get teased, ridiculed or dared. If you can't handle being less able than those you're working with, leave. If we hear about you trying something before we tell you that you can, we'll go straight to Isis. You do it more than once, and she might even lock your power away from you and send you home. Don't cross us on this; I'm not even close to kidding."

I looked at Liam, smiling slightly at being spoken to like a child but he simply crossed his arms, just as resolute as Alex. I understood that they were trying to protect me as well as everyone else, and I swore to them that I would not embarrass them or abuse their lessons, which reminded me of my similar promise to Isis. Then we agreed that mornings should be mine to go out and find some gainful employment to enable me to pay my way, but that afternoons would be devoted to my studies.

"Right," said Liam, uncrossing his arms and slapping the table lightly, "now that we've got that agreed, back to your practice. Move the rock." I worked at it for the rest of the afternoon, with a couple of breaks when Alex insisted, which I was glad to take to prevent my headache from worsening. The most I managed to do for the rest of that day was make the rock shimmy a couple of times. I clearly wasn't going to be flying items around the room any time soon. I also hoped that the headaches would lessen as I became accustomed to wielding the magick.

Later that evening, as I lay in bed thinking over the momentous events of the day, I suddenly realised that by absorbing the Veil, and with the silk crumbling to dust, I now had nothing to hand over to Angelica and her group. What the hell would I tell them? I didn't want them finding out about my magick, if I could ever learn to control it properly, and then demanding I use it for them. I certainly had no intention of being forced to lead some kind of group trip to bring them here to pester Isis for powers of their own. I would have to consider this carefully while I continued my education.

Chapter 20

The next morning I woke up early and went out after a cup of Alex's tea to see what I could find by way of employment while Gauvain went off to hunt. I took the few coins I had earned and purchased a toothbrush (they used natural bristles magically inserted into a carved and polished wooded handle). I wandered around through the city and thought about what I might have to contribute.

My biggest contribution would probably be my knowledge of Earth. Since I enjoyed cooking, I could maybe introduce a few new recipes to the people here. I went to a shop that seemed to be a combination of bakery, deli, and café, introducing myself to the man I thought was the owner.

It turned out he was just the guy who ran the counter while the owner was actually the young chef, whose name was Poppy. She was blonde with blue eyes and petite at only around five-foot-four, slim with almost elfin features set in a perpetual half-smile. He called her to the front, and I asked her if I could have a job in the mornings, in return for teaching her some recipes from my world that she might not be familiar with. She readily agreed, excited at the prospect of learning some new dishes.

When we went back to the kitchen, Poppy told me that she only used magick to do some of the mixing, fine grinding and chopping. The rest, she insisted, was always better if you took your time to do it by hand and didn't rush it, especially as the flavours took time to develop and mature the right way. Cooking was a magick in and of itself, so was better without outside magick contaminating it.

I could definitely appreciate her attitude and was excited to see what she had on the menu, to enable me to decide what to show her. She set me a few basic tests in the kitchen to see what I could do, but since I enjoyed cooking back home, I had no problem with any of them. Poppy saw how I coped and decided that I would spend two-thirds of my time in the kitchen and one-third up front. I also suggested that I could make a few lunch deliveries on my way home at the end of my morning shift. She readily agreed, since she had apparently been considering adding a delivery service but didn't have the staff to do so yet.

After seeing the dishes she had on her rotation, I showed her four of my personal favourite specialities. She already had a spicy burger type sandwich, so I showed her my special chilli. I included the tips of frying the chilli powder before adding the onions and garlic to the oil, then adding chocolate as a balance towards the end. I also showed her my boozy chocolate truffles, which she absolutely adored.

Poppy already had a fruit bread along with her savoury styles, but I showed her a simple brioche recipe which she promptly started thinking of ways to use with her own particular flair. I suggested a bread and butter pudding dessert made with chocolate chips, which she scribbled down to try later. Finally, seeing her home-made caramel, I showed her my chocolate chip chocolate brownies with salted caramel in the centre and salted caramel icing on top. The brownie recipe had her almost crying with joy, and she immediately named it as the new house speciality.

I was pleased that she liked my recipes and we had worked companionably in the kitchen, so I could definitely see this going well. I went out to the front where the guy at the counter, whose name was Roman, showed me the ropes. He was slightly shorter than me with mousey brown hair and stubble. He ran the front of the shop with an almost military efficiency, seeming more stand-offish than most people I'd encountered so far, although I couldn't quite work out why. Still, I couldn't expect everyone to like me, and I was quite happy to take time to get to know him. Maybe I'd figure him out better as time went on. My immediate instinct was to try to ignore him or walk away but

I had no idea how long I would require to learn my magick. I had got on well with Poppy, so I decided to build a friendship gradually if that proved possible.

I finished my shift by running some sandwiches across to a couple of other shops nearby. I also took some of the chilli I'd made when showing Poppy the recipe home to Alex and Liam for us to have for dinner.

As I returned I met a young girl, maybe thirteen or fourteen, coming out of the house. She had brown hair in a plait down to about the middle of her back and brown eyes. She had the slightly chubby cheeks of a child just about to hit their puberty growth spurt and was dressed in a simple homespun smock. She smiled when she saw me and waved, walking over to say hello.

"You're Gavan, aren't you?" she asked eagerly. "My name's Olistene, but everyone calls me Oli. I've been studying with Alex and Liam too. They told me that I'll be having my lessons in the morning while you're out. I used to have them in the afternoon but I actually prefer this, so I get my afternoon to myself. Have you managed to move anything yet? My mum knew my magick was waking up when I slowed a plate down before it hit the floor after I knocked it off the table a couple of months ago. I've always been a bit of a klutz. Oh, I'm sorry, I'm blabbering away, and you must want to have lunch then get to your lesson. It's so exciting isn't it? I can't wait to work with you –I hope you manage to learn everything OK. It must be a bit daunting, trying to learn all this as a human. Just ask if you want some help. Anyway, I'll let you get on. Bye!" She barely took a breath through the entire delivery, although I was sure I noticed a slight derogatory sneer when she said 'human'. She made it sound as though it was some disease or unwelcome bug. She turned and walked away, waving as she went.

"It was nice to meet you, Oli!" I called after her as she left, already less than enthralled with the idea of working with her after she had expressed such disdain towards me.

After a light lunch of salad and some cheese, I set to work on my magickal practice. I tried time and again to get the pebble to slide across the table, but met with no success. I was at least able to feel the flow of magick reliably, but I couldn't seem to push it towards the rock strongly enough to get the damn thing to move.

I took a break after an hour at Alex's insistence and walked outside, rubbing my temples and stretching. I felt Gauvain coming home from his hunt and turned unerringly towards him. He swooped down, landing on my outstretched arm, then hopping to my shoulder. We caught up on what we had done while we were apart, each happy with our achievements but glad be to together again.

He had managed to catch a young fledgling in flight, stooping on it from out of the sun. I could feel his pride at his success and his joy in his natural abilities. I congratulated him on his prowess, smiling inwardly as he preened at my praise. We agreed between us that while I was at work, he would hunt, but then we would work together to try to improve my magickal technique. I felt that our bond, combined with his natural instincts, might help me to more easily get used to my new abilities.

I carried him inside with me and sat back down at the table. Once again I reached for my magick and let it build. I channelled the light down my arm towards the rock, but it fizzled out before it even reached my hand this time. Gauvain shuffled on my shoulder and looked at me.

"You seem to be considering what happened yesterday too much," he said. "I am aware that you were shocked when the cup smashed, and then felt rightly concerned by what could occur if you propelled the rock with such force, but everything in life is a struggle of some kind. You must learn to relax and allow the power to flow, then guide it to achieve your goal. One cannot force a river to obey, but it can be subtly influenced towards the desired destination."

What he said was very true and was something I'd heard in different forms, from many sources. The question was always how much force to use to get the job done without overdoing it. It was like trying to pick up a bag without knowing what was inside it –too much force and you'd throw it over your head, too little and it wouldn't even leave the floor.

The question was how to pick it up with just enough strength. Thinking about it like that actually gave me a clue. When you picked up a bag, you hefted it and then used gradually more muscle until the bag lifted. What I needed to do was find a way to gradually increase the flow of magick I was aiming at the stone until it moved the way I wanted, rather than sending a single pulse that either fizzled into nothing or sent the rock flying through the air like a bullet.

Now I just needed to learn how to sustain my magick for longer periods, rather than building it up and releasing it like a sneeze. Liam came in from the sitting room, where he had apparently been reading if the book in his hand was any indication, to see how I was doing. I told him what I had figured out. He looked extremely pleased with me, although somewhat surprised at my insight.

"I'm impressed. That's an extremely useful metaphor, and not one I've ever thought of using when I teach," he said, rubbing his chin thoughtfully with his right hand while propping his elbow on the book in his left hand. "What you're talking about doing will take a lot more time and effort to learn and perfect but will eventually lead to much greater control over your abilities. As long as you're prepared to take that extra time, I think your method could result in you having greater precision than anyone we've ever taught. Usually the kids are too excited to get their magick flowing to slow down. Your added maturity will stand you in good stead in this case." I had an image of Oli in my head and imagined what her reaction would be if I ever surpassed her, and I smiled at the thought.

I decided to stick with my idea and try to build up my magick, then release it in a gradually increasing flow rather than a sudden blast. I chose to visualise a hosepipe connected to a tap in the wall around my imagined magickal reservoir. That way I could adjust the flow with both the tap and the nozzle of the hose, allowing for much greater control and gradual alterations in the flow. Gauvain definitely approved of my technique but was ready for a nap after his hunt, so fluffed up on my shoulder and closed his eyes, having spent the last ten minutes preening his wings to his satisfaction. I worked on building up my power and sustaining the stream for the rest of the afternoon. While I managed to increase the length of time I could maintain it, I certainly couldn't move the pebble yet.

Alex came in and also expressed her approval of my idea, which her husband had obviously told her, then told me to stop for the day. I protested at first, wanting to get the rock to at least quiver today, but she was adamant.

"You've been trying constantly since Liam came in here. That was three hours ago," she said firmly, picking up the pebble from the table and handing it to me.

143

"What? Three hours?" I was shocked. How had time gotten away from me like that? I thought about it and realised that I had been so internally focused that I had ceased to be aware of the outside world, including the passage of time. I stretched my arms upwards and heard a series of cracks, as my neck and back unlocked from being hunched up in one position for so long.

Alex laughed at the sound and gave me a typical mother's "I told you so" look while holding her hands up. I laughed along with her and rubbed my suddenly throbbing head.

"Wow, you weren't kidding!" Now that I had moved, the fatigue hit me in a wave. "I think this is the first time I've actually been really hungry since I arrived in Aaru. It just proves that mental effort can be more tiring than physical exertion." She nodded at me and smiled.

"Oh yes. I know a lot of people believe that sitting and thinking can never be classed as exertion, but I've never been more tired than when I learned to master my magick." She smiled again and patted my hand.

I got up and helped her set the table for dinner. We were going to have some crusty white bread with the chilli, which Alex was warming on the stove. The smell reminded me of home, but I was still glad I was here. We all sat down to eat, and even young Conor enjoyed it. I hadn't made the chilli too hot, but I had told Poppy about making different levels of heat to let people choose how spicy they liked it. I had even told her about some of the food challenges that some restaurants held to see if people could take the hottest levels.

While we were eating, I told my surrogate family the same thing and they laughed at the thought of people crying with the heat and begging for milk or yoghurt to ease the pain. I assured them that although I knew how to make a chilli that hot, I didn't see the fun in suffering for the sake of food.

We finished our meal and all pitched in with clearing up, Alex washing while I dried, Liam and their son putting things away. I was more than ready for bed, even though it was still early, so I said goodnight and headed off to my room. I got undressed and lay down in bed, Gauvain cuddling up to me as usual. I fell asleep in moments and I don't think I shifted all night.

In the morning I got up and washed, glad to finally be able to brush my teeth properly, then headed out to work. I was still stiff after sitting so long yesterday, but at least my headache had eased. When I arrived I said good morning to Roman, but he just grunted at me, continuing to set up for the day. I shrugged and went into the kitchen to help Poppy, and we got on with the baking.

The morning passed pleasantly enough, then I headed up front to help Roman deal with the lunch rush. I was starting to learn that despite being on a different plane of existence, the people of Aaru weren't all that different from those on Earth. Bearing that in mind, I tried to figure out why Roman might be unhappy with me being here.

It didn't take me long to reach an understanding of his attitude. I was spending time in the kitchen with Poppy while he was stuck up front. He clearly had feelings for Poppy but she had no idea, and he didn't seem to have any confidence or knowledge of how to approach her. I could definitely relate, and while I might not exactly be a Casanova myself, I could certainly give worthwhile advice for someone else to follow. As soon as there was a brief pause between customers, I went over to him and struck up a conversation.

"Roman, I just wanted to make sure you knew, I have no romantic interest in Poppy. I'm actually kind of interested in someone back where I'm from, plus I'm way too focused on learning to use my magick to get involved with anyone right now." He looked relieved but still a little down.

"I'm guessing you are interested in Poppy?" He nodded at me but hunched his shoulders and turned away slightly.

"I just don't know if she likes me." I smiled at him and patted his shoulder.

"I'll try to see what I can find out. Don't worry, I'll be subtle," I reassured him. This at least was a problem I thought I could deal with. We finished the lunch rush and I delivered to the same shops as yesterday, then headed home for more practice. Gauvain joined me as I walked home, having caught a couple of mice today. I looked at him and teased him gently.

"Don't go hunting every day or you'll end up too fat to fly!" He nipped my ear in disgust and cuffed me with his wing.

"I am still growing so I need the protein to increase my muscles. I am not getting fat!" I smiled at how easily I'd irritated him, but quickly stroked his head and reassured him.

"I know you're not, and you're definitely growing fast. Still, make sure you get enough exercise as well as enough food." He stared at me haughtily and clicked his beak.

"I spend most of the morning flying around. I need to build up my endurance, the same as you continue to do when working on your magick. I would remind you that since Isis linked us, I have access to your memories, so I am well aware of how to structure my training." I felt guilty, as I honestly hadn't considered his development in all the excitement of obtaining my magick and learning to use it. I apologised to him and he nibbled my ear more gently this time. Just like any two people getting to know each other, we still had a lot to learn, but we were nevertheless very glad to have been bonded. I had also never been in such a long-term relationship, so I was still getting used to how to behave and react.

I got home and gave Alex a pie that I had brought home for dinner, then settled myself at the kitchen table with the pebble again. I remembered my thoughts from yesterday and called up my power, opening the "tap" to ready the "hose". I let the pressure build up until both my head and chest felt full to bursting, then aimed a trickle through my index finger as the nozzle of the hose towards the rock. I gradually increased the rate of flow until I suddenly saw the pebble wobble.

Excited, I pushed more power towards the rock, increasing the flow a little at a time. The pebble shook more quickly, then finally shifted a fraction of an inch. I kept going until the pebble was slowly sliding across the table. After it had moved about four inches I was out of energy and gasping with the exertion. I heard clapping from the doorway and turned to see my tutors walk in.

"Well done," Liam said, "that was excellent. That showed some of the greatest control I've ever seen in a new magick user." His wife echoed the sentiment and Gauvain congratulated me as well. I think I felt more joy at my progress than I had in passing any of my exams at school. I beamed at my friends and then turned around to reset the pebble and try again.

The following day, on my way home from work, I ran into Oli again. She was a little less manic this time, but still very excited to be learning magick.

"Oh, hi Gavan! How are your studies going?" she asked me. "I managed to throw the pebble off the table four times in a row today. My mum's helping me practice, so I'm getting much more consistent."

"I managed to slide the pebble about four inches yesterday," I replied, knowing exactly what her reaction would be to my perceived lack of progress and readying myself to hear it. Sure enough, she didn't disappoint.

"Oh well, keep practising, I'm sure you'll get stronger eventually," she said, trying to be encouraging but sounding smugly superior instead. Clearly she was pleased that she was doing better than me, as I had known she would be, and her attitude was just one more spur for me to redouble my efforts. She ran off without looking back, and I saw her meet up with two younger children who looked a lot like her. Maybe they were her brother and sister?

Chapter 21

Over the next couple of weeks I began to suffer more with headaches and nosebleeds as the strain of using my magick began to accumulate. I started to feel that my mental imagery to control my power flow was more restrictive than it needed to be, causing excessive strain on my physical wellbeing. I saw Oli several more times as she left when I arrived back after work, and she became increasingly smug and derogatory at her continued progress ahead of me. I finally decided to sit down and create an entirely new mental framework for accessing my power.

I spoke to Alex one day when I got home and she agreed that I needed to alter my methods, commenting that she had noticed that I was struggling far more than she expected I would need to. She informed me that I needed to create my own imagery, otherwise it wouldn't feel natural to me and would still require more effort than necessary. With that in mind, she refused to make any suggestions regarding how to visualise my energy. She only advised me not to try to restrict the flow, simply to find a way to open myself to the power and then focus it as desired. I nodded and walked outside to stretch, leaving her to go back to her humming and dancing as she worked. I had noticed that she seemed to do it almost unconsciously whenever she focused on what she was doing.

I saw Liam coming back with some shopping as I went outside, so I smiled and winked at him, putting my finger to my lips and gesturing over my shoulder with my thumb. He grinned conspiratorially at me, immediately understanding what I meant –I'm sure he'd seen her doing the same thing many times. He crept in quietly, putting the shopping by the door, then I heard a shriek followed by a light slap and laughter. I smiled to myself as I heard their voices moving deeper into the house, then moved away from the door into the garden. Gauvain was approaching, and I reached through our link to try to feel him and possibly see through his eyes. We had been practicing daily in order to both cement our bond and respond to Isis' advice that we would determine the strength and flexibility of our link by how much we worked on it.

I was starting to feel the wind as he flew and see some of his view when he got closer, and I was hopeful this would become clearer and reach over greater distances as time went on. He landed on my shoulder and rubbed his head against my cheek, then turned to preen his wings –his favourite occupation when he wasn't hunting. I smiled inwardly and sat down to enjoy the light and warmth of the suns.

As I sat on the garden wall a new image suggested itself to me. I would view my magick as an internal sun on which I could open or close a door, then my hand would be a lens to focus with, like when I had used a magnifying glass to burn holes in leaves as a child. I visualised until I created a clear picture in my mind and then relaxed. Over the next few days, using my new technique, my practice started making significant progress. After a few days, I was able to push the pebble all the way across the table with hardly any effort. I then moved on to lifting it, first straight up and down, then moving it in patterns. After that came larger rocks, then two at once, then three. Each time I mastered an exercise, one of my instructors increased the complexity, determined to push my limits as far as possible.

I saw Olistene a few times over the next few weeks and each time she flaunted her progress, although she began to become sullen as I caught up and then surpassed her. From what she said, she was floating a rock before me, but she struggled with the precision required for some of the more complex patterns and didn't move on to multiple rocks when I did.

Meanwhile, my morning work at the shop was much more congenial now that I had spoken to Roman. I left it a couple of days, then casually mentioned to Poppy that she always seemed to be working. I asked if she ever went out and had fun and she laughed, saying she enjoyed her work, so it was all the fun she needed. When I asked about meeting anyone, I actually noticed her eyes flick towards the door of the kitchen that led to the front where Roman was working.

I smiled at her, then asked her if she liked him and she blushed peony pink. She said that she had had a bit of a crush on him since she was younger, which was why she had hired him to work here. She wasn't sure he noticed her because he always flirted with the girls who came in. I reassured her that he only flirted as a sales tactic to keep them coming back, but I had actually witnessed him turning down an offer of a date from a pretty brunette just the day before.

I told her I would talk to him (yeah right, like I needed to! I swear, magick was a piece of cake compared to relationships!) and see what he thought. When I went out to help him for the lunch rush, I told him that she had hired him because she had always liked him, but thought he wasn't interested. I told him to ask her out for a picnic on Sunday (they used the same day names as on Earth, or maybe that was just because I was there) as the store was closed and see how things went. Let's just say that there were lots of smiles and even a couple of hugs for me from both of them on Monday!

I also noticed another thing after that weekend –my power underwent a step up so I realised that, much like my journey to the city, good deeds were required to maintain and increase my magick. I had also enjoyed helping the two of them get together –I had always liked living vicariously through other people's relationships, since my own terrified me so much and were often such unmitigated disasters (my blind date being the perfect example).

Gauvain was growing fast. I didn't know if it was the natural rate of growth for his kind or whether his growth had been increased due to the magick, but he was soon the size of the largest of hawks on Earth and approaching the stature of a medium to large eagle. His daily flights were keeping him trim and strong, and he had plenty of admirers whenever we were seen together. His toes, when taken together with his talons, were now longer than my fingers. He had to be careful not to grip too hard when he landed, or he'd easily punch holes in my skin. Fortunately our link meant I was always aware of him, otherwise he could have staggered me from landing on my shoulder. His shoulder was now level with the top of my head from that perch. His grooming sessions extended to several hours, and I sometimes teased him about it by nicknaming him 'Vain' when he was preening or being admired.

Once I was able to hold three rocks —all roughly the size of a tennis ball —up in the air at the same time and move all three in different patterns, Alex finally said that we were done with those exercises and it was time to move on. Oli had finally managed the complex pattern with one rock, and Alex had reassured her that greater control and dexterity would come with maturity as she grew into her magick. She still sulked when she found out how far ahead of her I was, and that she was only moving on so that I would have a practice partner.

Our next area of study was the other side of the mental coin, telepathy. I was already used to contacting Gauvain with my mind, and we had strengthened our bond until we could contact each other easily even up to five miles apart. Beyond that, the connection became less distinct but no matter how far Gauvain had flown, we always remained at least aware of each other. Contacting other people would be a different challenge as I first had to identify who I wanted to contact. As Oli and I were both moving on to this stage, her lessons had been moved to the afternoons to coincide with mine, and we would work as partners to hone our abilities.

This would build on the awareness I had managed to create on that first walk from the main hall. Alex told me that this was always taught after telekinesis so that a novice didn't start using too much force and give their practice partner a headache or worse. I immediately saw what she meant and understood her caution. The first afternoon that Oli and I were to work together, she arrived just as I got back from work and joined us for lunch. After the meal, Alex, Oli and I went into the sitting room. We needed to be more comfortable and relaxed for mental exercises.

Alex told us to close our eyes and feel the surrounding area for different minds. When I reached out, I easily became aware of different ripples around me, but those were just the sense of a living creature. As I concentrated harder, the sense of life all around threatened to overwhelm me. I could feel insects, birds, worms and grubs in the soil underneath us, animals, and of course people, especially Oli as she was close by and reaching out in the same way. I had to shut off my mind as the noise set off another headache. My eyes flew open and I explained my problem to Alex. She was amazed at my sensitivity while Oli looked at me enviously for my greater ability.

"You must have had a degree of sensitivity even before you came here," Alex remarked in surprise. "Very few us are aware of as much as you just picked up. You need to try to be aware of everything around you but not listen so hard. It's like walking through a market. There's lots of voices but you concentrate on the one you want to hear and learn to pick it out."

Oli, on the other hand, was upset as she was struggling to sense anything, even me reaching out to her. I told her about my earlier image of removing my mental walls like a curtain and allowing my awareness to flow out over the area. She tried this, and after a couple of attempts was finally able to pick me up clearly, although she still couldn't feel as much as I could. She also resented being told how to do something by a "mere human", a disdain that I could actually detect as we connected. Alex told her to accept help from any source, and that this was why we were working in pairs; so we could learn from each other's progress. She apologised and we moved on, but this episode —although I didn't yet know it —was the start of things going truly bad between us.

I also saw Oli with the two younger children a few times around this time, and I noticed that she was getting much rougher with them. They even looked a little afraid of her at times.

I understood the theory of picking out a particular "voice" that Alex had mentioned, but the practice was going to take exactly that —practice. The first thing I had to learn to do was filter out the non-people noise. Just getting rid of the sense of the smaller creatures took me two whole afternoons of struggle. That first day I had gone to bed with a headache similar to what one might get from standing next to an amplifier at a Metallica concert for three hours. Oli had laughed at what she called my "limited human tolerance", which earned her a stern word from Liam on trying to be a little more sensitive herself, rather than mocking someone who was actually doing better than her.

After three days I was able to filter things down to larger animals, such as dogs and cats or larger, and people. Once I had that level of clarity, I was able to start differentiating individual "voices" from each other. Oli was obviously the easiest to hear, as she was trying to communicate directly with me. I soon learnt that even the awareness of different individuals felt different in my mind, so I was soon able to tell who was around even with my eyes closed.

Oli started to improve as well, although she tended to use more force than I felt was necessary. I wasn't sure if this was due to her immaturity, her lack of sensitivity compared to me, or her annoyance at my greater ability causing her to want to make me uncomfortable. It did have a benefit to me that I'm sure she didn't intend —I learnt to start shielding myself from her energy surges, which I knew would be helpful in the future.

The next stage was to try to hear more detail of each other's thoughts, which for me seemed to be the easiest part. Oli managed this part well enough, although when she saw my greater sensitivity, her resentment towards me grew even more and she would send bursts of mental energy at me while I was open to her, like a child kicking their fellow student under the desk when the teacher wasn't looking. Most of those got through my shielding efforts to begin with, until I started to identify the "twitch" in her thoughts that heralded an attack. Once I picked up on that, I was able to block her again.

We then learned to send our thoughts to another even if they weren't actively listening. This part was quite dangerous, as even if I didn't hurt them, my clarity was such that I could sometimes imprint my thoughts on someone else. Controlling another was obviously a frowned upon practice, and I could certainly understand why, although it was good to know I had that level of ability. I could imagine scenarios where it might be advantageous —mostly life and death, or at least great peril, in which case the rules be damned. I was keeping me and mine alive, thank you very much!

Oli, however, seemed to delight in taking control of a cat or dog and making it do what she wanted. Once she even made a cat jump into a bowl of water, then released it to find its own way out, laughing at its discomfort at being wet. That particular event earned her a suspension from lessons for three days when Alex found out. During her suspension, I saw her playing with her cousins a couple more times —I'd found out that that's who the younger children were. I became even more concerned about her when I saw the boy running away from her in tears once, and the girl looking at her in genuine fear. I mentioned it to Liam and he said he'd speak to her mother, but I heard no more about it.

Around the time I was coming to the end of my telepathy training, a new face appeared among the lunch crowd at Poppy's. She seemed to be in her late teens, although here that could mean she was seventeen or seven hundred. Look at Isis —she appeared to be in her mid-thirties, and she was well over four thousand Earth years old!

The girl was solidly built, with short dark hair, deep coffee-coloured skin, full lips, a broad nose and dark expressive eyes, but surprisingly delicate hands. She was chatting about her work one day and said that she was a new apprentice at one of the jewellers nearby. She asked if we delivered, as it was easier than coming across. Her mentor was apparently quite set in his ways, so preferred to have the same thing for lunch every day when working. He had become very partial to a particular cheese we carried, which he like on a crusty white roll.

She, on the other hand, liked a little more variety so left a rotating order of three different sandwiches. Her only constant was a small piece of the brownie with salted caramel that I had shown Poppy, which was becoming a big hit in the area and sold out completely every day. I spoke to her about the sort of items that her mentor sold, and by her description of some of the pieces it sounded like the stock of the stall where I had seen the twin pendants that I had wanted to get for Summer and Emily.

The next time I did deliveries, I made the run to their shop and sure enough, there were the pendants on display in one of the windows. When I went in I remarked on them and asked if the shop had some sort of lay-away scheme. The young assistant didn't know what I meant but once I explained the idea she said it was a common practice, but she had just never heard that particular term before. I paid a first instalment, and the pendants were taken out of the display and set aside for me.

I headed home for lunch and practice with a particular spring in my step knowing that I had finally found and started to pay for the gifts I wanted to take home for the girls. I continued to make weekly instalments out of my wages over the next few months.

Meanwhile, my magickal studies had moved on. Oli had returned from her brief suspension even more sullen. She had, however, progressed enough in her telepathy to be allowed to move on with me to energy manipulation. This was different from simply building up a surge of magick and then using it to push a pebble. For this we had to first learn to collect energy from outside ourselves. There were two different overall classes of energy we would learn draw on –life and elemental.

Life energy is what powers animals and plants, down to the smallest bacteria. While collecting this energy is easier, it is finite as doing so weakens or kills the life form you take it from. Many magick users never progressed beyond using this form, which is why they never learnt higher magickal abilities. Those required much more power and refinement, so hurting other lives to do so was unacceptable. Only those who could learn elemental energy manipulation could go on to learn the higher levels of magick.

Once I heard this, I was determined to progress to elemental levels, no matter how long it might take, not only because I wanted to go as far as I could and learn higher level abilities, but also because I refused to hurt others all the time to fuel my magick. I felt that it was not just unfair, but to take energy from a life form you had to connect to it (hence learning telepathy before moving on to this stage), which meant you then felt its pain and death as you stole its life. No way was I subjecting myself to that repeatedly!

The actual collection was something that both Oli and I found quite easy, but for very different reasons. She delighted in exerting her dominance over other creatures as she had already exhibited, so simply treated them much as she would a candy bar or sandwich. I, on the other hand, looked at them as a separate sun. In the same way as I viewed my own internal one, I could focus the energy as needed but try not to pull too much. Liam was careful to have us only do small things with the collected energy at first, only drawing from larger life forms that could handle the limited drain.

I did, in my early attempts, cause the death of a family of mice by mistake which reduced me to tears. Oli laughed and berated me for my display of human weakness. Gauvain eventually pulled me out of my depression by simply eating the mice, thanking me for the snack and loudly proclaiming that they would have died anyway had he hunted them. It took me two full days to overcome my aversion to trying again, but my instructors informed me that I would be unable to progress any further unless I overcame my regret.

They understood my aversion and agreed with me to a degree, even looking somehow pleased at my distaste for my carelessness, but simply advised me to be more cautious in monitoring the life forces I connected to. I also managed to further alienate Oli in our later exercises by accidentally rendering her unconscious when I pulled more energy from her than she drew from me during an exchange lesson. This did not, however, seem to give her any insight into how she made "lesser creatures" feel when she harvested energy from them.

Once I had learned to collect energy, I had to do something with it. I had to learn to change it into physical shields, as opposed to the mental shields I had developed against Oli (that was less than fun as Liam hit me in the stomach five times in a row with a ball of electricity before I got it). There was also electricity, fire, ice, wind, pure energy (kind of like an energy donation in case someone was weak) and various other things. Oli and I obviously didn't spar as we were viewed as being too inexperienced to do so safely. I was very glad of this when I once saw her collect so much energy that when she released it into the ground, she reduced an entire corner of a field to ash. It still had not recovered by the time I went back to Earth.

Elemental energy was apparently a whole different ball game. It was virtually unlimited (unless you wanted to try to absorb the sun. Just let me know before you try that so I can vacation in another dimension). It was so different from life energy that it took a different technique and indeed a whole different mindset to collect and use it. This is why many magick users never learn to make the leap.

It is possible to absorb energy from light, heat, motion (kinetic energy), even the electromagnetic field that birds use to navigate. Absorbing that energy could even be useful. For example, a weaker magick user might have to try to redirect or catch the rocks in an avalanche. This would be nigh impossible and leave them exhausted, if not dead. An elemental energy user could simply absorb the kinetic energy, which would then give them the power of that avalanche to use elsewhere.

All of that sounds fantastic, right? Yeah, well, in practice not so simple, and the transition was when my relationship with Oli finally went to hell in a handbasket, with a side order of groin kick for good measure.

Chapter 22

Before we moved on to elemental energy forms, Liam set us an exercise to build a stack of bricks using only the energy around us, then walked away so we couldn't take from him. We were up in the main hall, so there were no other people nearby, nor any larger animals. There were only the bugs and small rodents present in any city, plus the underground life forms. I could tell that drawing enough energy to complete the pile would kill at least some of these creatures, so I refused to do the exercise, especially after having already inadvertently hurt Oli and killed the mice during the earlier incidents. Oli, on the other hand, simply drew in what she needed to and completed the pile in seconds, then sat on her stack and looked at me pityingly for my weakness and over-emotionality.

When Liam came back he looked at both of our piles of bricks –mine unchanged and Oli's assembled into the prescribed stack –then sent Oli to see Alex. She sneered at me on her way out, clearly thinking that I had failed. Liam asked why I hadn't finished, and I explained. He told me that there were three kinds of people at this stage. Those who just did the exercise and were found next to the pile ready to move on were taught no more and watched carefully, as they lacked sufficient feeling for others. Fortunately, these were few in number in Aaru (I wasn't so sure about back home, Ciarán's face coming to mind). He was surprised that Oli had fallen into this group, and I tried to excuse her by saying that she was just young and trying to compete with me. Liam said that if that had been the reason, she would have fallen into the next group. This consisted of those who were found next to a completed or partially completed pile, but in tears for what they had felt when the lives they were drawing on were snuffed out. They could go on, and usually mastered the basics but rarely much of the advanced teaching as they lacked the subtlety of understanding required.

The final group didn't move any bricks, despite having established the ability in earlier lessons. They refused, as they had already thought through the consequences of their actions, knew what would happen, and refused to cause death for the sake of an academic exercise. Those were the ones who appreciated the subtlety of the magick and understood the world around them, often going on to be among the most powerful and talented magick users. He looked at me proudly, knowing that I had fallen into this third group. He explained that Oli would obviously be told she had completed her basics and sent home, so I should try to be careful not to engage with her if I saw her around.

"Now we can move on to elemental energy usage," he said, "and it's best done outside where there are plenty of sources. Being in a house and making everything dark and cold isn't particularly helpful." He laughed and I joined in, realising the limited sources of elemental magick indoors. Moving onto another stage in my studies once again reminded me of getting home. I hoped that Ciarán hadn't hurt Gonpo or Yeshe. I also wondered what I was going to tell Angelica about the Veil. I still hadn't figured that one out.

I struggled when I first tried to access element sources. With life energy, the practitioner uses their mind to locate another life force. They then tap into it and draw some across the link into themselves, using it as needed. I did this by utilising my focusing lens imagery. As well as harming the source, this method also limits how much power can be stored by the user's body, unless you have a way to store it. Intellectually I knew there had to be a way to do that, I just hadn't learnt it yet.

Elemental energy has no consciousness to feel for or detect, it just existed. I tried standing out in the sun and while I did get nice and warm, I wasn't able to do anything with it. I put my hand near a candle and almost burned myself, went out on a breezy day and just had my clothes blown about —nothing seemed to work. It was starting to look like I had the mental capacity and temperament for higher magick, but not the ability. I started to feel depressed that I was going to fail and let down myself, my teacher, my friends, and my patron. My self-doubt started nagging at me again, despite all my earlier successes.

Then I gave myself a stern talking to. Isis wouldn't have brought me here to be a weak or mediocre magick user! She had faith in me; I needed to have more in myself. The problem I had was that Isis was busy, and there just weren't that many higher-level users around. Those that were had important things to do. Or they were already teaching someone else who had earned that right by getting past this stage.

I tried to meditate like I had seen some of the monks doing in the monasteries I had visited, to see if I could feel the energy of the universe and draw it into myself. After forty-five minutes of my mind questioning everything and being distracted by every breath of air, I gave up on that idea. Clearly I wasn't the 'meditate-for-three-days-naked-in-the-rain-standing-on-one-foot-on-top-of-a-pole' kind of guy.

To try to clear my mind, I decided to practice my katas. I stretched a little, then started. I always worked from the most basic upwards through the levels, as the more complex ones needed me looser and more focused. As I was moving, my mind kept thinking about energy, but now went in a new direction –chi.

As anyone who has done martial arts (or even just watched a Bruce Lee film) knows, chi is the term for a person's vital force (or life force, material energy or energy flow, depending on your preference). It can be controlled, directed, and used for multiple purposes. There is also chi in other things, such as the layout of a room or home, the balancing of which is known as Feng Shui. There were many other forms and uses of chi that I won't list here (although the study of chi is fascinating, and I highly recommend looking into it) but those two particularly stuck in my head.

If it was possible to direct chi around the home to improve Feng Shui, then moving it myself to do other things should be possible. I let my body flow through the katas almost on auto-pilot while I felt for the energy flow of the elements around me. I visualised it flowing towards me then being redirected by my forms to create shields over my blocks and energy balls from my strikes.

I deliberately locked down my own energy, otherwise I'd be sending fireballs out without using external energy. I then felt for any wind, as I reasoned that redirecting kinetic energy might be the easiest to start with. Feeling the breeze was easy, now I had to try to redirect it. I couldn't cheat and simply whirl my hands and cup them to deflect the wind, I had to make it follow me and then go where I wanted.

After a few hours, I had gone through all my katas several times with no perceivable change in energy flow. I decided to get a fresh start tomorrow and just focus on my most basic kata, so as not to distract myself with complex forms. It was just eight blocks and twelve punches in a pre-arranged pattern. At least I had a plan. Now to see if I could get the damn thing to work! At dinner that evening I relayed my frustrations to my teachers and they smiled at me.

"To be honest, I'm actually a little relieved," stated Alex. "You've made such rapid progress through the rest of the basics we've taught you, if you'd have got this straight off I'd have started being afraid you might be too capable for your own good. You've mastered everything else so easily that it's good for you to have to work for this." I was amazed at her comment.

"Wait, you think it's been easy?!" I said, aghast. "I've been getting headaches and nosebleeds from straining every day to learn these abilities! You think I enjoyed getting sucker-punched in the gut by Liam's electroballs?" Liam actually laughed at my remark —whether at my name for the technique or the memory of my discomfort, I wasn't sure. Possibly both.

"No, of course not, and we know how hard you've been working," he replied reassuringly. "What she meant is that you've been able to learn everything up to this point in just ten weeks. Most people take six months to get to your level!"

I stopped with my fork half-way to my mouth.

"Six months?" I whispered, stunned. "Are you serious?" They looked at each other and smiled. They appeared to have one of those telepathic communications that spouses can have when they've known each other for years —of course, for these two, it could be actual telepathy.

"Oh yes," said Liam, "I took almost four weeks before I first made anything move. It was over two months before I could break a cup."

Now I understood their surprise and concern when I had shattered the mug on my first try.

"Why did you allow Oli to move on with me if she wasn't ready then?" I asked, astounded.

"She started before you and she had the basics, plus Isis wanted you to have a study partner," Liam replied. "If she hadn't shown her true colours the way she did, we would have continued to work with her to improve her abilities more as she got older."

"I had perceived that your progress was above average, but I was unaware of just how proficient you were and how well you were acquitting yourself. My congratulations," said Gauvain, rousing himself from a rat that he'd caught earlier and had been eating in the corner. I'd had to build a stand for him a while ago —I refused to let him sit on my shoulder with a fresh kill.

I set my cutlery down and sat back, re-evaluating everything I'd done and learned in light of this new information. Each time I'd struggled with a new skill, I thought it was because I was human rather than from Aaru. I'd had no idea that I was basically a magickal prodigy!

"I guess I should give myself a day or two to master elemental energy manipulation then?" I joked, at which my friends joined in a stress-relieving burst of laughter.

"Yeah, that should be plenty!" gasped Alex in between giggles.

"Then next week you can master the advanced skills!" her husband chimed in.

It was a relief to know that I wasn't about to be kicked out of magick school for being too slow (there was a Hogwarts and squibs joke somewhere there, I was sure). I certainly wouldn't slack off from trying to do my best, but I would be a lot less concerned if I didn't get anywhere for a day or so.

"A day or so" turned into over a week, and I still had no luck using elemental energy. At least my job was going well. Poppy and Roman were so happy together it was almost embarrassing to be around them at times now. I was glad they had gotten past their awkward shuffling around each other phase, however, and my relationship with Roman was definitely more congenial now.

I was also making good progress on paying for my souvenir pendants. The young apprentice girl, whose name I found out was Soraya, was always grateful when I brought their lunch order over to save her from having to get it. I had noticed their shop was always quite cool. I had expected that if they were making jewellery, they would need some kind of forge for melting gold and silver and therefore the heat would bleed into the shop. I happened to remark on it one day to Soraya as I delivered their food, and she smiled.

"Oh, Master Harfi doesn't use a forge," she informed me, happy to talk about something for which she clearly had such passion. "He has a magickal affinity for precious metals, so he shapes them with magick then sets the precious stones in the right places to complete the designs. That's why I wanted to be his apprentice —he's generally thought to be the best in the city. He tests every applicant and won't accept anyone who can't work with metal in that way. I'm the first apprentice he's taken on in over three hundred years."

I now understood how he could create such beautiful designs, and I congratulated Soraya on impressing her mentor enough to be taken on. I had had an idea in the back of my mind for a while, and I was thinking that Soraya and Master Harfi might be able to help me bring it to fruition, but I needed to get a handle on using elemental energy first. I would, however, start sketching some ideas down in preparation.

That thought prompted me to talk to Soraya about my struggle. She clearly was able to use elemental magick if she could manipulate precious metals with such precision, so I asked her how best to get started. I explained what I was doing, and she smiled again.

"I can see why you thought the way you did. It's actually quite a logical idea and many people try it at first. The problem with using kinetic energy from the wind is that it's very fickle and impossible to see. You need something that's easier to connect with first. My advice would be to try using water, and to start off, you're best off actually standing in it to connect as closely as possible, at least until you get used to the feel of elemental energy and can tap into it more naturally. Just don't try and use the same connection techniques as you did for life energy, because it just doesn't work that way."

It was like she had flicked a lightbulb on in my head, and I thanked her profusely before dashing away to get home, eager to have lunch and start my afternoon's practice. Liam and Alex noticed my excitement —not least because I was bolting my food to get done —and asked what was going on. I explained the chat I'd had with Soraya and they smiled and nodded.

"We were wondering when you might get there, but it's not even been two weeks, so we were content to let you keep trying a while longer. We've obviously been used to dealing with teenagers —they're a lot less eager to admit they can't do something, so they take much longer to ask for help. They also tend to think they're always right, so it's not until they've struggled with their way and got nowhere for a while that they become receptive to suggestions."

I smiled and said, "It sounds as though teenagers are not much different wherever you find them. The ones on Earth are exactly the same. It's almost a running joke that they should all move out and get jobs while they still know everything before it wears off and they realise just how naïve they really are." Liam started laughing and his wife, who had just taken a sip of water, sprayed that sip onto her sandwich and started coughing as she tried to breathe, laugh and swallow at the same time.

After lunch I changed into a loose shirt and drawstring shorts. I'd bought some clothes once my wages had started coming in. I was tired of wearing the same thing; they needed washing and weren't the easiest to do any exercise in. I headed out of the city to the nearby river; time to see if water would cooperate better than air.

Chapter 23

I walked across the purple grass in front of the city (it was amazing how quickly I'd become used to that; green grass would look almost weird when I got home) and soon came to the river. Near the bank there was a large flat stone that looked to have either been set there for this use or had been worn smooth by years of students doing the same thing as me. Either way, I felt I was in the right place.

There was a nice large tree nearby, with its branches trailing into the water, something like a willow from Earth, and Gauvain found a nice sturdy branch to sit on to watch my attempts. I took off my sandals and stepped onto the stone.

The water was not as cold as I was expecting, for which I was grateful since I hadn't much fancied developing numb legs from freezing cold water. The surface of the rock was smooth enough not to hurt, but rough enough to give a firm grip, so I felt quite secure in my footing. There was no way I'd be able to do my full kata on it, as I'd soon run out of space. I decided instead to get into a low stance and just do the arm movements of blocks and strikes without stepping through the pattern.

I closed my eyes and started moving, trying to feel the water flowing past at the same time so I could tap into its energy. I could certainly feel the water but couldn't feel anything different than before I arrived at the city, when it was just a source of a drink. I thought back to what Soraya had said about elemental energy being so different from life energy.

Maybe that was my problem — I was still reaching out with my mind in the same way I had before.

I decided to go back to focusing on my chi, feeling the energy flow of my movements, while I once again locked down my internal magickal energy to prevent it contaminating things. I kept at it for a good hour and a half, falling into an almost zen-like calmness. I let myself simply be in the moment and relaxed my mental constraints, my consciousness simply aware rather than focused. By the end my legs were starting to shake from holding the stance, but I thought I had felt something nearby.

I got out of the river and dried my legs, then put my sandals back on for the walk back. Gauvain flew overhead, stretching his wings after watching me from his branch. He joined me as I neared the gate, landing on my shoulder lightly for such a large bird. He nibbled my ear fondly and looked at me.

"What degree of success did you experience today? Did you find things any easier with water?" he asked. I thought back to that strange sensation I had felt at the end.

"I'm not sure," I replied cautiously, "I might have felt something as I was finishing, but it wasn't strong enough to tap into." He stretched his wings out and resettled them with a flutter.

"That may not be a complete success but it is a distinct improvement in comparison to your earlier efforts." he reassured me. I stroked his head while I thought back to my kata practice from the days before. I had never felt even a hint of what I had noticed in the river. Maybe this would work.

I arrived home and saw Conor was outside playing with his ball, so I stopped and played catch for a few minutes until Alex called him in to wash up before dinner. We walked in together and I saw her dancing gently at the counter to a tune she was humming softly.

"Oh, Gavan, I didn't realise you were back. How did it go?" she asked, startled as she turned around. I relayed my experience in the river as we set the table and served up the food — fish tonight, with some fried root vegetables similar to potatoes. Not quite fish and chips out of greasy paper, but I appreciated the thought and effort.

"It sounds as though you might be making some progress," said Alex, "just remember that elemental energy isn't like life energy. You can't hurt what you're drawing from, so don't be afraid to pull hard and make it do what you want."

"Is there something I should try to do with it once I've got it?" I asked. "I don't want to end up with a huge store of potent energy and nowhere to put it. Wait that sounded wrong..." I realised how it sounded as soon as I said it, but Alex just laughed.

"Well I've not heard it put quite like that before" —she laughed— "but why not try making the river obey you in some way?"

"Ah, good idea," I replied. With that, we sat down to eat, and I munched distractedly through my food while I thought about what I could make the river do. For the next few days I kept returning to the stone in the river for my practice. Each time, I felt the river a little more clearly but was still unable to tap into the flow of its energy. I was pleased that I was at least making progress in detecting the energy, even if I couldn't use it yet.

As I walked back to the city one day after my practice, I saw a group of children on the roof of one of the houses just inside the gate, Conor amongst them. They were daring each other to try to jump across the alleyway to the roof of the house on the other side. The gap was about six to eight feet, so probably looked achievable in the hubris of youth. The thing they had forgotten, that was clear to me from my angle as I walked towards them, was that the roof across the alley wasn't empty like the one they were on but had been planted as a garden of some kind.

As I opened my mouth to shout to them, Conor took a short run-up and made the jump. When he landed, the loose soil shifted and his foot slipped back. He landed on his stomach with his legs hanging down over the edge and scrabbled for grip. The plants he grabbed were too weak to support his weight and he toppled back and fell.

I froze for a split second, wondering what to do, then reacted out of pure instinct. My senses still attuned from my practice in the river, I reached out with my mind. I felt the kinetic energy of his fall as a building pressure I could touch, almost like the jet of water in a whirlpool bath. I reached out to it and simply pulled it away like a stage magician with a tablecloth, freezing his fall and leaving him hanging in the air. I folded the energy into a cushion and put it below my young friend so it would catch him, then eased him slowly down onto it. He picked himself up off the floor and stared at me.

"Thank you!" he said, clearly shaken by what had just happened.

"Just wait until you learn magick before trying to fly next time," I said kindly. He giggled nervously, then ran off to re-join his friends. I felt like I was the one floating now —I had done it! I had taken the kinetic energy and used it! I also felt a swell in my internal stores as the good deed fed back to me. I made my way home like I was walking on air. As anyone who has been the victim of gossip knows, rumour is the only thing known to man that moves faster than light and it seemed like Aaru was no exception to this. By the time I got back, Conor's parents were there waiting for me with huge smiles on their faces.

"We already heard, and we're so proud of you!" gushed Alex, pulling me into a hug so tight it almost cracked some ribs. "Not only did you access elemental energy, you saved Conor from a nasty fall. We couldn't be happier for you, as well as extremely grateful."

"It was just a reflex. I didn't plan it, or even think," I said honestly, still not completely sure how I had managed it.

"Exactly, that's the point," said Liam. "Elemental energy doesn't respond to thought and reason, it's too primitive for that. It requires instinct, emotion and reflex. That's why your kata helped. When you reached your state of zen, you stopped thinking. Now you just have to learn to react on instinct deliberately, which I know is a complete oxymoron, but it's the only way I can explain it."

"Deliberate reflex; considered instinct. Great," I quipped. "At least I know how it feels to use elemental energy now. It's almost like knowing what you want to do, then getting out of your own way to allow your body to accomplish it."

"That may be the best explanation of the technique that I've ever heard," said Alex, glancing across at her husband. "If you can explain it that well, then it already makes sense to you. Now it's just practice." I hoped she was right. If I could nail this, I could move on to the higher abilities and then get home.

Over the next few days I went back to my stone in the river each afternoon to try to stop thinking. Trust me, it's not as easy as you might think —pun intended. If someone tells you not to think about cuddly puppies, what's the first thing you think of? Exactly, "Aaaww how cute". That's precisely why meditation is so hard for most people, and why it takes years of practice to master it.

I could at least reliably feel elemental energy now, having felt it when Conor was falling from the roof. It was all around in various forms, almost like being surrounded by water but being given a sieve to use to drink out of. I could sense the energy, see its effects, but not collect it. Part of the problem, as I saw it, was that I wasn't sure what to do once I had it.

I decided to start a project that I would use the energy for, to see if that made a difference. My hope was that once I got used to using elemental energy, just like creating muscle memory by doing my karate techniques over and over again, this might create "magick memory" to teach my body how to access it routinely at will. I mentioned my idea to my instructors, and they were very encouraging.

"It usually takes people a long time to even start to feel elemental magick, never mind use it, so you're still way ahead of the average," Alex told me.

"In fact," added Liam, "I don't even think Isis was as fast as you in reaching this stage, according to what I've heard. Then again, she was only eleven at the time."

I was greatly reassured by his first remark, although his qualification did take some of the wind out of my sails. Still, being noticeably faster than average was definitely a good thing. Now to see if I could maintain my progress.

Since I needed to keep doing good deeds to help boost my power, I decided to build a small pier in the river for people to fish from and tie up boats. I also thought about modifying my practice spot to give me more space, so that I might be able to do the legwork of my katas. The first couple of days had a number of hilarious mishaps, including me somehow launching myself headfirst into the middle of the river. Gauvain was always ready to either support me or laugh at my slapstick fails (usually the latter), but as time went on my magick grew stronger and smoother.

I also noticed that as time went on and I got more accustomed to reaching for elemental energy, I increasingly began to notice different visual distortions around various energy sources. It was like the wavering in the air you see above a hot road except from other, normally invisible sources. Light was obvious, heat had the shimmer in the air, and kinetic energy from a physical object was again obvious.

The most noticeable extra energy that I started to see was the aura around living beings. This changed according to mood, intention, level of fatigue, and various other factors. I also noticed pale green streamers in the air of the kinetic energy from the wind. While this new degree of my vision certainly made it easier to detect and access energy sources, the first few days of trying to focus my eyes in a new way brought back the headaches of my earlier studies. It felt like what I imagine someone must feel when they get new glasses with a new prescription, so I was very glad when I adjusted and the headaches faded.

Once, about ten days into my project, Gauvain's sharp hawk eyes caught sight of Oli watching me from some trees a short way back from the other side of the river, and he alerted me via our link. When I looked over, I caught a flash of her plait as she whisked out of sight, but Gauvain said that she had been crying and looked angry as she was watching me. I knew she was upset at not learning any more, and I doubted this would be the last time she might try to spy on me. I would have to be careful, as I didn't know if her mother might try to teach her in secret, now that she was off the official learning program. I also wasn't sure just how much resentment she might harbour towards me, or how long she might nurse that grudge. After that, Gauvain flew periodic circuits over the area, and if he saw her, I would stop what I was doing.

A few days after I saw Oli by the river, there was a panic in the city as I returned one afternoon. I soon learned that Oli's cousins had disappeared, and their mother —who was Oli's father's sister —was utterly frantic. Given her earlier behaviour with the kids, I had a horrible suspicion. I didn't want to believe that Oli would genuinely hurt the children, yet I couldn't think of another reason why they would have disappeared.

I joined the group that was gathering to look for the kids, thinking that more eyes could only help. We quickly broke up into teams, each team having at least one advanced magick user. Each team headed in a different direction from the city gate, spreading out as we went to try to cover the most ground. I opened myself to as much energy as I could, trying to think of Oli's distinctive personal signature. I had become well acquainted with it while we were working together, but I had no idea if I would be able to track her movements by it. Still, it was worth a try.

I adjusted my vision into what I had decided to call the magickal spectrum and tried to find Oli's unique signature. All I was able to see were the energy sources around me. Even the advanced magick user in our group didn't leave any kind of trail of energy behind him, so there was no chance of tracking Oli like that. I closed my eyes, instead reaching out to try to feel for Oli's presence. I felt nothing nearby, so it looked like this was going to be an old-fashioned visual search.

Oli had been conspicuous by her absence during the initial kerfuffle in the city, so no one had been able to question her regarding her cousins. The rest of my group had headed off in our prescribed direction, so I hurried to catch up with them.

They had crossed over the river and started walking in a spread out line, trying to cover as much ground as possible. I joined one end of the line once I caught up with the group. We swept the ground between us for over two hours, the landscape gradually becoming rockier. Gauvain flew ahead, using his raptor's vision to help us search.

As the first sun was setting, we reached an area where the ground was broken by cracks. Some were only a couple of feet deep, some went down almost thirty feet. There also looked to be areas where the cracks led into caves.

We gathered together and discussed how to proceed. Three people volunteered to head into the caves, the advanced magick user among them. He and I linked our minds so that the two groups could stay in contact, just in case the children were found. The cavers set off into the cave system, and the rest of us picked our way between the crevasses.

Around half an hour later, I heard something that lifted my spirits: a child's voice, shouting for help. I sent Gauvain in the direction I heard the shout from, closing my eyes to see through his instead. He rapidly covered the distance, soon seeing the two children at the bottom of one of the deeper ravines.

I asked him to circle above them to guide everyone, then sent the cavers a message to say to head back. The magick user, whose name was Varion, asked me to look around. I did so, following which the three cavers suddenly appeared next to us. Varion had transported them out of the caves.

We all hurried towards Gauvain, soon enough reaching the ravine. Varion reached out to the other magick users involved in the search, and the other groups started appearing around us. Man, I couldn't wait to learn that. While the groups were arriving, I used my telekinetic abilities to help me climb down into the crevasse and comfort the kids.

Fortunately they were only scared, not hurt, so I let Varion know and he teleported himself down after asking me to look around again. We each picked up one child and he moved us back up to the top of the rock face. The magick users formed a circle around the rest of us and teleported the entire search party back to the city gates.

The children immediately ran to their mother, who had been waiting near the gates in case the children turned up by themselves. Through their sobs, they told everyone how Oli had led them to the rocky area as an adventure. Then she'd lifted them into the ravine using her magick, saying they could explore the deep crack in the rock. Then she had simply left them there and run off.

Oli's mother hugged her niece and nephew, then her sister-in-law, promising that Oli would have no further chance to put the children in jeopardy. She would also punish her severely. Fortunately, since the children were not physically harmed, Oli did not have to go before the city council. Her mother was warned that any further incidences, however, and Oli's discipline would be taken out of her hands and become a council matter. Everyone headed home, relieved beyond measure that the outcome had been so good. I went straight to bed, eager to get back to my training the next day.

After another three weeks I had the quay finished and I could use elemental energy at will to accomplish a task, but I found that unless I had a purpose in mind, I had great trouble hanging onto a store of it for more than about ten minutes. I decided that the practice area was actually quite sufficient for one person, and this sort of thing was better done alone rather than in pairs or a group, so I left the rock as it was. I decided it was time to see what my next step was, so I called Gauvain, and said goodbye to my rock, then headed home to see what Alex and Liam had for me next.

Chapter 24

When I got back, both Liam and Alex were out with Conor, visiting Alex's sister on the other side of the city, so I had the house to myself for the evening. I had a light dinner as I wasn't particularly hungry, then wandered into my room feeling slightly bored. Normally we would spend the evening chatting about magick, or perhaps playing a game of cards with Conor.

As I sat on my bed, my eye fell on the gem that Isis had given me after awakening my magick. It was resting on the nightstand, on top of the sketches I had been making. She had called it my heart-stone, telling me it would be useful as I learned to use my abilities. Thus far, however, I'd found nothing special about it. I had examined it with my magickal sense but not detected any unique attributes to it. So, what was it supposed to do?

It was called a heart-stone, so it must be linked to me in some way, I reasoned. I picked it up and headed outside. The sunlight struck the polished top of the stone, making the six-pointed asterism blaze brightly. I thought back to an earlier experiment I had done with a gemstone, trying to see if I could store energy in it like Eragon did in The Inheritance Cycle books, but the stone had shattered with the power. I had never tried with this as I didn't want to risk something that I had been told was important, but I couldn't see what else it might be for.

What I did know was that I wanted a way to keep it on me and protected at all times, so I had thought of setting it into a ring, which was what I had been designing. I had the evening free, and I knew Master Harfi always worked late, so I decided to take it over to him and see if he could help me. I also had the last payment for the pendants ready, so I could kill two birds with one –*ahem* –stone.

"Was that really necessary?" Gauvain groaned as he overheard my horrendous pun in my mind, and I laughed.

"Come on you, let's go see Soraya, get the pendants and then see if Master Harfi is willing to help me make a ring for my heart-stone." I held out my arm to him and he soared over from where he had been sunning himself in a nearby tree.

I strolled across the city towards Master Harfi's shop, just enjoying the late afternoon sunshine. When we arrived, Soraya was setting some new pieces in the window display, so I took the time to admire them. Then I went in and told her I had the final payment for my pendants. She smiled brightly at me and went to get them.

She wrapped them in a small piece of cloth, and I put them in my pocket, pulling out my heart-stone at the same time. I placed the gem on the counter and Soraya looked at me curiously. I told her I wanted to have it set into a ring, so she assessed it with a professional eye. She asked me where I had got it but when I told her it was my heart-stone, given to me by Isis, she backed away in shock.

"I can't help you," she told me, sounding almost afraid. "I'm not advanced enough to include the protection wards required for a heart-stone. Let me go and get Master Harfi." She turned and hurried into the back of the shop, where I heard Master Harfi working. The noise of him tapping and filing ceased as Soraya interrupted him.

"I'm far too busy to take on a new commission, Soraya." I heard her softer voice murmuring an explanation to him, and then, "What?!" He came hurrying out and eagerly walked over to me. He was probably the oldest looking individual I had seen in Aaru. He had curly black hair, wrinkled, deep brown weather-beaten skin, and a permanent hunch from working on his jewellery. His eyes, however, were light blue and alive with interest.

"You told Soraya that this is your heart-stone?" he exclaimed.

"Yes," I replied, "Isis gave it to me, but she just told me it was important, not what it was for or how to use it."

"Hah, that Isis, always trying to be so mysterious!" He grunted, unimpressed. "One of these days she's going to be so mysterious about something, even she won't know what she's talking about!" I snorted at the image, and his eyes twinkled at my amusement.

"So can you tell me what it's for, sir?" I asked politely, hoping my manners might get me the information I needed.

"Just call me Harfi, young man," he replied with a kind smile. "A heart-stone is a gem that can only be created by magick. It is attuned to the one for whom it was created, usually the same one who created it. It is the only way to store elemental energy" (I knew it! I thought to myself) "but even more importantly, it changes the stored energy to a form unique to its owner. It becomes even easier to access than life force from others, basically becoming an extension of your own body's energy. The difference being that the amount of energy the heart-stone can hold is almost limitless. It therefore needs to be protected by powerful wards, attuned to you. Otherwise, if it were to be damaged while holding that much energy..."

"Hiroshima, Nagasaki, even Tunguska all in one!" I whispered, awestruck at the level of power we were talking about.

"I don't know what that means, but let's just say a supernova wouldn't be far off the mark," he replied. I stared at him in shock.

"I'm almost afraid to ask how much it would cost to commission you to create a ring for my stone after hearing that," I said tentatively, "but I will do anything I can to pay you for it. Would you at least consider it?" I asked hopefully.

"To create a piece to house the heart-stone of Isis' prophesied chosen one?" Harfi replied, looking reverential at the prospect. "It would be the crowning achievement of my career, and my honour. It will be my gift to you, as thanks for including me on what I am sure will be an epic journey for you. Do you have a design in mind?"

"Yes, actually, I do," I replied, getting out my sketches and laying them on the counter next to the gem. The top of the ring was a circle of runes, divided into four by equally spaced circles. Each circle contained a symbol –a Triquetra for heart, a Valknut for binding and inspiration, a Vegvisir for way-finding, and a Triskele (Horns of Odin) for further inspiration. The runes between each symbol meant Power, Protection,

Binding, and Victory. "I thought that the circle I've sketched could be the pavilion of the ring, with the heart-stone in the centre, and then another Triquetra on each shoulder." I showed him the design in my sketches and explained each part as we discussed it. He smiled as he saw the design I had drawn.

"That is a beautiful, truly unique piece. The symbols and runes can be woven into the protection for the gem, enhancing your connection to it," he said. "In order to truly attune it to you, you should be involved in the making. Fortunately, since I work with magick rather than a forge, as I understand Soraya told you, we can get your ring finished in just a couple of hours."

"I don't know how to thank you for your kindness, Harfi," I said. He smiled and winked at me.

"Just wear your ring proudly and tell people who made it for you when they ask," he said, smiling at me. I laughed in turn, immediately understanding his thoughts.

"Nothing like advertising and a good recommendation to help business!" I joked, and Harfi patted my hand in approval and smiled.

"Well, we better get started!" Harfi clapped his hands together and rubbed them, then motioned me around the counter. I scooped up my heart-stone and sketches, and followed him into the back of the shop where he created all his pieces.

"Soraya, it's about time to close, so can you shut the shop while we get ready? Then come back through. It's not often anyone gets the chance to work on a heart-stone, so you should see how it's done." Harfi started getting his work-bench ready while he sent Soraya to lock up. She did so quickly and smiled at me as she came back through, clearly excited by the chance to learn such a rare part of her trade. Harfi pulled a gold ingot towards himself and settled onto his work stool.

"I'm going to link to you so that your energy infuses into the metal as I shape it, and your power creates the wards," he said to me. I nodded and reached out with my mind towards him, offering my energy to him to use as he needed.

Since we were so closely linked, I was aware of the wards and protections Harfi wove into the gold, defending it against both physical and magickal influence. Over the next hour and a half, he recreated my mental image even more perfectly than my sketches were able to convey in the gold. Then he set my heart-stone into place, folding it into the wards until there was no way anyone but I could touch it.

The second sun was setting as we finished, and he polished the ring one final time before handing it over to me ceremonially. I slipped it onto the middle finger of my right hand, where it felt as though it became a piece that completed me in a way I hadn't even known I was lacking. I thanked him again, and Soraya thanked us both for being allowed to watch. As I left to walk home, Gauvain admired the ring as it flashed in the dying light of the sun.

I knew my next exercise would be stocking the gem with as much elemental energy as I could, to help me when I started learning the more advanced techniques. Hopefully, with the added power at my disposal, I would be able achieve the required mastery. It might also mean that I wouldn't suffer from the headaches and nosebleeds that had plagued my earlier studies. I was sure it would come in useful for dealing with future threats, even ones that had previously seemed significant but now would certainly be less so, thanks to my new abilities. A certain annoying doctor sprang to mind, making me wonder again what had happened when he woke up in the cave to find me gone.

My friends were home by the time I arrived, and they immediately noticed and admired my new ring. I told them that Master Harfi had helped me create it, along with explaining about heart-stones and their use. They looked shocked, and Alex became immediately apologetic.

"We didn't even know you had a heart-stone, or we would have told you about it sooner," she remarked. "You never mentioned it, and even among us, not everyone has one. Those that do usually create it much later, in private, so we never even considered it as part of your basic instruction."

"Isis had just told me it would be important in my training, so I just waited until it was time to work with it. I thought it would be a natural stage, so I simply set it aside until the time was right. I designed the ring on paper and took it to the jewellers, since I was picking up the pendants I bought as gifts. I thought I'd get a quote on having the ring I'd sketched made while I was there. It wasn't until Master Harfi told me that not everyone had a heart-stone that I realised how rare they were." I apologised in turn.

"It's fine," said Liam, "we're just glad you know now, and have it so well protected. I'd suggest you take some time to store some energy in it."

"Yeah, that was my plan for the next few days." I smiled, glad I had reached the same conclusion.

"Once you're happy with your store, you'll be ready to move on to your advanced instructor. Finishing the pier was your 'basics graduation piece'. By the way, it's very nice. We're taking Conor fishing there this weekend." He smiled at me in approval, and I felt a surge of pride at his praise.

I couldn't believe it —I'd finished my training in basic magick. My next few days would be like a brief holiday, during which I would gather as much energy as I could for the next phase in my education. I had a feeling I was going to need it.

Chapter 25

As planned, I spent the next several afternoons, after I'd finished at Poppy's for the morning, heading out of the city to sit in the countryside and draw in as much elemental energy as I could to store in my new ring. Bearing in mind how that sounded even to me, I was going to have to come up with a name for my heart-stone ring soon. Otherwise I'd end up sounding like a cheap porn star. I decided to head in a new direction so that I was away from the new fishing pier. It was already very popular with the youngsters, and children could be seen there daily with their fishing poles. At least they weren't falling from rooftops now! Conor had been grounded for a week after that little stunt, then had been made to promise he would never do something so stupid again.

I reached out to the elemental energy and drew it towards me, then focused it through my mental lens at the gem. As the energy bathed it, it glowed briefly, making the image of the wings that I had noticed when I first looked deeper into it stand out more prominently, eclipsing the natural asterism. Then the light would be sucked into its depths like water into a sponge, and the wings would fade back into the straight rays once again.

On my second day I came across a waterfall, so was able to collect heat and light from the suns, plus sound and kinetic energy from the waterfall. It was fascinating to watch the water fall more slowly in complete silence, with a twilight-like dimness. Collecting the heat also made some of the water turn to ice and snow, and the first time I did that resulted in a large patch on the pool's surface freezing, which killed several fish. I felt sickened by what I had done, causing suffering and death for no reason, and I cut my efforts short for the day.

I thought about what I had done all evening. I knew it had been an accident and I could tell I wasn't becoming like Oli by the fact that I felt so awful about what had happened, but it made me realise that even 'safe' energy collection could still cause damage. If I collected sunlight, plants couldn't photosynthesize for example. Everything had an impact on something else, and I would just have to be that much more careful in future. The Law of Unintended Consequences in all its glory.

As I stocked the heart-stone, I noticed that the energy forms were not equal. It took hours of elemental energy collection to create even a small amount of life energy. That explained why some people never bothered with elemental energy —it may be limitless but was not as dense an energy as vital energy. No wonder Master Harfi had said that the heart-stone could absorb an almost unlimited amount of elemental energy. I had once tried doing my kata to generate kinetic energy to store in the ring, but all that happened was that I ended up frozen in place. It felt like I was trying to push against a mountain, exhausting myself for minimal energy gain in terms of what I could store in the ring.

After ten days, the amount of energy I had stored in the ring was maybe as much as I might get from around twenty cows, or thirty people. The heart-stone wasn't even one millionth filled. It could take a thousand years of constant energy collection to even make a dent in the energy storage capacity of the stone. I resolved to make deposits whenever I could, but what I had would at least make a start for my training.

That evening, I tried putting some of my own energy into the stone, focusing the light from my own internal magickal "sun" towards the gem, and I found that as long as it came through my body, life energy could also be put into it. I just had to make sure to do it slowly —if I let the stone start absorbing too quickly, it could simply keep absorbing my energy until I fell unconscious or worse. I decided I'd also spend a couple of hours per evening putting some extra energy of my own in there, as I'd then be able to restore it as I slept. I would not, however, start draining other animals to fill it. Rule one, after all.

The next morning Liam told me that I was expected in the main hall after lunch to meet my advanced tutor. He also advised me not to be late, as this individual was known not to tolerate fools, and hated tardiness. If I was late, chances were I'd be dismissed without even a chance to start. Also, I needed to devote all my time to my education now, so I would need to leave my job at Poppy's shop.

I headed to my job for the last time and explained to Roman and Poppy that I needed to leave because of my educational commitments. They understood and hugged me, thanking me for all my help and for helping them get together. Poppy gave me a bonus as thanks for the new recipes, and they wished me luck in my studies.

I helped out as usual but headed off slightly early to do the lunch deliveries so that I wouldn't be late for my appointment. My last stop was Harfi and Soraya, who also wished me luck on the next stage of my studies. I thanked them again for their help and told Harfi that several people had already commented on my ring during the lunch rush. I had pointed them all his way, and they both beamed in anticipation of the extra business. Soraya kissed my cheek and Harfi shook my hand, then I headed home. I ate lightly and quickly on my own, as Alex and Liam were out teaching some new students on the basics. Then I headed up to the hall, Gauvain joining me as I walked.

When I arrived, I knew I was early. I had always believed, however, that to be early showed respect for the time of the person you were meeting. Conversely, being late indicated that you felt your time was more important than theirs. Therefore I always made sure to be early to any meeting or appointment. Plus sitting and waiting often gave me time to read, which I never minded.

As my new instructor wasn't here yet, I decided to try to meditate. It was always a difficult skill for me as my mind was usually too active, but this seemed like a good time and location to try. I knelt down, seiza style as if I was in a dojo, and closed my eyes. I allowed my mind to reach out to be aware of my surroundings, but I felt no one other than Gauvain near me. As usual, thoughts started running through my head —who would my instructor be, what would I learn —but each time I tried to push them away and centre myself again.

Soon enough I felt two individuals approaching. Out of politeness I withdrew my consciousness back within the confines of my own head and opened my eyes to see who was arriving. To my surprise Isis walked into the hall, smiling as she saw me kneeling there. Gauvain stretched his wings then settled back.

"Greetings Isis," he said conversationally, "I had wondered when we might see you again. How fares the city?"

I looked at him in amazement, feeling a little uncomfortable at his casual manner with someone so important.

"Gauvain!" I remonstrated. "I know she said people here were more equal, but she's still a goddess, and head of the city council –show a little respect, will you?" Isis, on the other hand, simply laughed.

"It's fine. As I told you before, we don't stand on ceremony here." She came over and stroked Gauvain's head, then held out her hand to me to help me up. I took her hand and stood up. As I did, I felt the other individual who had arrived with Isis, although I still couldn't see who it was.

"I've been kept updated on your progress by Alex and Liam, and I have to say I'm very pleased that you've done so well." Isis smiled as she discussed my studies thus far. "You even surpassed my expectations. I already knew you'd do well because I felt your potential when your power awakened, plus you absorbed my Veil, but your progress has been remarkable.

"You have managed to avoid giving in to your baser instincts, despite provocation from your fellow student, so thus far you have not slipped down the dark path. You must be prepared to find the balance between light and dark, though, as the world will not always allow you to walk away and keep your hands clean. I am aware that you also have your own inner demons, as do most of us, but those are yours to overcome.

"Now it's time for your education to go to the next level. I will warn you now, your new instructor is not like those you've had before. Basic magick was your right simply for being who you are. Now that you have that, you have to earn everything from here on out. If you do as well as you have so far you should be OK, but if you try to coast even a tiny bit your teacher will simply walk away and that will be it —no appeals, no do-overs. Now, let me see your ring."

My mind reeling from the implications of what I had just heard, I dazedly held my hand out to her, too stunned even to snigger at the thought of 'showing her my ring'. She took hold of my fingers and lifted my hand closer to her face. She looked closely at the ring and I could feel the wards around it as she reached out towards my heart-stone. She smiled as she was repelled and released my hand.

"Master Harfi really is extremely talented," she said. "Whose idea was the design?"

"Mine," I replied distractedly, still thinking about the implications of not learning the advanced techniques I wanted and needed. "I'd been thinking about it since you handed me my heart-stone and said it would be important." That thought snapped me back to the present. If there was no standing on ceremony, it was time to ask a question.

"Oh yeah, how come you never told me what it was actually for? I had to find out from Master Harfi when I asked him to set it into the ring." Isis smiled, not insulted in the least by my attitude.

"Although I was almost certain you'd do well, there is nothing certain in the universe..."

"Except death and taxes!" I quipped. Her smile and lack of response made me pause, but she moved on without addressing my comment.

"As I was saying, I didn't want to tell you in case you weren't able to achieve what I hoped for you. You were, after all, starting much later than most. You had a lot of preconceptions to overcome. I'm so very glad my caution was unwarranted."

I understood her reasons, but her caution indicated a degree of doubt in my abilities that, while understandable on an intellectual level, still stung a little. It gave me just one more reason to work as hard as I could on my advanced studies, to prove just exactly how wrong she had been to doubt me. The fact that even a goddess could be wrong removed the last of the awe I had for her, and I was able to see her as just another person at long last.

"Can I ask a couple of questions please?" I requested and she nodded to me. "You said when my power was unlocked that I had the potential to be among the most powerful magick users." She nodded again with a tolerant smile, so I continued. "Is there some kind of scale? Are there levels that I could aspire to?" She looked at me rather pityingly.

"Not everything in life has to be set to a scale! This is the same as you asking what to classify yourself as. You are Gavan and you are powerful. The most I can say is that very few magick users have ever been, or will ever be, more powerful than you have the potential to become. Though they may be more knowledgeable or capable in certain areas than you. There is a difference between raw power, and education in a particular technique." I nodded in understanding and proceeded to my other query.

"Now that I have arrived here, is Aaru vulnerable to others from Earth? I was sent to find your Veil by a group who wanted it, and now it's inside me. Have I opened a door that anyone can walk through?" She shook her head even before I finished speaking.

"Even with my Veil within you, we could still deny you entry to our realm if we wished. If you tried to bring others, we could allow you in and block them out. We have full control over who comes in and when." Her comment reassured me greatly and I relaxed. Now I could go on with my studies with renewed focus, although I still hadn't figured out what I was going to tell the group when I finally made it home.

"So, are you going to be my advanced tutor?" I asked. "I thought you would be too busy running the city."

"Oh, I am," she replied, smiling at my more conversational tone. "I just wanted to come and see you, as I haven't spoken to you since your awakening. Your instructor is... Well, let's just say different. Have fun!" With that cryptic statement, she turned and walked out of the hall, waving as she did so.

I once again felt the presence of the other mind that had approached with Isis, but it seemed to be both mildly familiar and yet totally unlike anyone I could remember meeting. It was the sort of familiarity one might get when remembering a dream once you woke, and yet I knew this wasn't that. I looked around, trying to home in on the presence I felt, finally spotting a pair of eyes high up in the rafters at the top of one of the columns.

Once I had seen them, the eyes blinked and then moved down the column, resolving into the shape of a cat. At the top of the column it appeared to be a small tabby, but as it descended it seemed to grow larger and larger, surpassing a Maine Coon or even a Norwegian forest cat, until it reached the ground as big as a cheetah.

It sat there and looked at me, Gauvain seemingly unconcerned with the large feline so close by. I reached out towards it with my mind very cautiously, encountering that semi-familiar consciousness once again. The eyes changed from feline to human, and I recognised them from a girl I had seen a few times in the lunch rush at Poppy's. Then the presence altered slightly, and I remembered feeling this awareness when I was reaching out during my first energy siphoning lessons. Finally, the nose changed to human for a moment, reminding me of one of the stallholders in the market.

All the features reverted back to those of a cat, but I realised that this individual was a talented shapeshifter who could be anyone or anything it wanted. It must have been watching me at random times over the weeks of my basic lessons. The knowledge that it had spied on me removed my trepidation and I looked it straight in the eye.

"I would like to thank you for agreeing to try to teach me," I started. "I'm guessing Isis herself asked you, as you probably consider teaching a mere human to be a waste of time, to judge from the way you're looking at me —or is that just the standard feline disdain resulting from your current form?" I heard a voice in my mind as the cat cocked its head.

"Are you saying you think you deserve my time and knowledge? Just how arrogant are you?"

"That's not what I'm saying at all… Sir? Ma'am? What should I call you, by the way?" I enquired. "No, all I'm saying is that I did pass all of the basic training, so have I not at least earned a chance at the advanced lessons?" I fought my natural inclination to back down, as I got the sense that if I did, my new instructor would happily turn tail and leave.

"A chance, perhaps, but no more, and you will have to prove your worth at each stage if you wish to keep progressing," the voice stated, confirming what I had just thought. "As to who I am, I have been around as long as there has been coherent thought. To the Sumerians, Etruscans and Hittites I was variously known as Nidaba, Menrva and A'as. To the Mongols and West Africans I have been Mergen and Orunmila. The Japanese call me Fukurokuju, and the Celts knew me as Ogma. I have been many names to every race, but I am still me, here from the first thought and enduring still, on this and every other plane, unlike many others who have withered and faded.

"For the purpose of your lessons, you may call me Danu. Search for that in your reference library when you get home!" she finished imperiously.

Chapter 26

The name Danu rang a bell in my memory, from when I had been doing some reading into my Welsh roots.

"The mother goddess of the Tuatha de Danann?" I asked, hoping to surprise Danu with my knowledge of Welsh lore. The raised eyebrows on the feline face told me I had succeeded in my attempt.

Something else clicked in my head at that realisation. While Danu had no other specific mythology that I could recall, I recognised at least a couple of the other names used as gods and goddesses of knowledge and wisdom. Also, if this being was choosing to identify with a Welsh goddess, that could explain why the city name also had a Welsh connection. Danu was clearly listening in on my thoughts, as she remarked on them sarcastically.

"Oh look, the penny drops. Have you not yet realised that we on this plane don't actually need physical surroundings? That much of what you see was brought into being for your convenience during your visit? Once you go home, a great deal of this will disappear, and those of us who choose to will be able to go back to the comfort of our formless existence. Of course, some choose to remain physical. Learning magick of various types even requires it at times." I could sense almost a distaste for the physical from her as she made her remarks. She seemed to consider it as a lower state than the formlessness she had mentioned.

Several coincidental familiarities from my visit now became clear. The Welsh link also suggested a name for my ring –Seren, the Welsh word for star, for the asterism of my heart-stone. At least now I wouldn't want to snigger every time I thought about my heart-stone's new home.

"Then surely, if you want me gone as soon as possible, would it not behoove you to either refuse to teach me at all —" I started, but Danu interrupted me impatiently.

"Then someone else would simply volunteer, and they would no doubt take much longer to drill the knowledge into your thick skull," she snapped, flicking her tail in irritation.

"Fair enough," I continued, refusing to rise to her insult. "Well then why not work with me, to help me learn as quickly and effectively as possible, rather than being antagonistic?" Danu's tail switched back and forth again, in the classic feline indication of irritation. I took it that she didn't like my reasoning her into actually helping me.

"Fine," she ground out, "but the second you don't measure up to my standards, you're done, finished, over, caput, finité, gone, terminated, discharged. Just like Isis said." I could tell I wasn't going to be given any leeway, and I'd have to work hard to even have a chance of being adequate.

"Gather your things," Danu continued, "and meet me at the front gate in half an hour. You're not staying where you have been up to now. We're heading out of the city to stop your incompetence from being a risk to anyone here." So saying, she turned around and bounded out of the hall with a disdainful flick of her tail.

I rushed back to the house while Gauvain soared off to wait by the gate. I gathered my things up into my trusty backpack, including my new working clothes and toiletries. I left a note on the table, apologising for not saying goodbye in person and explaining Danu's insistence on leaving the city for my studies. I promised them I would come back to see them before I headed back to Earth. I propped the note on the kitchen table and rushed off towards the gate.

I got there in good time, and Gauvain flew down from his perch on top of the wall as he saw me approach. After meeting Danu and seeing evidence of her shapeshifting tendencies, I had a funny feeling she might already be here watching me. I extended my consciousness and sure enough, she had disguised herself in the form of a large, bearded man in a blacksmith apron, watching me from where she/he was leaning against the wall outside one of the resident forges with her/his arms crossed.

This time I was the one to cock my head and give an old-fashioned look, complete with raised eyebrow. Had I not already proven that I knew appearance didn't matter with her? She (I decided I was sticking with that; it would get too confusing to switch between him, her and it all the time) walked towards me, shifting as she did into the attractive young woman who had once asked Roman for a date.

I made a firm decision to completely ignore what she looked like and just respond to her consciousness. She smiled slightly, clearly having no reticence in reading my thoughts. I then realised that as a goddess of wisdom, all knowledge was hers, so she might not even need to read my mind. Her eyebrows raised at that, and she nodded, almost looking impressed in spite of herself.

"Follow me," she said brusquely, and I had to stop myself breaking into the inevitable Arnie quote.

"...if you want to live. Get to da choppa!" I murmured under my breath, giving in to my childish impulse once she had passed me. She was turned away from me at the time, but I swore I heard a snort. Maybe there was hope for me yet.

Danu led the way out of the city with me following in her wake. She headed off in the direction of the waterfall where I had been gathering elemental energy to put into Seren. We didn't stop there, though, and headed further away from the city. The landscape gradually changed, becoming rockier and harsher. It was vaguely reminiscent of the Giant's Causeway at one point, indicating a possible crystalline structure to the rocks. If I thought about it, I could almost convince myself that I could smell salt and hear the sea.

The terrain changed back again to a more verdant look, and eventually we came to another waterfall. There was a rough pathway leading behind the cascade and Danu didn't even slow down as she headed along it. The pathway led to a cave, in which the echoing thunder of the fall threatened to deafen me. Gauvain was no happier than I, and his screeching simply added to the din.

Danu headed deeper into the cave system, proceeding around a tight bend into a new cave. This one was lit by an oculus in the roof which had a few vines hanging over the edge into the cavern. Thankfully the bend in the path cut almost all of the waterfall's noise down to just a soft rumble, and I yawned to clear my ears. Gauvain screeched once more, then settled back on to my shoulder.

"Good grief, that was unpleasant!" he said to me. "I think I may have had to abandon you had you remained in there!"

"I know what you mean. I don't think I could've heard myself think in there, never mind anyone else, and I certainly would have struggled to concentrate on any new studies." I looked at Danu, and she eyed me with a knowing gleam.

"I'm guessing that one of my tests to see if I've mastered some of the techniques will be to do them in that first cavern?" I asked, knowing and yet dreading the answer.

"Hmph. Good guess." Danu looked impressed despite herself that I'd figured out my final exam conditions. "Still, you have a long way to go before you get to that stage. I still need to see if you can even manage any of the advanced techniques." She almost sneered with seeming scorn for my abilities. What exactly had I done, or not done, to cause such enmity? Everyone else here had been so nice, and I'd replied in kind. Maybe that was it? Maybe she wanted to see if I could be more than just a nice guy? Surely, if she knew everything, she'd know about my confrontations with Ciarán, the mugger at Kings Cross, or the bullies from my childhood? I was careful to keep my mental walls up so that she couldn't simply read my thoughts if she wasn't already aware of those episodes. I would make it one of my missions to try to really shock her. Let's see just how much of a knowledge goddess she really was.

"So, what are the advanced techniques I need to learn?" I asked with some asperity, wanting to get on with this and show her I was no milksop. "I already know about translocation, clearly shapeshifting is another, so what else?"

"Shapeshifting is just one aspect of the discipline, properly called transmogrification." Danu's voice took on the lecturing tone of a teacher as she began my advanced instruction. She wasn't going to be the friendly style of teacher like Alex and Liam; she was more of the 'further education, prove yourself or get the hell out' style of professor. "It includes alchemy –the changing of one element into another –and form changing of living beings, both others and yourself. Form change and location change are the essentials of the advanced skills. Pretty much everything beyond that is a specialisation within one of those disciplines, combined with some of the basic energy exchange techniques."

"What about spells?" I asked cautiously. "As you are no doubt aware, Earth has whole libraries of magickal volumes devoted to various forms of spell-casting. Some of them are clearly fakes and misdirects, some are mere fiction. There are a precious few, however, that have been proven to contain genuine magick. The different disciplines amongst them seem far more numerous than those you just stated. Are they merely different aspects of the same thing, wrapped in mystery to hide the true power they involve, or are they genuinely separate?"

Danu looked at first disdainful of my question, then grudgingly impressed at my extrapolation of her explanation. She refused to acknowledge that I'd shown any signs of intelligence, instead continuing to treat me like a child. I let it slide as I wanted to learn from her, but I wasn't sure how long I would be able to do so before I finally lost my temper.

"Of course, humans always feel the need to write everything down," Danu scoffed. "Your underutilised primate minds require as much assistance as they can get. Spells might be useful to guide you when learning a new aspect of your magick, I suppose, but you'd be better off understanding the underlying principles associated with whatever you want to do. Then you can dispense with all that primitive mumbo jumbo and direct your energy where it needs to go more efficiently."

I clenched my fists to help me keep control of my temper, which flared at her ongoing insults, and I tried to simply pick out the useful information from the stream of abuse. Goddess or not, teacher or not, she was pushing my buttons in a way few ever had, and I wasn't sure how much more I could take.

It was getting late so I located a couple of rock shelves that would serve as sleeping areas and put my pack down on one of them. I didn't have any more of my trail mix or jerky as it had all been consumed over the months I'd been here. If it hadn't, it would almost certainly have spoiled by now anyway. I wasn't truly hungry, but I knew I'd need some form of sustenance if I was going to be studying magick. No wonder she'd brought me out here —not just for everyone else's protection from my ineptitudes, but to see if I actually would kill an innocent animal if I had to. I knew that at the least, I would never let Gauvain starve, so I might as well kill a large enough animal to feed us all if need be. For now, I decided to get some sleep and see what tomorrow might bring.

Chapter 27

When I woke in the morning, I could tell by the darkness of the cave that it was still early. The first sun was barely high enough to shine into the oculus, striking only the rim. There looked to be some quartz or metallic flecks in the rock which reflected the sun into the cave like a disco laser ball.

I lifted myself on one elbow to see that Danu wasn't on her shelf. I looked around the space but couldn't see her, so I reached out with my consciousness. I immediately located her, disguised as a chameleon and observing me from one of the overhanging vines in the opening above. Did she really think that I couldn't detect her? Had I not already proven I knew her energy even in other forms? Her continued disrespect for my abilities and education along with her general condescension towards me was going to just make everything harder as I had to learn these new techniques. Isis had also told me that I couldn't always walk away, I would have to fight sometimes, and this was definitely something worth fighting for. All those thoughts had been churning around my mind since I had met my new instructor yesterday, and this final unnecessary test brought it all to a head and I let her have it with both barrels.

"Oh, come on! Haven't we moved past this yet?" I yelled up at her, allowing my frustration to overcome any respect or reticence I had. "I showed you yesterday I could find you as a bearded blacksmith, I saw you change into a woman, plus I'd already seen you as a cat in the hall. Your energy is the same regardless, and I know you can shapeshift, so just pick a damn form and stick with it! Or are you so fucking insecure yourself that you have to keep proving to everyone how clever and capable you are?!" Gauvain wasn't happy with the echoes of my angry voice bouncing around the cave and flew up out of the hole in the roof to go hunting.

For a moment, I feared I'd gone too far, then I caught myself before I could start to apologise. What I had said was true, and I'd stand by my assessment of her personality until she showed that she was more than what I had seen. Respect had to be earned, after all, and while I had respect for her abilities, her personality thus far had left a lot to be desired.

She let go of the vine and dropped into the cave. She rapidly changed into a small bird to flutter down, then into the same young woman as yesterday. For the first time since I had met her, she gave me a grudging nod with a slight upturn of the corner of her mouth. On anyone else it might go unnoticed; on her it seemed like a beaming smile.

"So, it wasn't all smoke and mirrors in your mind, you actually do have some fire in there. Good. The universe isn't a nice place. Darwin got it right —dog eat dog, survival of the fittest, however you want to say it. All I've seen since you arrived was your Mr Nice Guy side, which is great, and we were all glad to see that you were caring towards others and didn't think only of yourself. However, you can't just rescue an animal or build a pier to get out of every situation. Sometimes you have to fight." She sounded approving at last, but I wasn't done just yet.

"What, you think I do karate for the style points? Martial arts have fighting built into the name, for God's sake!" I said heatedly. My blood was still boiling, and I wanted her to know just how pissed off I really was. She wanted to see my spirit —brace yourself, bitch, 'cos here it comes! "I have fought outside of competition kumite, you know —or you should know, if you really are the goddess of knowledge!"

"True, but your encounter with Ciarán was a perfect example of your lack of willingness to follow through and do what was necessary." She spoke in a more reasonable, conversational tone now that she wasn't trying to deliberately antagonise me, though she was still resolute in her attitude. "You only did the minimum at the time; you never keep going to fully destroy your enemy. That kind of reluctance just leaves you open for them to recover and come back at you harder and stronger in the future, as Ciarán did in the cave in Tibet. One day, for the benefit of all, you may have to follow through and actually finish the fight. Can you do that?"

"I won't harm the innocent, but I'm not stupid!" I snapped, still fired up and not done with standing up for myself. "If someone threatens those I care for, you should already know my attitude. Just because I haven't up to now, if I had to do it to protect the innocent, I'd view ending a life as removing a cancer —painful but necessary. I still refuse to take pleasure in it, or celebrate the taking of a life, as I think it should only be done as a last resort. I'm also aware that sometimes it is the only option to prevent a worse threat in the future. I'm not a child! I know the world isn't a nice place and that sweetness and light aren't the predominant approaches. That doesn't mean I can't try to balance the scales a little. Yes, sometimes you have to take away from the negative side, but if you don't add to the positive, both within yourself as well as in the world as a whole, all you're left with is just a different shade of bad."

My shoulders were heaving as I panted after my impassioned speech, but I definitely felt better for getting it all off my chest. Danu finally nodded at me, rubbed her face in a motion that looked suspiciously like wiping away a tear, stepped over and put her hand on my shoulder.

"I must apologise. You're right, sometimes I do put too much stock in my knowledge, and I forget that not even I know everything. I can't know the depths of your heart unless you tell me. Unfortunately, breaking down walls is violent." She looked genuinely contrite, but I decided to finish driving my point home —she wanted me to finish a fight properly, after all.

"Oh, now who's being naïve and simplistic?" I retorted sarcastically. "Walls don't have to be smashed down, they can be lowered voluntarily as a gesture of trust. Have you never heard of catching more flies with honey than vinegar?"

"Honey does work, it's true," she replied with another sharp nod, stepping back and crossing her arms, taking on the air of a teacher once again, "but shit works even better and faster, and I didn't want to waste time developing the necessary trust. If you want to quote banalities, then the hottest fire makes the strongest steel." She was tapping her foot impatiently as she finished. I couldn't help myself; when she came out with that line about shit I burst out laughing, feeling my anger drain away in its aftermath.

"Now that we've gotten past that and you've seen my spine, can we just get on with things?" I still had a little smouldering resentment, but I was ready for a fresh start. I would certainly be watching for any further testing, though. "I've already been here for quite some time, several months of this plane's time. I have no idea how that translates to time on Earth, but I have to get back. I'm not sure how Gonpo and Yeshe managed with Ciarán when he woke up, so I need to check on them. I also need to work out what to do about Angelica and her group, plus I know Summer will be wondering what's happened to me."

Danu raised her hands placatingly. I was starting to get used to her less combative attitude and approval, but it still felt as though she was setting me up for something. I wouldn't relax around her for a while yet.

"You're right, we do need to get going on your studies, but I can at least put your mind at rest on one score." She was clearly trying to build bridges and mend fences now (damn, my mind was stuck in analogy mode). "We have the ability to vary the time difference between here and Earth, just like some of those fairyland legends you've heard back home. I know Alex let slip a hint about how we've set it up while you're here but let me be clear. We've currently set it so that one month here is the equivalent of one minute on Earth. So one year here will be only twelve minutes on Earth, but if you manage to learn what I have to teach you at even close to the same rate you've picked everything else up, you won't be here even that long."

Wow, a compliment? I almost staggered and looked for a place to sit down. She saw the look on my face and smiled at my expression.

"Yes, I can actually be nice, you ass, but only if you earn it!" She shook her finger at me, and I laughed, finally relaxing and letting go of my bad mood.

"Of course, now that we've had this discussion and you've recalled your reasons for wanting to get home, you've set your own deadline on countdown, so let us begin." Danu clapped her hands and walked over to her sleeping shelf, sitting down, ready to instruct and observe. "First, you'll learn transmogrification, split into inorganic first and then organic, including yourself. After that comes translocation, first on this plane and then, finally, dimensional gateways." I immediately felt my pulse pick up, as my determination to learn these advanced abilities set my mind on high alert.

"So how do I start?" I asked eagerly. I thought about what I was being asked to do and tried to think how it might work. "I'm guessing it's something like changing one energy pattern into another?" Danu looked at me in approval of my understanding and settled into a lecturing tone.

"Exactly, so to be able to do it, you have to be intimately familiar with the energy signature of what you want to turn the item into. That's why many people just have an affinity for one or two things, like Master Harfi with precious metals and gems. It took him centuries to learn the energy signatures of just gold, silver and platinum, then diamond, ruby, emerald, sapphire and pearl."

I understood immediately. To understand the intimate differences between energy signatures —how the hell could you remember them all?

"I'm thinking you won't be teaching me every energy signature in the world, just how to achieve the change? After that I have to keep learning new signatures as I go along, right?" I said, hoping to show her that I wasn't a novice expecting to be spoon-fed my education; that I was prepared to put in my own ongoing effort after she had given me the tools to use.

"Exactly." Danu nodded approvingly. "Capable you may be, but even with an eidetic memory, I have neither the time nor the inclination to teach you every energy signature in the universe. Learn a couple of simple ones to start with, then learn more as you come into contact with new substances."

"Any suggestions for my basic target substance?" I asked, excited to get started. "I'm thinking water, since that would be both a simple molecule and useful for various reasons —thirst, fires, cooling..."

"Exactly right, that's always the first one taught," Danu replied. "So, let's go out to the waterfall and you can get a feel for water. Just remember, you're not trying to feel the energy of the flow, you're trying to feel the energy of the water itself. It's the difference between recognising someone's voice or face, which could be imitated or replicated, and recognising their energy when you reach out magickally."

"In that case, would I be better off studying standing water rather than flowing water? Maybe put some in a bowl and reach out to that? At least remove some of the distractions, like the motion and sound." I thought that any edge might help me speed up the process, getting me that much closer to completing my 'basic advanced' studies, and Danu actually looked slightly shocked at my comment.

"You know, since we don't have your desire to get things done as quickly as possible, we're usually happy to take our time and accept that things are as hard as they are," she told me. "I have never had a student look to simplify their studies, they just get on with the river as is. This is one time I will actually say that the human condition puts you one up on us."

I jumped up and down, pumping my arm and shouting out loud.

"Yes! Homo sapiens for the win, baby!" Danu gave a deep sigh and shook her head at my juvenile outburst, but I swore I saw a slight smile as well.

"Yes, very good, just don't let it go to your head. As you might say, even a stopped clock is right twice a day." Now I smiled, aware that she was absolutely right. I then realised that as brilliant as my idea might be, I hadn't exactly come equipped for a dinner party out here. No bowls. I looked at Danu, and she immediately understood the issue.

"I can make you a bowl, don't worry," she said, with the barest hint of sarcasm. "I'd hate to have your brilliant idea ruined for want of something so simple."

Chapter 28

Danu and I went out through what I nicknamed "Thunder Cave", and as we did so I had another flash of genius. I reached for the sound and simply collected the energy, storing it in Seren. As I did so, Danu spun to stare at me in shock at the sudden silence. I grinned broadly, happy that I'd achieved my aim of surprising her along with storing some extra energy.

"Again, my previous students have just accepted the noise as a price of their education," she said. "Just know that you can't do that for your final test. You have to be able to work magick with precision despite distractions, or you'll be useless in a fight or any other kind of emergency." I nodded in understanding.

"That's fair enough, but until then I'm avoiding a migraine as often as I can," I replied. "Besides, it all helps stock my heart-stone with energy." At that, she nodded and looked at my right hand.

"Agreed, and you should take every opportunity to do just that. You never know when extra energy might be needed."

I smiled inwardly at the knowledge that I was gradually earning her approval.

As we went out past the cascade, I decided to do as she had just said, so I took the kinetic energy from the fall, holding it still as we went past. (Hey, who wants wet feet if you don't need them?) Danu nodded absently and then walked past, scanning the bank of the catchment pool. She found a rock about the size of a basketball and touched it delicately.

Meanwhile I let go of the falls and the noise burst forth again as the water pounded down once more.

The rock quivered, becoming a clear crystal bowl. I picked it up and dipped it into the water, filling it to the brim. We then walked away from the falls to get some peace so I could concentrate more easily. I set the bowl on a fallen tree trunk, straddling the log to sit down, and looked into the depths of the bowl. The water was pure and clean, clear of any debris and only distinguishable by the occasional ripple caused as I shifted on the log.

I reached out with my magickal senses, easily feeling the abundant life around and under the bowl. I tried to tune out the extraneous energy and feel for the water, but it felt like a dead spot by comparison to the cacophony around it. At least it gave me a frame of reference, so I focused on the dead spot and tried to feel for its unique energy signature.

I felt nothing, but I wasn't overly surprised. I was used to feeling for energy, not molecular structures. As I thought that, I thought back to my A-level chemistry classes. I knew a lot about water as a molecule. It was two hydrogen atoms covalently bonded to an oxygen atom, forming a wide-armed 'V'. Then those molecules were held together by weak hydrogen bonds which was what gave water its surface tension and cohesive properties.

I decided that I would insert a little human science and ingenuity into my studies again. It had worked before, so maybe it could help me this time as well. By removing some of the magickal mysticism and inserting something I understood in its place, I might be able to MacGyver my way through this.

Holding the structure of the molecule in my head, I reached out towards the bowl once more, this time feeling a sensation akin to two magnets pulling together as I encountered the surface of the liquid. The structure in my mind fitted perfectly with the energy in the fluid, like puzzle pieces slotting together. I could feel the attraction between the individual molecules, as well as the molecular bonds between the atoms. It was unlike anything I had encountered up to now and I suddenly understood; if the bonds between atoms in a molecule were this strong, how much stronger must the internal forces in an atom be? No wonder splitting an atom released such a devastating explosion. It was a good thing I wasn't trying to absorb this energy, merely remember the pattern so I could use it as a template to replicate in the future.

I poked and prodded at the energy I felt with my mind, testing the pattern in reference to the structure I held in my head, until I knew I had it fixed in my memory. The other benefit to this was that I now knew the different type of energy that I was feeling for, which would make it that much easier to feel for other substances in future. When I stood up from the log after less than half an hour, Danu looked at me as if I was crazy. I smiled at her and winked.

"Human ingenuity for the win again." I smirked. I opened my mind to her and showed her both what I had learned and how I had got there, all the way back to my chemistry class with H2O on the whiteboard. She stared at me with her mouth open in the purest image of shock I think I had ever seen, and I just couldn't help myself –I burst out laughing.

"I'm sorry Danu, no disrespect, I just never expected to see that particular look on the face of a knowledge goddess."

She closed her mouth and gave me a very old-fashioned look.

"OK, I'll admit it, you actually impressed me on that one." She finally smiled, the first real smile I had seen from her, then the rest of her face lit up. "I have never, in all my millennia of existence, seen anyone combine such disparate ideas at the speed you just did. To use science to understand magick was a leap I thought you might eventually make, although not this soon and certainly not so easily."

"Hey, you're the one who said my deadline was drawing in." I smiled back, truly flattered by what she had just said. "This was the only way I could think of to make sense of what you asked me to do. By the way, while I was assessing the water, I had a thought. The energy of the bonds within a molecule is significant, correct?" Danu nodded, looking at me curiously. "So then, the energy within an atom…" Her eyes went wide as she suddenly understood where my train of thought was taking me and she held both hands out to stop me. "I'm guessing trying to reduce any substance completely to pure energy is a bad idea, then?" I said.

"Well, there's bad ideas, then there's really galactically stupid ideas, then there's world-endingly galactically stupid ideas, which is what you just suggested." Then she smiled. "So please don't try it." I grinned at her understated phrasing.

"Yeah, I thought as much. Atomic fission via magick, bad: check." I thought she might actually break into a genuine laugh at that point, but she restricted herself to a wry smile.

"OK, in all seriousness, if I'm not breaking the atoms, how do I change a silicon or calcium atom into oxygen, or especially a hydrogen atom, to make water?" Danu nodded at me, seemingly glad that I couldn't figure out everything on my own.

"Well, that's where the magick comes in," she replied. "You need to think of the energy pattern of the water and use your magick to press it onto what you're trying to change, forcing it to conform and change to follow the new pattern."

"So sort of like pressing a mould down onto dough or clay, to make the shape you want?" I asked, picking up the general idea easily enough, but seeing a problem.

"Exactly," she replied.

"OK," I continued, "in that case, would it not be easier to start with something closer to what you eventually want? For example, start with a plant that's already got a high percentage of water in it, and the remaining material is carbon-based which is quite close to oxygen, as opposed to trying to start with a big ol' lump of lead?"

Danu nodded at me. "Oh, most definitely, especially when you're starting out. As you get more advanced in your studies and your power stores increase, you'll be able to make more dramatic changes. Even so, if you can stick closer to your original material, it's always easier. That's why I made the bowl out of quartz rather than changing it to glass or plastic, and why ancient alchemists always started with lead when trying to make gold. Now, you understand the theory and you have the pattern for water; let's see what you can do."

I reached over and pulled a leaf off of a nearby bush and cupped it in my hand. I held the energy pattern of water in my head then called on my magick and used it to push the pattern onto the leaf. I imagined it like a lump of cookie dough being pressed into a seasonal pattern tin before baking, then pushed more magick at it to make it stay in that shape. Suddenly the leaf quivered and then water splashed over my hand. I was certainly more tired than with some of the basics, but it was by no means impossible. My head throbbed a couple of times afterwards but then eased, nowhere near as bad as my earlier study headaches.

Danu clapped, and said, "That was excellent. I've only known a few others to get it on their first try. As we said earlier, the rest is just learning new patterns and practice. Since you're now in a rush, I think I can leave you to practice on your own. Just remember, the bigger the item you're trying to change, and the bigger the actual change, the more energy it will take." I had another thought at that comment.

"What about just a status change?" I asked.

"What do you mean?" Danu asked, clearly not reading my mind now.

"Well, rather than turning a big lump of rock into a crystal bowl, what about melting the rock and just reshaping it into a bowl? Or taking mud and making a pottery bowl? Would that be less energy as you're just changing its shape, rather than its elemental structure?"

"Oh, absolutely. Just because you're using magick, there's no reason to waste energy and make things harder for yourself than it has to be."

Chapter 29

I practiced changing various pieces of foliage into water for the rest of the day, each time finding it a little easier as I got used to the technique. I was still exhausted by the end of the day, and definitely hungry. My headache had come and gone through my exertions, but the energy I had stored in Seren had kept it from turning into a migraine. Gauvain joined us as we walked back towards the waterfall, and he had caught a couple of rabbits while he was out hunting. I skinned and gutted them with magick, then we roasted them for dinner. I was glad he'd done the hunting, so I hadn't had to kill anything. I'm still a softie and I don't care. We went to sleep quite early as I was definitely ready for bed, and the following morning I was woken by Gauvain greeting the sun with a screech.

"Mmmnh, morning bud," I said as I stretched. I turned, and Danu was also just sitting up on her shelf and stretching. I had to snigger –it was nice to see even goddesses suffered from bedhead! Gauvain sniggered in my mind too, then flexed his wings.

"Nice look. I'm off for a wash in that pool outside," he said, then he once again headed off to leave me to my studies.

"So, shapeshifting today?" I asked eagerly. I couldn't believe I'd managed to get alchemy in one day. I was determined to keep using some of my human knowledge to help me get through this as quickly as possible. I'd been here for several months already, and while that might be only around five or six minutes back on Earth, the sooner I got back the better.

"I'm going to take another human leap and guess that as I'm a mammal, sticking with mammals is going to be easier at first? Dogs, cats, and horses, rather than birds, fish, and insects until I get the hang of it?" I was still riding the high from yesterday, but it seemed logical to me.

"You know, maybe I've been dismissing the human side of your equation too quickly," replied Danu thoughtfully. "It seems to be giving you an insight into the advanced studies that people from Aaru just don't have. Maybe we could stand to learn a thing or two from you for a change. A little basic chemistry and biology might just stand a few people here in good stead. Yes, mammals first. You need to understand the intimate workings of the creature you're trying to change into, so you'll have some studying to do once you get home.

"For now..." she continued, dropping into lecture mode again while discretely trying to finger-comb her hair under control. She gave up and grabbed a pebble, changed it to a smooth cylinder of stone about the size of a chopstick, then looped her hair up and shoved the stone stick through to hold it in place. I giggled and she smiled in return. "Ahem, yes, as I was saying... For now, you need to picture what you want to change into and imagine your body conforming to the picture in your head. You are not trying to turn yourself into an actual cat or dog. Think of this more like putting on a costume. On the other hand, if you're trying to do the whole 'turn your enemy into a toad', like witches in Earth's middle ages, then it's much the same as the transmutation you did yesterday."

"OK, so personal shapeshifting is basically magickal Halloween?" I kind of liked the idea, and it actually sounded easier than true transmutation, as it was just an external image change, not a change in the underlying energy configuration. I had always been more of a dog person, so I decided to go for a canine. Plus, if she changed into a cat again, it would be fun to chase her. The idea of such a disguise, allowing me to be me, but not me, was also quite appealing.

"So do I just picture myself as whatever animal I choose, and then force my energy into that shape?" I asked. "I know you said it's not an energy form alteration, so I guess I don't need the energy signature of whatever the animal is, just an understanding of its inner biology?"

"Actually, yes, that's pretty much all there is to it. I just hope you know as much about animals as you think. There can be some unexpected differences, you know," Danu replied.

I nodded, already thinking of a couple.

"You mean like a cow having several stomachs instead of just one, that sort of thing? Or animals having tails?"

She nodded in reply.

"Exactly, and you need to hold all those things in mind. Also, keep in mind what markings you want to have. I would suggest one solid colour first, as it's easier. Once you're used to the process of changing, then you can go for spots or stripes."

Again, it all seemed perfectly logical. A nice grey wolf it was, then.

"Should I undress first?" I asked, and she shook her head.

"No need," she replied. "Your clothes should become your fur, scales, shell or whatever." I nodded, glad I wouldn't have to stand in front of her swinging in the breeze as I tried to shift. I looked at Danu, and she sighed.

"Close your eyes and call to mind everything you know about the creature you want to turn into. Then take a deep breath and focus your entire being on becoming that animal." I did as she said, closing my eyes and thinking of a wolf. I called to mind the ears, the snout, the teeth, the paws, the tufted tail —every external feature I could think of from pictures and videos. Then I thought of its internal workings, so similar to a human's but configured differently. Once I had it all in my head, I imagined pouring myself into that image, taking it on as my own skin. Absolutely nothing happened, and I opened my eyes to look at Danu.

"Am I doing it wrong?" I asked, aware that she was probably monitoring my mind to make sure I didn't do something stupid and kill myself, or more importantly her. She thought about it for a moment, trying to analyse what she had seen in my mind during my attempt.

"When you tried to become your animal, how hard were you holding on to your sense of self?" she asked me. I thought back and realised that I had been rigidly holding on to "me" for fear of taking the transformation too far and ending up as a full wolf.

"Pretty tightly, actually. I was worried about making the change too complete." She nodded as I said that.

"I thought as much. Going too far is actually harder than you think. You would have to willingly surrender your humanity and give yourself over to whatever you had become. That's totally different from someone else forcing your energy to change if they tried to trap you as an actual animal. You need to release you fear and surrender to the change."

"Easier said than done –this isn't exactly a normal, every-day experience for a human," I replied, then closed my eyes to try again. I tried several more times with no success, then finally felt a change wash over me. I opened my eyes to see myself covered in fur instead of clothes, but no other change. Danu shook her head.

"You're still holding on too tightly to who you are." She closed her eyes and I felt her in my mind, looking through my memories. She opened her eyes again and continued. "Think of the sensation of slipping into a warm bath at the end of a long day, that sensation of relaxing and surrendering to the feeling."

I understood what she meant, and called the sensation to mind, feeling myself relax as I did so. I then tried again to make the shift into a wolf form, thinking of it like slipping into a bath as she had said. I felt my joints shift and my muscles along with them like a pleasant stretch, and I felt the stone of the cave floor under my paws.

"Excellent!" Danu said, but her voice sounded much louder. The smells in the cave became so much sharper and clearer, and I could smell the vegetation above us, along with hearing the sound of the water from the falls. I opened my eyes and looked. Sure enough, I had fluffy paws, a furry snout, a tail –I was a wolf! I barked and chased my tail a couple of times, then sat on my haunches and looked at Danu.

"OK, so how do I change back?" I asked –or tried to. A wolf's vocal cords aren't exactly set up for talking, so it came out as a sort of gargled bark-howl. Danu smiled at the sound then covered her mouth to hide her laugh and reached into my mind to hear my thoughts.

"Oh, changing back," she said, understanding my query. "You simply need to reverse the process." I thought back to her original comment regarding getting into a hot bath, so I pictured myself standing up out of a bath, and the water as the wolf's skin simply sliding off me as I stood up. I felt my body shift, then heard Danu gasp and snort. I opened my eyes to see her turn away, then looked down to see my clothes at my feet. I immediately spun away and grabbed my shorts, pulling them on quickly. I then snatched up my shirt and turned back.

"Sorry about that," I said, embarrassed. "You can turn back now, it's safe." She turned around and gave me a withering look.

"Safe?" she scoffed. "Do you really think I've been around this long and yours is the first naked body I've encountered?! I've been both sexes; there's nothing you have that's new to me. I was simply allowing you a modicum of dignity to correct your error. Next time, think of your clothes remaining on your person when you change back."

I thought back to my mental image and made a note that I should view my change back imagery as staying wet when I stood up out of the bath, and the water would therefore be my clothes. I tried again, changing more easily both times, but kept my dignity intact the second time around.

"Transmogrification basics learned in two days? OK, I'm officially impressed. Even Isis took longer than that, and she was the most gifted I had ever taught before you," Danu said in reluctant amazement.

"Wow, thank you!" I replied, actually quite impressed with myself. "Do we move on to translocation tomorrow, then?" I continued, now eager to get done so I could get home. Aaru was great, but even heaven can get tiring after a while. I'd definitely come back in the future, though, if only for a holiday to see my friends.

Danu smiled and nodded. "Absolutely, but you should get some rest tonight, and you might also want to store some more energy in your heart-stone."

We relaxed for the evening and got an early night in preparation for a fresh start the next day. In the morning, Gauvain went off hunting and we prepared for the next lesson.

"For this, you need to be able to focus clearly on your destination," Danu told me. "That's why this is always taught last —we need to be sure that you can keep an image in your head and not get distracted. The obvious danger is that if you get distracted mid-way through, you could end up inside a tree, in a rock, up in the air —the end result being death."

I stopped smiling in anticipation and paid very close attention at this point. I suddenly remembered Isis' panic when I suggested I translocate us out of the windowless room as my first lesson. Now I understood.

Once again, what Danu was saying made sense. Hey, I'd watched Star Trek, I knew that the transporters could go horribly wrong.

"So can you only translocate to places you've been before and know well?" I asked. "Otherwise how would you have enough of an image to keep it clear in your mind?"

Danu looked at me seriously.

"It's definitely better to start like that. Once you're clearer in your abilities and the technique, you can get an image out of someone else's mind and go somewhere they know well. You must have a clear image, though, however you get it." I glanced at her sideways and grinned.

"I guess this time, being a knowledge goddess really does come in handy, huh?" I joked. She actually rolled her eyes and sighed at that one, then smiled slightly with a gentle tilt of her head, silently admitting that being "merely human" had actually given me a leg up in the last couple of exercises.

"Please don't tell me you have a PhD in quantum entanglement theory," she said sarcastically. I looked at her, completely lost.

"I've watched some sci-fi shows, and I know that it's been used to try to explain teleportation," I replied nervously. "Then again, it's also been quoted as the theory behind twins linking, along with several other ideas. I have a vague idea of the kind of thing it says, but I wouldn't even dream of thinking I had even a basic understanding of the actual science."

"Oh good, I actually get to teach you the way I'm used to!" Danu said, crossing her arms with a satisfied nod. I laughed in response, which definitely helped ease some of the tension I'd been feeling. The thought of ending up in the middle of a mountain definitely scared the shit out of me, so I wasn't going to joke around on this one.

"So I should think of somewhere I know intimately well, like my home or my shop?" I asked. I wasn't trying this one until I had it straight in my head, so I wanted to clarify every point in the process first.

"No, you can't use this technique across dimensions, only on the same plane," Danu replied. "We'll get to cross-dimensional travel later. The first thing I want you to do is simply try to translocate from one side of this cave to the other. Look around yourself now, remember everything about where you're standing. Remember your location in relation to the wall, to me, your sleeping shelf, everything you can to enhance your mental picture."

I looked around carefully, glad that I had always had a good memory as well as a good imagination. I mentally measured the distance from various points nearby. When I had it fixed in my head, I looked back at Danu.

"Now stand on the other side of the cave." I walked over as told and stood next to the opposite wall. "OK, close your eyes and picture everything you can about where you were standing." Again, I did exactly as I was told and nothing more, keen not to try to rush into this one. I pictured everything I had committed to memory, even the sensation of a small ridge in the rock floor that had been under my right heel.

"Now, open yourself to your magick and command it to move you where you're imaging. You need to be very positive and not let yourself panic." My eyes flew open and I stared at her.

"Yeah, that last bit won't be quite so easy after all your warnings of the potential catastrophes," I replied. "I'm not looking forward to overshooting and ending up in the wall."

Danu nodded understandingly.

"If you weren't feeling that cautious, I'd be less keen for you to try," she said kindly. "Being a little scared means you understand the risks properly, and your fear also kicks up your adrenaline, which helps your mental picture be that much clearer."

I nodded and closed my eyes again. I recreated my mental picture once more, took a deep breath, opening myself to the magick in Seren as well as myself to ensure I would have enough to complete this properly, then moved. I felt that ridge under my heel again and knew I'd made it. My eyes shot open and I let out a whoop as I jumped for joy.

"I did it!"

Danu smiled broadly and applauded vigorously.

"So what did you feel?" she asked.

I thought about it carefully and realised I hadn't actually felt movement.

"It was a surge of magick, a split second of feeling weightless as if I was floating, and then that floating sensation went away. That was it." I looked at Danu as I recited my experience and she nodded.

"Excellent. When you do it right, that's all you should feel. The magick does the movement, your body should just be picked up from your starting point and gently placed where you're picturing. As long as you keep a clear picture, that's all there is to it."

I spent the rest of the morning practicing until I knew I had it set in my head. I was going to have to start taking pictures with my phone of new locations when I got home, to help me commit them to memory. I was reminded of a film where the character could teleport and had pictures all over his apartment. Maybe then I could even get rid of the car. That brought a question to mind.

"How do I take someone with me? I guess if I'm holding onto them, they come automatically if I choose, but Isis took me in and out of a windowless room without touching me."

Danu nodded and said, "It's all about your focus. If you can picture whoever you're wanting to take with you in the new location with you, and command your magick to include them, it will work. Just make sure to picture things very clearly, or you might end up splicing yourself. Think The Fly movie."

"Yeah, I'll practice a bit first, thanks," I responded.

"And I shall ensure that I grip tightly to you!" called Gauvain as he soared in through the oculus to join us. I laughed and stroked his still damp head.

"Probably a good call, buddy," I told him. "Also, something else just occurred to me. If I'm standing still like I just was, I arrive standing still. What if I'm moving at the time? Say, for example, if I'm in a car that's about to crash and I teleport out, will I arrive at my destination still doing seventy miles an hour? Or if I fall off a cliff, same idea."

"Excellent question," she said, "it depends on your clarity and your intent. In the example of a vehicle crash, do you want to save yourself or move the whole vehicle out of danger? If you're running, do you want to simply go past an obstruction and keep going or do you want to go somewhere completely different? Intention is everything in magick – well, once you take the ability and power side of it away –which is why you need to be able to keep a very clear image in your mind. If you want to move something large, sometimes movement can help as the kinetic energy can assist in the power requirement for the translocation.

However, until you are more experienced, I would definitely recommend doing your translocation from a standing start whenever possible."

I nodded in understanding and resolved to be very careful with all of my initial efforts.

"Now for the final step. Trans-dimensional travel," Danu said.

Hoo boy, this was gonna be a doozy, I was sure.

Chapter 30

"Right, cross-dimensional movement is actually safer than the last exercise because you're not moving yourself with magick. You use your magick to basically open a door to where you want to go, then step through the portal," Danu instructed.

"Could you not do that within the same dimension if you didn't want to teleport?" I asked, curious as to why two different methods were required. Danu nodded approvingly at me.

"Of course, and some people do prefer that. The benefit of the first method is that no-one else can see where you've gone or follow you. A portal lets others see through, and if they jump through before you close it, then they're still right with you."

"So the first method is like the stealth travel and emergency escape version?" I asked. Danu smiled at my levity.

"If you like. Opening a portal also takes more energy, as you're creating a temporary magickal passage between two places. Another reason to use translocation."

"So a portal is a kind of magickal wormhole, a rip in the fabric of the universe?" I asked, somewhat awed by the implications.

"Exactly, that's a good way of thinking of it," she replied.

"OK, now I get the need for the first method for simple transport. Although for every day, I may still stick with my car!" I joked, but Danu simply nodded.

"Indeed, especially for the weekly groceries!" she said, surprising me with a joke. The references she made definitely made it clear how much she knew about modern-day Earth.

"So how do I go about this, exactly?" I asked.

"You need to think about where you want to go, then aim your magick at a point in front of you to create the portal," Danu instructed.

"Sort of like sticking a needle into the dimensional boundary, then inflating it to open up the hole?" I asked, trying to reduce the technique to my level again.

"You could do it like that. Alternatively, you could use your magick like a knife to cut through a curtain between realities. You could even create an actual door with your magick, then open it to your destination. Personally, I like the 'knife and curtain' analogy," Danu replied. I decided to stick with her way and pictured my shop.

"Should I just go for it?" I asked. "No warnings about things to avoid?"

"Uhh…" Danu looked like she was about to say something, then changed her mind. "No, you've shown you can focus well; I'm not worried. Plus, you're not going through just yet, you're just trying to open the gateway."

I wondered what exactly she had been thinking about, but thought that if it had been important, she would have told me. Thinking about things that were important brought to mind getting home once again. I was still wondering what would happen when the group that had hired me found out that I couldn't give them the Veil. Even worse, that the quest they had sent me on had resulted in me getting this kind of power. I hoped I could repay them in some way without them getting overly upset. There was nothing for it but to get home and deal with this as soon as possible.

I thought of my office in the shop, brought to mind as much detail as I could, then accessed my magick to cut a neat slit in the border between this reality and my own. As I forced it open, almost staggered by the effort required to do so, I saw my office with Summer and Angelica sitting in chairs opposite each other, both looking utterly terrified. A voice from somewhere behind the portal spoke in a deep voice.

"One or the other, Mr Maddox. This is your doing, so you have to choose."

I screamed, "NOOO!" and my magick slipped away from me, the rip closing in its wake. I dropped to my knees in shock at what I had just seen and heard. How had the owner of the voice even known I was there? Danu ran over to me concerned at my distressed reaction.

"What happened? What did you see?" she asked me, placing her hand on my shoulder. It took me a couple of tries to explain, and Danu looked stricken at what I said.

"I'm sorry, I thought you were too focused for this to happen," she said, clearly distressed. "When you pierce the veil between dimensions, people often forget that time is a dimension. Humans call it the fourth dimension, and that's actually close to the truth on any plane of existence. On some planes it's more flexible, as it is here, but it's still a dimension that can be traversed. Time travel is always strictly prohibited because of all the problems that could ensue. Fiction has created multiple stories about time paradoxes and causative events, and they're not wrong. You can't change the past without multiple unintended consequences you might never have considered. Even time-viewing, which is what you just accidentally managed, is strongly advised against due to the fact that what you see is only one possible outcome. Having seen it however, you might strive to either avoid or create the particular scenario you witnessed, causing new outcomes that otherwise would never have happened.

"No matter how upsetting the situation you saw was, I urge you to consider it no different to a dream and discard it just as easily. No more practice today, you're far too upset. You need some distance from this. Let's go for a swim and take a complete break."

Gauvain snuggled up to me and preened the hair on top of my head trying to comfort me, but my heart was still racing over what I had heard and seen.

Danu headed out towards the waterfall and I quickly changed into some shorts suitable for swimming, then followed her. I silenced the waterfall again but didn't bother catching the water as we were going to be getting wet in a moment anyway. Gauvain went and perched in a nearby tree as he had already had a wash today. I dove into the pool and swam down deep. It was cold and calm down there, although I could still hear the water pounding down the cascade.

I came up and swam towards the falls, then under the pounding water itself. I let it push me down to the bottom of the pool and used the activity of fighting the tumbling action to help clear my head. I got my feet under me and pushed out of the churning cauldron into the calmer water, then came up gasping for breath. I also felt I'd deserved a bit of punishment for the stupidity and lack of control I'd shown in my last exercise. I caught my breath again, then swam to the edge of the pool. Gauvain yelled at me as I got there, his careful speech slipping for the first time in his distress.

"What the fuck, Gavan? Are you insane? What were you trying to do, drown yourself?!" He flew down to the edge of the pool as he spoke. Danu, on the other hand, looked supremely unconcerned –I had a suspicion that she was quietly monitoring my mental state, so knew what I had been doing. She had probably also kept track of me under the water, ready to pull me out if I had truly got in over my head. I raised an eyebrow in her direction, and she nodded slightly.

"Sorry bud, I didn't mean to scare you. I just needed to do something physical to clear my head," I replied. He stomped across the rock to get right into my face and stared at me.

"You do something so insane again and I shall shit in your ear when you're asleep!" he threatened. I dissolved into fits of giggles at the image.

"Eeewww!" I responded. "Gross!" Danu rolled her eyes but did laugh lightly at the image. The laughter was the final stress relief I needed to settle my equilibrium.

We swam around for a while more, occasionally splashing each other or Gauvain, who had stayed on the nearby rock, until the second sun lowered in the sky. We got out and lounged in the light of the dying day, air-drying and just enjoying the rest. I felt centred again and accepted that although what I'd seen had been distressing, it was no more real than a particularly vivid nightmare and should be treated as such. Once we were dry, we headed inside, and I got myself ready for bed. For the first time, Danu stroked Gauvain and then kissed my forehead.

"Sleep. You can try again tomorrow," she said, sounding almost motherly in her concern over my earlier mistake. I appreciated the sentiment and closed my eyes.

I fell asleep so quickly, I wasn't sure whether she might have used a hint of magick to help me drift off. Regardless, I had several disturbing dreams while I slept, possibly triggered by my experience with time-viewing. I saw Summer and Emily getting married, then getting divorced; Angelica tied to a chair and branded; my shop in flames...

I woke up with tears running down my face at the visions, but I was able to dismiss them more easily this time, as they were clearly dreams –right? Anyway, if I wanted to get home to try to prevent these futures, I needed to get this final ability down pat. I also needed it if I ever wanted to bring myself back here. The Veil might give me permission, but I saw it like a train ticket –it allowed me access, but I had to be able to get here or the permission was worthless.

I dashed my tears away and sat up, determined that I'd have this learned today. Danu looked over at me, stretching as she sat up and tied her hair up again. I swung my legs off of my shelf and stretched, Gauvain jumping off my shoulder as I lifted my arms. He just dropped onto the shelf rather than flying off as he had the previous couple of days, and I looked down at him curiously. He returned my look and blinked.

"I'm sticking around in case you need me today," he said simply and Danu looked at him approvingly.

"You are linked, after all. Maybe his being here will be an additional grounding force to help guide you through this final step," she said. I nodded, grateful for anything that might make this go more smoothly. I stood up and took a couple of steps away from Gauvain.

I remembered what Danu had said yesterday and focused on my office, this time thinking very clearly of the date it had been when I was in the cave in Tibet. I reached out with my power, including Seren as before. I used it to tear through the fabric of reality, picturing a clean and discrete archway. Danu came and stood next to me and looked through as I opened my eyes to see my office bright and empty as ever.

I held it for a few moments, noting the different feel of the portal compared to yesterday. That had felt like trying to stretch a hosepipe open with my fingers. This was more like just pulling a door open that had a firm spring on it. Once it was open it took much less energy to keep it in place, while yesterday's opening had slammed shut as soon as I relaxed even one iota.

I looked through one more time, Danu expressing her approval by resting her hand on my shoulder, then released the energy and watched the gate rapidly seal itself. I looked over at Danu and she beamed at me.

"Well done! That was the final stage of your education. Now you just need to pass your final test," she said, pleased that I had managed the portal so cleanly and without errors today. I remembered the conversation we had had upon arrival about proving I could handle distractions. I readied myself to deal with the noise of Thunder Cave while trying to use the skills I had learnt.

"OK, let's get this over with. I've got places to go and people to see," I said, only partially in jest. Danu came with me, and we walked into the cave behind the waterfall.

"OK," she shouted, as I strained to hear her over the echoing din. "You have to change this leaf into water first." She held out a large waxy leaf to me, and I took it from her. I held it in my hand and stared at it, calling to mind water's energy signature and pressing it onto the leaf. It shook briefly, then splashed onto the floor as pure water.

"Good," yelled Danu, "now change into your wolf again." This was easier, and I changed smoothly, immediately cowering from the increased noise. I changed back quickly —this time without giving Danu a Full Monty show —shaking my head to clear my ears, but confident I'd passed that step.

"Last one. Translocate out of this cave back into the other one!" Danu shouted, then turned on her heel and walked out to watch for my appearance. I remembered my mental image from before and closed my eyes, moving as quickly as I could to get out of the racket. The drop in the noise level and the feel of the small ridge under my foot told me I had succeeded even before I opened my eyes, combined with Gauvain's welcoming screech and Danu's applause.

"Marvellous! Superb performance, well done!" shouted Gauvain in my head. Danu came over and put her arms around me and hugged me hard.

"I've never been prouder of a student, nor more impressed with the speed of someone's learning," Danu stated. "You can be justifiably delighted with everything you've accomplished, but now it's time to head back to the city and get ready to return home."

Chapter 31

I gathered my things and packed everything into my bag again, then Gauvain flew up onto my shoulder. As I was packing, I had what I can only describe as a vision of a darkened room. It had stone walls, and a being with a face of ash was staring at me. It was only for a second, then it vanished, so I dismissed it, but the memory stuck with me. I looked over at Danu and asked the obvious question.

"So, are we walking back, or are we doing this the quick way?" I raised an eyebrow as I asked, almost feeling like a superhero as I did so. The magick I had learned since I arrived here was the stuff of legend, abilities I had only read or dreamed about. They made Heffernan's little electricity ball look like a simple static shock.

Danu smiled, and said, "Just because you can use magick for something, doesn't mean you have to use it. Sometimes it's good to take a little time and enjoy life. You need to save your energy for when you actually need it, and store as much as you can in your... heart-stone." She looked at me as she paused and appeared to be fighting a smile.

"You were going to say ring, weren't you?" I giggled, and she shook her head with a smile.

"You are so juvenile," she said, desperately trying to keep a straight face.

"Hey, it crossed your mind too," I replied, still laughing.

"Fine, so it's funny." She gave in. "Anyway, let's get going."

We headed out through Thunder Cave and I silenced it for the last time, stilling the falls again as well as we made our way out. I released everything once we were past and watched as the built up water dropped in one massive splash into the pool. I turned to follow Danu back towards Dinas Affaraon while Gauvain soared up into the sky to stretch his wings. As he left my shoulder, I had another flash vision, this time of Gauvain fighting with another bird, this one made of smoke and flame. Again, it was gone in an instant.

As we went, I took every opportunity to store extra energy in Seren, so we were walking in an almost perpetual twilight and cooler temperature, with sounds being far more muffled than normal. Every little helps, as the saying goes, but I knew from my previous collection efforts that this wasn't even a drop in the bucket. Danu looked at me approvingly but took the opportunity to add another warning.

"Doing this is fine here, but you'll have to be more careful when you're home. On Earth, magick is rare and unusual as you well know. Most people, what many magick users there call 'mundanes', have no idea about that world. They view things to do with magick as only myths and legends, often even less than that. The Veil was a perfect example." Talking of the Veil reminded me that it was now a part of me, and that I had nothing to give Angelica when I got home. I really needed to come up with something to tell her; something substantive that she could pass onto the people she represented.

"If I want to come back to Aaru, do I have to access the Veil and channel power through it in some way? Or is it just like some kind of intrinsic password, colouring my magick so that this plane recognises me automatically and allows my portal to open?"

Danu glanced over and nodded.

"The Veil's energy is now inextricably tied to your own, so yes it flavours your magick. You'll learn to access it for certain purposes in the future, however it can't be removed from you. To answer your next question yes, you're going to need to think of something to tell this mysterious group that hired you to find it."

It was uncanny the way her comment echoed what I had just been thinking. Something occurred to me when she mentioned the group – she was a knowledge goddess, so did she know who they were? Maybe she knew why they were after the Veil in the first place? I had so many questions about them and from her comment, Danu seemed to know all about them. Maybe she could answer some questions for me. I looked over at her and she was already shaking her head, although she did at least have the grace to be sorry about it.

"Some things you have to find out at the appropriate time in the appropriate way, otherwise events can spiral in a way they were never meant to do." As she said that, I had a third vision, this one more intense than any of the ones before. I saw myself standing outside a city, watching as it burned, and in front of it was an army of creatures from myths, legends and horror films. I saw horns, animal heads, wings, weapons of every conceivable description, and some that had never been described. Then it was gone. If these were visions of the future, triggered by my accidental time-viewing, just how bad was this future war going to be that I had to be selected by a goddess and trained by heaven for it, and what exactly were they expecting my role to be? To cover my shock and disquiet, I lit into Danu for keeping things from me. I was so distressed, my temper got away from me and I was harsher on her than I meant to be, fuelled by my fear of such demands being placed on me and my worry over potential failure.

"Seriously?" I shouted, "You're telling me that viewing the future isn't allowed, but there is a plan of how things are supposed to go, I'm just not allowed to know about it or even try to get some information? What the hell kind of bullshit is this? You're a knowledge goddess, for fuck's sake! How can you tell me that knowledge is a bad thing?" Danu stopped and looked at me during my tirade, but despite my swearing at her, she didn't look annoyed at my outburst.

"I can understand your position," she replied ruefully, "and yes, as the knowledge goddess I do appreciate that information is important. You should know by now, though, that even the right information at the wrong time can end up being very dangerous. As the saying goes, knowledge is a double-edged sword —it cuts both ways. Try to grip it at the wrong time and it can cause more damage than good."

I knew that what she said was true, and I could even think of examples where the wrong piece of information, however correct and well-intentioned, could utterly destroy a situation. It didn't make me feel any better knowing that, when I was the one stuck twisting in the wind with no idea what was going on. Nor when I knew that, if I mentioned my visions, she was liable to reach into my head and rip the memory of them clean away. I decided I would keep them to myself. I wanted as much warning and advanced information as I could get. I made a mental note to write down as much as I could remember once I got back home.

I stormed off, pulling all the light and heat for a moment to leave Danu in the freezing dark as an expression of just how I felt. She simply tsked and muttered under her breath. I released all my collection efforts, not wanting to cause undue suffering to anything else around in my fit of pique. I stomped off, and Gauvain landed on my shoulder as I did. Due to our link he was aware of everything that had been said.

"Calm yourself. We shall come up with something to tell them. Don't concern yourself about it." He preened my hair again as he spoke in my mind, trying to be comforting. Feeling the weight of him on my shoulder was actually very reassuring, as it reminded me that I wasn't alone in this.

I soon passed the waterfall where I had done my earlier energy collections. I gradually slowed down, my temper easing and my common sense returning to remind me that Danu was actually right. She came up beside me and put her hand on my shoulder.

"I'm sorry."

We both said it at the same time, then smiled at each other, already understanding what the other was sorry for —me for my childish display of temper, her for not being able to tell me things that she would otherwise like to in order to make my life easier.

We walked on, now in companionable silence, until the city walls finally came into view once again. I had a few other questions I wanted to ask Isis when I saw her, and I also started to think about Gauvain back on Earth. Walking around with a big white hawk on my shoulder wasn't even inconspicuous here on Aaru. On Earth, I might as well put a big flashing light on my head and announce my power to every magick user in the world.

As we got nearer to the walls, I started to feel a little despondent at the thought of leaving my new friends. I knew that the entire city was only here to make things easier for me, that my friends usually spent their time in an incorporeal state, but it still felt real, and I had grown used to everything over the last few months. Still, at least I had tonight before I had to go back.

As we drew near to the gate I saw Oli walk out of the city and stand there with her arms folded, staring at me. I looked at Danu and motioned her to wait as I went on. She nodded and I continued towards the angry adolescent waiting for me. As I approached, Oli uncrossed her arms, put one hand on her hip and shook her fist at me in rage.

"I bet you think you're so clever, leaving me behind and going off to learn more magick," she shouted angrily. "You made Alex and Liam throw me off the course and refuse to teach me!" She broke into tears of frustration.

I felt sorry for her, but she was her own worst enemy as her actions during training had demonstrated. I had no hand in how she had been treated −I'd even stood up for her to Liam after the brick-stacking exercise, but the rules were what they were.

"Oli, I didn't have anything to do with what happened to you," I said calmly. "You completed the brick pile and felt no remorse at having to kill to do so. That was why you were removed from the classes. That's the test we took, and I had no input into writing the rules."

"Oh come on!" she yelled. "Bugs and rats? They don't mean anything!"

"It's the principle, and how you react to taking a life," I said. "You have no consideration for others, which is why you were denied the opportunity to learn the more advanced techniques. You proved that again when you trapped your cousins in the ravine."

"I HATE YOU!" she screamed, and I felt and saw her reaching out to try and draw power from whatever was around to use against me, the energy of her reaching flaring to my newly developed visual spectrum. I reached out and blocked her by cutting the streams and setting a barrier around her, isolating her from any external sources. She stared at me in fury, then drew upon her own internal stores to send a blast of energy at me like she had during our lessons. Since we were not linked in the way we had been then, I simply caught it and funnelled it into Seren which made it flare briefly as it absorbed the power. Oli sent one last blast at me, weaker than the first, so I reflected it back at her. It hit her as a slap across the legs, like a parent might give a naughty child having a tantrum, and she yelped, then turned and ran back to the city.

"You'll be sorry you did that!" she shouted back to me as she ran off. Danu walked up to me, placed her hand on my arm, and sighed.

"In a purely magickal technique sense, you handled that well. I can understand you not wanting to take it any further since she is only young," she said sadly. "You need to realise, however, that even though she is a child now, she will grow and will likely harbour this resentment for the rest of her life, which is likely to be a significantly long time. Be on your guard, as you have made an immortal enemy here." My irritation at being treated like a child again made me speak more sharply than I otherwise might have done.

"I'm well aware of that but she is still young!" I said hotly, still worked up from my brief confrontation with Oli. "I'm not powerful enough to finish every fight, plus I'm not going to kill a child! Unfeeling bitch!" I muttered, finally turning away.

Danu grabbed my shoulder, swung me back and slapped me across the face, making me stagger. I was so shocked, I reacted without thinking and blasted her in the face with a ball of energy, knocking her down. She looked up at me from the ground, touching her nose cautiously and wiping a drop of blood away. She got up carefully and looked at me.

"So much for not being powerful enough," she said. "At least you're willing to fight though. That's a start."

"I'm sorry, you surprised me," I replied. "I know she may come for me in the future, but she also has a chance to change."

"I appreciate your position; I just hope for your sake that you don't come to regret your leniency." So saying, we walked on towards the city.

As we walked through the gate, Danu nodded to me then turned and walked away. I had expected more of a goodbye to be honest, but maybe I'd see her again before I left. I went to Poppy's to say hello and Roman came around the counter as soon as he saw me.

"Gavan!" He shouted gleefully. "I'm so glad you're back. You have to come. You will come, right? You have to!"

"Hey, slow down Roman!" I laughed at his eagerness. "It's good to see you too, but try telling me where I'm supposed to come, it might just help."

He laughed brightly. "I'm sorry," he said, "I'm just so excited. I asked Poppy to marry me and she said yes! It's all thanks to you. We're getting married tomorrow. I know it's short notice, but after you go back to Earth, much of the city will go away and many of us will go back to our normal formlessness. There's nothing wrong with it, but we don't have weddings there. We do form pair bonds and have families, but there's no big celebration like humans have. I want that for Poppy."

"After all your kindness, how could I refuse you your day?" I smiled. "Of course I'll come."

"Good," he said. "I understand from my research that I need a 'best man' to stand up with me." He winked at me and I stood there in shock with my mouth open.

"Uh… um... OK, do I need to organise a bachelor party?" I started to panic slightly at the thought of trying to be a best man for a wedding in one day, not least speaking in front of a large group. Roman laughed at the anxiety on my face.

"No, just stand up with me and look after these." He handed me two gold rings covered in beautiful scroll-work, with 'Roman and Poppy' engraved on the inside. I recognised Harfi's handiwork and smiled, putting them in my pocket. I nodded at him.

"If a month here is one minute on earth, one day is about two seconds –I'm sure I can spare a couple of seconds for the sake of friendship." I joked, and he beamed at me.

"Liam and Alex are expecting you for tonight. The wedding will also be your send-off, so you'll head back to Earth afterwards. Isis will perform the ceremony for us, and Danu will be there to record our union, so you'll be able to say goodbye before you go."

I hugged him and told him I'd see him tomorrow, then headed off to spend one more night with the family that had first taken me in. When Conor saw me coming, he squealed in excitement and shouted for his parents. They came running out to see what was wrong, then smiled and clapped when they saw me approaching. Alex ran up and threw her arms around me.

"We're so proud of you. To learn the advanced magicks that fast is unheard of, even amongst us. You were meant for this," she whispered in my ear and I hugged her back.

"I'd never have got anywhere without your help, both of you. If you ever need anything from me, I'll be here. All you need to do is call."

She beamed and stepped over to Liam, taking his hand.

"We're honoured to have been involved in your training." Liam said, reaching out with his other hand to shake mine. We went inside and had a quiet dinner. We didn't need anything more in view of the wedding tomorrow. Afterwards, when I was in my room and lay on my bed for the last time, Gauvain and I discussed going back to Earth.

"If we're out in the countryside, you can fly around and no-one will bat an eye. Even in my shop you could sit and be admired. Walking around a city however, you'd be far too conspicuous. We need a way for you to be near me, but not seen," I said, stroking his head. Gauvain thought about it for a while, then told me his idea.

"You need something to represent me that you can have on you all the time. I could transfer my energy into it when I shouldn't be seen, then emerge when needed or it's safe," he suggested.

"Nice idea. What are you thinking of?" I asked. "It's your idea, and you'll be the one spending time in it, so you choose."

He thought for a moment, then fluffed his wings.

"Well, a feather would work, I suppose —you could get one tattooed somewhere. Your hand, maybe?" he proposed.

"Nah, that's been done," I said. "What about one of your talons?"

"That could work," he replied. "You need to find some way to keep it on you at all times."

"I've got an idea for that," I said.

He nodded and pulled at one of his claws that was a bit long, biting off the end, and dropped it into my hand. I imbued it with energy, and it grew until it was as large as any of his other talons. I took a piece of leather strapping off of my rucksack, then plaited it until it was long enough to go around my wrist. I then fixed the plait to more of the leather for reinforcement, finally fixing the talon to the bracelet. I then put the strap around my wrist and sealed the ends together with a piece of gold-coloured steel taken from a buckle on my bag that I reshaped. I recalled some of the protection runes used in my shop and magickally imprinted them on the leather and metal, protecting the bracelet from any damage or tampering. Satisfied we had a plan, we snuggled up together and went to sleep.

Chapter 32

The next morning I got up and washed myself. I still couldn't believe I hadn't had to shave the whole time I was here —maybe my beard was still on Earth time? When I came out of the washroom, Alex had laid out a new set of clothes on the bed for me, with a note saying it was a gift from Roman to his best man.

I got dressed while Gauvain finished his morning preening, then we went out. The market square was already set up with chairs and flowers, ribbons and archways. A raised platform was at the end near the fountain where I had first seen the people. An archway was set over it, ready for Roman and Poppy to join hands underneath it.

Later that day, with Isis there to join their hands and wrap them in a ribbon, Roman and Poppy exchanged their vows and rings, merging their lives into one. Danu stood by to bear witness and record the proceedings, and I stood next to my friends to share their joy. Almost the whole city was present to celebrate, although I looked around for Oli and couldn't see her anywhere. Then after the wedding feast came the dancing and games. I said my thanks and my goodbyes to the newlyweds as well as Master Harfi and Soraya as the day progressed, then later I managed to step aside to talk to Isis.

"Now that I know you're real," I said, "I wanted to ask, are the other gods and goddesses from Egyptian mythology real as well? What about other pantheons? What about demons? Have I just opened myself up to a whole new shitstorm of problems now that I have magick?"

Isis laughed loudly (personally I think she was a bit drunk) and threw out her arms.

"You've stepped into a much bigger world, it's true," she said. "As to who is real, and the challenges you have yet to face, well, Danu already warned you that knowledge has to come in its own time. You'll just have to wait and see." She winked at me. "For now, it's time for you to go home." I turned to see Danu standing just behind me, and next to her were Alex, Liam and Conor.

"I don't know how to thank you all for what you've done for me," I said, feeling a lump in my throat in gratitude to my friends and sadness at leaving them, blinking to clear my eyes (damn, I'd been here for months and my allergies start up again now?) "You've given me back something I only dreamed I might have lost. I am forever in your debt." Danu smiled at me, as did the others. I sniffed quietly, wiping my tears away with one of my handkerchiefs.

"One day, we may call on you to repay that debt," Danu replied with a wink, "but you still have much practicing to do and much to learn before then. Study hard and remember who you are —don't let the magick control you and turn you into someone you're not."

I nodded at her, then went round and hugged them each in turn.

When I hugged Danu, she held me at arm's length and gave me one more cryptic piece of advice.

"Just remember, caution and kindness are good things, but too much of anything can be a bad thing. Even order may not be beneficial." As she said that, stressing the word order, Isis looked over at her sharply. Danu looked as though she wanted to say more but refrained. I was confused but filed it away to think about later.

Finally I came to Conor and dropped to one knee next to him.

"As for you, my young friend, the one who first showed me that I wasn't alone here, just remember —not all strangers are kind. Listen to your parents, study hard, and maybe someday I'll be able to come back for a visit so we can go fishing together. Remember, no more rooftop shenanigans." I hugged him tight, then stood up. I nodded to them all, then went and changed back into my original clothes from when I arrived. It wouldn't do for Ciarán to see me in a different outfit and wonder what had happened. Mind you, if he tried to use magick on me when he woke up, he'd get one hell of a shock.

I walked out of the city with Isis and Danu, waving to the rest of my friends as I went. Once out of the gate, Gauvain merged himself into the talon on my wrist, then I reached for my magick and opened a portal, thinking of the cave where I had left Gonpo and Yeshe. Isis put her hand on my chest, and I felt a surge of energy. I looked at her questioningly, and she simply smiled at me.

"For the altitude," she told me. I nodded, then stepped through and released the power.

Heffernan was still on the floor, and Gonpo was talking to Yeshe. I cleared my throat and they spun to look at me. Yeshe immediately rushed over to me.

"What happened?" he asked me anxiously. "Where did you go? You were gone for almost ten minutes!" Gonpo on the other hand merely raised his eyebrows at me questioningly, and I simply nodded in return. He beamed at me, then patted Yeshe's arm.

"We'll leave you to deal with your friend when he wakes up," Gonpo said. "We'll be in my hut when you're done here." I nodded and knelt down to wait for Ciarán to wake up. I gave it about ten seconds, then got bored.

Why does he deserve a nap? I thought to myself, then called up a small charge of energy, just enough to wake him up, and slammed it into his chest. He jerked up and scrambled away from me, stopping when his back hit the cave wall. He looked about for Gonpo and Yeshe. Seeing they were gone, he sneered at me and pushed himself to his feet. I stood up as well, dusting off my knees.

"Give me the Veil and you won't get hurt," he demanded. "I don't care what kind of charm that bitch gave you, it won't help you now. Either give it to me, or I'll go after your little guide and the old monk." I weighed the options, then put my bag down and pulled out the box with the Tyet symbol on it. I opened it and showed him that it was empty.

"Just a fanciful legend," I said. While he was distracted, I reached out with my mind and did something I'd been dying to try. He swore vigorously and called up another of his balls of electricity. Having sparred with Liam using a similar technique, I noticed how much weaker Ciarán was in comparison.

"You're lying!" he snarled. "I can feel the residual energy from here. What did you do with it? Send it off with the monk?" I realised I would have to reveal at least a portion of the truth, both to him and to Angelica's group, so I thought quickly.

"Fine, so it was real," I admitted. "What can I say? I touched it and it crumbled to dust. What do you expect me to do about it now?"

"You destroyed it? You MORON!" he yelled. "How could you be so careless with such a valuable artefact? Do you have any idea what that could have meant to the world? Genuine evidence of a goddess on Earth!" His control slipped during his tirade as he became increasingly irate, finally throwing the ball of electricity at me as he lost his temper completely.

I caught the energy, remembering to look appropriately shocked at my apparent sudden development of magickal ability.

"Holy crap!" I said, feigning fear at the sight of the electricity in my hand. "The Veil must have done something to me! Looks like I'm not as defenceless as you thought." The sight of me wielding magick seemed to be the final straw for Ciarán, and he started flinging fire and electricity indiscriminately.

I managed to simply dodge most of his spells, as his aim seemed to have degenerated along with his grip on his temper. The few that did come close I simply absorbed and funnelled discretely into Seren. He quickly ran out of energy and his spell-slinging ceased, so I decided to taunt him a little more.

"Looks like you can't keep it up, Doc," I snarked, watching as he panted in exhaustion. He growled at me, then turned to storm out of the cave in disgust. He promptly fell flat on his face as his stride was arrested by his tied-together laces. What can I say? I loved Looney Tunes cartoons.

"Team Roadrunner for the win. Meep meep, motherfucker!" I laughed loudly as I walked out. I paused at the mouth of the cave and turned back. "Oh yeah, leave my Tibetan friends alone. Otherwise we'll see just how much power the Veil gave me." I turned away again, heading after my recently departed friends.

"You haven't heard the last of this!" he yelled as I walked away. "I swear, I know people who can put you in your place!"

"Whatever," I muttered to myself, then set off along the goat path. I quickly caught up with Gonpo and Yeshe and told them how I'd shown Ciarán the empty box, related his temper tantrum and my trick with his laces, at which they laughed. Gonpo handed me my necklace and I put it back on. Yeshe and I left Gonpo in his hut and we continued on our way through the monastery. As we left the hut I saw Ciarán stomping down the mountain, heading to a different part of the city rather than going through the monastery. I was happy Gonpo wouldn't be bothered by him.

Yeshe drove me to my hotel, where I thanked him and paid him a bonus as thanks for all his help. He proffered his hand and I gripped it tight, looking deep into his eyes as I did. I could see the realisation dawn in his eyes that there was something different about me, and I nodded to confirm his suspicion. He smiled, then got into his car and drove off.

I went into the hotel and went up to my room. I gathered my things, repacking all my luggage, and then made my way down to reception and checked out. I went out and walked around the building, finding a quiet spot. I pictured my home and willed myself there —no more airports, thank the gods.

I set my things down and flopped onto the sofa, letting Gauvain know that we were home. He flew out of his talon on my wrist and landed on the back of the couch, looking around at my place.

"This will suffice, although some adaptations may be required now that we are living here together," he said, and I scrubbed at my face with my hands.

"We'll get things sorted out starting tomorrow buddy." I promised him. I considered what to tell Angelica when I contacted her tomorrow from the shop and decided to go with what I had told Ciarán about the Veil crumbling after I had touched it. Since she would likely be aware of the change in me, I would admit that the Veil had unlocked my magick but simply not disclose the degree of power I had been given or the extent of my training. I would also mention nothing about Aaru.

That decided, I texted Summer, then went to bed and slept deeply, waking to a bright morning. After showering and shaving, I dressed and headed to the shop. As I arrived, I felt a presence behind me and heard a familiar voice.

"Morning boss. Any luck?" I smiled to myself, then turned.

"Well..."

Gavan Maddox will return in

"The Order of the Nine Seals"

Acknowledgments

There are a number of people I need to thank for their help in making this book a reality. First and foremost, my beautiful wife Melanie for her undying love and support, without whom this book would never have been completed —or would at least be much more boring and full of errors.

Secondly, I need to thank Tammy and Larry for their patience in rereading my first efforts, and their invaluable suggestions on improvements.

Thirdly, Brittany, for her encouragement and enthusiasm. Also her artistic interpretation, painting a beautiful suggestion for the front cover.

Next, Shayne Silvers. His professional encouragement and suggestions kept me going and showed me how to step my writing up to a whole new level.

Lastly, as promised, I need to thank Mark for finally leaving me alone long enough to get the book finished!

About the Author

Alex Polak is a qualified doctor who lives and works in Yorkshire. He went to Harrow School and then Leeds University where he studied medicine. He lives with his loving and supportive wife Melanie, her mother and their two cats, Samson and Delilah.

Alex has practiced GKR karate and is a licensed instructor. He enjoys reading, watching films and playing computer games on several platforms, as well as swimming and cycling. He loves cooking – and eating! – and he and his wife spend much of their time together in the kitchen.

He has always been an avid reader, even as a child, and has read everything from comic books to Tolkien, Douglas Adams to Tom Clancy. Over the last few years he focused more on urban fantasy, eventually finding the books of Shayne Silvers and becoming deeply involved in his Facebook fan group. Alex finally met Shayne in 2019 at Shayne's 'Friendsgiving' event, and upon returning to the UK became inspired to try his hand at writing his own book.